Grim Tales of Hope

by

Finn Clarke

Published in 2008 by YouWriteOn.com

First Edition

Published by YouWriteOn.com

To my father

John Francis Gay Clarke

31st May 1931 – 3rd October 2006

Acknowledgements

Thanks to Im Ahmad for all her help with the chemistry, Élise Michaud-Pomerleau for the fantastic front cover, mum for the proof-reading, Pip Harris for her last minute setup support, and all those enthusiastic friends who helped with the blurb.

Grim Tales of Hope

Pénélope

In the pathway of the sun,
In the footsteps of the breeze,
Where the world and sky are one,
He shall ride the silver seas,
He shall cut the glittering wave.

I shall sit at home, and rock;
Rise, to heed a neighbor's knock;
Brew my tea, and snip my thread;
Bleach the linen for my bed.
They will call him brave.

Penelope by Dorothy Parker

"More, Doctor?"

"Merci, Monsieur Ramsey. I don't mind if I do."

"James, please. I don't believe in last names after the second round of port."

"Well – in that case you must call me Arnauld." The doctor looked him in the eyes, making it a challenge.

"Thank you sir." Ramsey met the look easily, smiled and passed the port. "Although there are always exceptions to such a rule. Too quick a familiarity with one's seniors could be seen as bordering on disrespect." His voice rose, making it a query and Frenet smiled in acknowledgement, before shaking his head.

"No, James, you cannot have it both ways. Either we are both familiar, or we are both formal. Besides – who knows? I may be speaking to a man of great future power. I would be best to get my familiarity in quickly, to be on the safe side."

The men around the table laughed, including Ramsey, though a gleam of recognition told the doctor his point had been noted. "In any case," Frenet continued, enjoying himself, "doctors are too well-versed in failure to accept special treatment. And all men are equal in the eyes of our Lord, hm?" He paused and looked round the table to make his point.

There were eight of them in all. Ramsey along with his deputy manager and head foreman formed the contingent from Montréal, while Dr Frenet headed up St Léopold's main dignitaries of mayor, lawyer, priest and the town's homme d'affaires. They were dining in the latter's hotel, the best St Léopold had to offer, in a private room at the back – and while it fell short of Ramsey's Montréal standards it was a cosy scene, the relaxed atmosphere no small tribute to Ramsey's skill. The table was in disarray, remains of dessert and coffee littering the cloth, discarded cutlery gleaming in the soft gas light and chairs pushed back for comfort – the business of getting to know each other properly had begun.

His point made, Frenet moved on before the Protestant incomers could become ill-at-ease. "Though despite my failures," he added, "I can admit to one particular success I am proud of."

"Oh yes?" Père Martin obliged. "What was that?"

The fellow guests leaned forward, curious despite themselves. Dr Frenet was not prone to boasting, though his skill was respected throughout the area. Were they to learn some privileged information?

"My daughter."

A chorus of approval and disappointment greeted his announcement. The doctor was not perturbed.

"Of course I am very proud of my sons too," he continued, addressing himself to Ramsey. "But my daughter is special. To be intelligent, beautiful, wise – and feminine – and all this without the aid of a mother. That, I declare, is a small miracle. Her mother died you know," he added for the newcomers' benefit, "when Pénélope was a baby."

He sat back and sipped his port, waiting for Ramsey's response. Instead Père Martin cut in.

"She has her faults too," he added. "I remember when she was ten – we all do – blowing up the barn. The whole barn, pouf! at only ten years old. Now *that* is a miracle."

The table laughed again. The Catholics, old friends of the doctor, with an indulgent familiarity; the English with curiosity. Ramsey looked at the doctor for enlightenment.

"I'm afraid," he explained obliquely, "that my Pénélope will not win her way to a man's heart through his stomach." More laughter. "She is what you might call an amateur chemist," he enlarged. "A lonely girl must have a hobby after all. I tried to stop it in favour of cooking and sewing – but after the barn episode I was forced to concede defeat. Better, I felt, to have her under a watchful eye before she blew herself up too. Since that time it has been a comparatively harmless hobby."

"The doctor is modest on his daughter's behalf," Charles Longrin, the lawyer, put in from Ramsey's other side. "If she were a man she would be well on her way to fame. I believe she is a most intelligent and thorough chemist."

"But what a waste!" Ramsey was spontaneous the doctor noted approvingly, with a young man's disrespect for form over content. "A chemist is a chemist, whatever their sex. If she's that good she should be given opportunities and the world allowed to profit.... What is her field?"

"Something to do with metals," Frenet said vaguely. "Indeed, you two may have something in common – your reputation as a chemist precedes you, James. All of us are very anxious to find out what a man so dedicated to change and new discoveries will make of our traditional saw mills with your pulp and paper industry." He left the merest pause to underline his point, then, before it could stretch into a confrontation, continued. "But as to the details... I don't understand a bit of them. You will have to ask her yourself."

Pénélope was waiting up for him.

"Puis?" She gave him a kiss and took the medical bag he still carried everywhere just in case.

Frenet rubbed his hands and turned to face the fire. The night was clear and icy, his old horse slow, and despite the blanket over his legs and the short sleigh ride home, the chill had got into his bones.

"Puis?" he returned with a smile. "You should be in bed."

"And sleep sweet dreams while you plot my future?" she returned without rancour. "Far more interesting surely, to wait up with a good book and a night cap."

"A girl should not drink," he reproved automatically, while picking up Durham's *Report on the Affairs of British North America* that lay on the sofa.

"Nor should Benoit," she retorted, "at least not in the quantities he does. But you don't go on at him."

Frenet ignored her. "Have you truly been reading this all evening – or did you get it out to impress me?"

The girl laughed and fumbled under the sofa cushions to bring out Henry James's *The Portrait of a Lady* in French translation.

"It's new out," she told him. The doctor studied it curiously.

"It is a good choice," he said finally, "but –" he threw it deftly into the fire. "In English."

"Papa!" Pénélope went to the fire but it was too late. She sounded more exasperated than shocked. "I was enjoying that."

"And so you will, ma chère." He touched her cheek in a gesture that robbed his vandalism of all hostility. "In English."

"That means waiting until our next visit to Montréal."

"For business, yes. For emergencies, no." The doctor took off his heavy coat, gave it to her to hang up and sat down. "I have a contact who can get it for us. You will have finished the book by next week."

"Papa! I'm impressed." She poured her father a large glass of water and sat down next to him. "Though I must say that for a man who fights so desperately for our culture, our rights and our language – your enthusiasm for me to master all things English sometimes seems a little ... bizarre."

"The perfect spy," he retorted, "blends in perfectly. And you may need to start blending in more quickly than you think."

"Ah." She stood up and went to the drinks cabinet, her hand hovering by the cognac. "So, we come to the debriefing. Is he handsome? Is he strong? Will he kiss well?"

A flicker of pain twisted Frenet's face. For a second his lips opened, vulnerable, then the moment passed and they closed, the words unsaid. When Pénélope turned back to him, glass in hand, his eyes held the same amused, sartorial gleam she was used to.

"I think he will," he conceded. "Yes, I think...."

She waited, forgetting to breathe, unable to conceal her nervousness while he searched for the right words. He found them. "I think ... he is perfect."

"I see." She gulped back half the cognac, her hands shaking. For once he didn't mention the alcohol.

"Come here," he said instead holding out his arms to her, and when she did he folded her slim frame onto his old bony knees as if she were still a child.

"I think he is a kind man," he told her, settling her head on his shoulder and beginning to stroke her hair in rhythmic comfort. "And I think he is an honest man too. I am sure he will be very successful – who knows – maybe even one day Prime Minister? And he is well-intentioned towards us. Of course his intentions, at present, are to exploit us well, but with the right woman by his side, the right voice in his ear, the right influence standing beside him, speaking up for the French cause in oh-so-perfect English. I think he could be brought to do us a great deal of good."

A sob shook Pénélope's body. She sat up to rub a tear angrily from her cheek but he forestalled her with a kiss. "It is never easy," he said, "to be a maker of history, a provider of dreams – to know your fate. But that doesn't mean you won't be happy."

She sobbed again and he held her to him tightly, as if she too were to be wrenched from him like his wife. But she pulled away, her need for comfort in conflict with the pain his words were causing.

"So it is decided then?"

"Yes," he let her go. "It is decided. All that remains now is for us to make it happen."

The next step came more quickly than the doctor had hoped for. The spontaneity of youth, often to be curbed and reprimanded in his own children was, when it came to Ramsey, an admirable affair.

The following morning being Sunday, Frenet was back in his favourite chair after church, a coffee in his hand replacing the water of the night before. Church had been a surprise. A surprise for everyone, to be sure, but the doctor was not used to being caught unawares and he was annoyed at his reaction. Ramsey had been there – at their church, the Catholic church – and he Frenet, so sure the other was a Protestant, had only stared and nodded coldly, his astonishment evident for all to see. It was a tedious error and one he'd have to rectify quickly, but in the long term it would make things simpler. Despite a missed opportunity therefore, his initial problem remained unchanged – how to incorporate Ramsey into an informal meal without subjecting him to the vitriol Benoit was sure to pour on him after, if not before, his second glass of wine. It was an enjoyable challenge that offered several interesting solutions so it was with a curiosity tinged with regret that he received the news.

"Papa! L'Anglais! Il arrive!"

"English, Michel," he replied wearily. Then, "What Englishman?"

"The one you saw last night. The one at church. The Ram." Michel laughed at his joke.

Frenet looked at him. Michel, tall, strong, loyal, with the black hair and eyes of his sister and father but without their quick intelligence, was someone to be relied upon, but not kept informed. He, like all the family knew his sister was to be offered up to the cause of freedom and justice, as in their own ways they all were. This was a fact known from birth, a reality of their world – not a choice to be questioned – but Michel in particular could know no details. He was too clumsy, too obvious. In fact he, in his naiveté, would be the perfect man to show Ramsey how innocent and straightforward a family they were.

"Then go and meet him," Frenet said. "And invite him in."

Ramsey came in full of energy, noise and bulk, blowing the cold from his hands, and stamping the snow from his feet while taking off the thick coat he wore against the freezing weather outside.

"The winters here, Dr. Fren–, that is – Arnauld," he started while shaking hands, "are *not* what I'm used to. Thank God the factory is warm."

"God and his plentiful resources that create our energy." The doctor smiled.

"That's right. And which may create a lot more if this new hydroelectricity stands the test of time." If Frenet was making a discreet religious gambit Ramsey had missed it completely. "They are running a railway on it, did you know, in Ireland? Imagine!" Ramsey caught himself and shrugged. "Still, I didn't come here to talk industry with you. You must be wondering what brings me here so soon?"

"Well, naturally I had assumed it was the irresistible pleasure of my company – unless, that is, you have need of my professional services?"

"No, no, not at all. Not yet anyway," he amended, blowing on his fingers. "Though no doubt I shall be suffering from frostbite before too long."

"Perhaps we can offer you a coffee? Michel made it, so it is not particularly good. But it is hot, which is perhaps the main criteria?" And on Ramsey's enthusiastic agreement, "Michel? If you would be so kind? So, James," Frenet continued slowly, "you were saying what brought you here?"

"I was." Ramsey smiled. "And I confess that while it was not strictly for the pleasure of your company, your conversations give me great enjoyment – not to mention practice."

"Practice?" Frenet raised an eyebrow

"I shall need to engage in many battles of wits if I am to succeed here," Ramsey explained, "as you must be well aware. And I have a feeling, if you don't mind my saying so, that if I can hold my own with *you* – then I shall do very well with everyone else."

"You flatter convincingly."

"I do? Good. Perhaps because it's true." He looked Frenet in the eye for a moment to underline his sincerity, then moved on. "But to the point of my visit. Your comments last night left me with a great desire to see your daughter."

"My daughter?"

"Not with intentions – don't get me wrong – well, not with *those* intentions, anyway. With scientific intentions. I'd like to find out for myself quite what she's up to. If her interests do lie in a similar field to mine – well, her knowledge could be very useful."

"Indeed?" Frenet's tone said all that was needed. "Well, in that case let us waste no more time. Michel," he continued, as the latter returned with a steaming café au lait. "Do you know where Pénélope is?"

Michel looked surprised. "In the barn I should imagine – or her room. Why?"

"I shall go and find her." Frenet got to his feet. "Perhaps you would be so good as to entertain James meanwhile."

"Not bad for an old man of over 70?, hein?" Michel said as soon as Frenet had gone.

"Is he?" Ramsey was surprised. "He seems much younger." He sipped his coffee. "So you and Pénélope," he pronounced her name tentatively, practising the French way, "are the babes of the family?"

"Pénélope, yes," Michel agreed. "Myself, I am the unmarried, eternal bachelor. The son who never leaves home. I look young because I avoid responsibility, but in fact I am eight years her elder."

"How many of you are there?" It could be touchy to discuss numbers of children with a Québécois, Ramsey realised, but if Michel was eager to talk then why not take advantage of it? Any information was useful at this stage, when he needed all the insights possible into this new community he was adopting.

"There are six of us left – five brothers and little Pénélope. There were ten in all. Mathilde, the first born and only other girl, died at birth. Then boys, nothing but boys." He smiled as though it were a joke. "Until Pénélope. Lucky they got her in, hein? Five months more, and it would have been too late."

"Yes?" Ramsey couldn't help feeling he was getting a rather more details than he required.

"A measles epidemic," Michel enlarged. "Carried off my mother along with several hundred others. And my father, a doctor, wasn't even here. Non, he was off with his political friends chewing over the British North America Act – making sure it contained everything necessary for our new Québec's special preservation. Ironic hmm?" For a moment he looked sad, his face changing from jolly bonhomie to something altogether more insightful. "I don't think he ever forgave life – or himself – for that. So you must understand, eh? If he is sometimes a little prickly...."

"On the contrary," Ramsey's enthusiasm was sincere, "I find him most invigorating. Dr Frenet is – "

"Allo."

Pénélope stepped into the room to find the English stranger red-cheeked by the fire, animated, gesticulating dangerously with the coffee in his hand. He wasn't handsome, not even a well-wisher could call him that, with his broken nose and florid complexion. Nor was he her type – blonde, pale-eyed men striking her from the mature profundity of eighteen as somehow superficial, lacking an appropriate air of mystery. But he was, well, vibrant. His enthusiasm seemed to emanate from his skin as disdain or hatred might from another.

"I am Pénélope." She went forward, light on her feet, smiling politely and offering her hand as she moved. "You wished to see me?"

"Yes. James – James Ramsey. I met your father last night. I say – " he added as he took in her stained skirts. "I hope I'm not disturbing you."

"Actually I am about to start something. But I have a few minutes now, unless...."

"Why don't we talk in your lab." James correctly guessed her hesitation. "Then you can get on with it – unless it's private. I know to my cost that some experiments shouldn't be made public too soon."

"It's true." She inclined her head in agreement. "But this one is no secret. Indeed, it is the village joke. I want to produce aluminium through electrolysis. Sainte-Claire Deville's work is obviously a vast improvement on Wöhler's, but I can't help feeling that there is a much better way yet, if only...."

"Electrolyse aluminium!" Ramsey had come prepared to meet a competent chemist, but hadn't expected this. "You must be –" he'd been going to say *rich as Croesus*, but curbed himself in time. "That is, you must have a sophisticated laboratory."

"Unfortunately not." She smiled politely. "Still, it does me well enough. Would you like to see it?"

"I'd love to." He glanced at Michel. "That is – if you would excuse me...?"

"Chemists!" Michel dismissed them with a grimace. "A beautiful day like today, perfect for skiing – and they shut themselves up in their workshop." He wiggled his finger against his head. "You, James, have at least the sense to do it for money. But Pénélope –"

"Would do it for money if she could." Pénélope interrupted. "Unlike some I might mention, who would do anything in their power to avoid earning money at all."

Michel was undeterred. "It is true money is not my strong point," he confided to Ramsey. "But then, we cannot all be good at everything, hmm?"

"I would love to come skiing with you one day," Ramsey side-stepped. "If you wouldn't mind. Since I'm doomed to these snowy wastes I might as well make the most of them."

Following Pénélope down the narrow, wood-panelled hallway to the back door, Ramsey had a chance to study her more openly. She was medium-height, slim – almost wiry – with a tensile strength to her grace that made him think more of a lynx than a delicate woman. Her thick black hair, Indian straight, was tied in a casual knot off her face, revealing glimpses of the back of her neck as she walked. It was a tight, competent figure rather than feminine, that went well with her tight, competent face that had smiled so charmingly beneath suspicious eyes. The doctor had not been exactly right about her beauty, he mused. She was not beautiful – she was striking.

Pénélope opened the back door, annulling his thoughts with a blast of cold air, and hurried them across to a barn the other side of the yard.

"Here it is." She stood back for him to enter with proprietorial pride.

Ramsey surveyed the lab, taking in all the various equipment. The usual vials, bell jars, pipettes, retorts and tubes cluttered up a long work bench on which were also a Bunsen burner, a voltameter, and even a spectroscope. To one side a battered-looking Bunsen battery, a voltaic pile, and a clay crucible lay ready for use – or rather not quite: closer inspection showed the clay to be cracked. Next to it was a wine glass. Ramsey lifted his eyebrows, but continued his visual inspection without comment. In the middle of the barn, set on stone slabs that had been added to the earth floor and as far away from the wooden walls as possible, was a small old bellows-driven furnace. Currently it was giving out barely enough heat to combat the drafts that seemed to enter from all sides.

"Very nice," he said. "You have a lot of space to work in – and," he shivered, "I imagine you are glad of the drafts when the furnace gets going properly."

"I am," she nodded, putting on a pair of gloves. "But today being Sunday I am not really here. Papa permits me to 'play', as he calls it, but proper work is strictly forbidden. Naturellement. Besides, a boiling furnace would alert the neighbours."

"There is that." Ramsey found himself smiling in response. There was something charming about her directness, with its assumption of complicity. "Though I should imagine that in a small town like this the neighbours have little need to be alerted."

"Père Martin finds me a great trial," she acknowledged. She looked as if she were going to say more, then her expression changed as she remembered something. "And you? You were in Church today. What is your opinion on such things?"

Ramsey was prepared. He wouldn't have been there if he wasn't.

"I wouldn't work myself on a Sunday, naturally," he said without hesitation. "As manager it is my job to set a good example and fit in with the community – not to mention the commands of our Lord." Then he paused, so that a twinkle in his eyes had time to belie the pomposity of his words. "But I hardly think it is my place to judge others, do you?"

"No," she answered simply. "But then that's what everyone says. We shall see."

She poured some water into a flask, lit the Bunsen burner, and placed it to heat up before going over to some shelves in the far corner that he hadn't noticed before. She came back holding a very small white rock which she dropped gently in the water, then moved back over to the wine glass while she waited for it to dissolve. Ramsey used the moment to shift his position so that he could get a better look at the shelves. They were well stocked. He could make out a fair quantity of prepared aluminium oxide, along with sodium, carbon and iron. Then a huddle of lead vessels caught his attention. Without being impertinently curious it was hard to get close enough to be certain, but he was fairly sure he could make out the formula for hydrogen fluoride. The previous night's conversation came sharply back to him.

"Is it true," he asked, "that you blew up a barn when you were ten?"

She blushed, and he cursed himself for his clumsiness, but she rallied well.

"It is true that Bunsen lost his right eye in an explosion," she retorted. "But that did not in any way lessen the value of his experiments."

"True." He turned his attention more tactfully back to the experiment in progress. She had connected the wine glass up to the electrodes, and Ramsey watched intrigued as she poured in a small amount of the solution.

"Ingenious," he said as she stood back to wait. "Quite ingenious."

She flashed a look at him, but he appeared sincere. Indeed there was something about his fleshy, open face that seemed congenitally trustworthy. He felt her relax an iota as she shrugged.

"Need is the father of invention – isn't that what they say?"

Ramsey nodded. "More or less. And today you are electrolysing …" She hadn't told him deliberately, he knew, and it was time to hazard a guess. "Aluminium fluoride?"

"Yes." She gave him her first real smile. "It's true then – you are a proper chemist?"

"I try to be. It is certainly where my interests lie."

"Oh me too." And for a moment all her defences dropped. "Aluminium fluoride is the obvious next thing to try – as far as I *know*, no-one has tried it before. It won't work of course, but if only…."

"Yes?"

She hesitated, torn between the wish for secrecy and pride in her ideas. Loneliness won over. For years her experiments had been the subject of at best indifference, at worst mockery. To be with someone who understood, who cared – it was an opportunity she was too hungry to pass up.

"If only I had the heat! The answer, I'm almost sure, will not be in an aqueous solution. If I could experiment with using fused salts as solvents …."

"I see. It's been tried before, to be sure – and failed many times. But then perhaps they didn't…." Ramsey was talking more to himself than to her, turning the idea over in his mind. He seemed to come to some conclusion because he suddenly said: "What kind of fused salts?"

Pénélope heard the eagerness in his voice and taking it for greed, clamped down again.

"I don't know." She bent over her equipment, effectively avoiding his gaze and hiding her face. "But then, why would I? I'm just a girl."

The bitterness rang out like a slap and for a moment Ramsey was quiet, discomforted. He had been warned, to be sure, of the prickly nature of the Québécois with their eternal complaints, grudges and feisty politics, but this was not that. This was to do with character: she was defensive yet determined, hopeless yet combative.... Ramsey smiled to himself. He was just as curious about the workings of human nature as the mysteries of science – indeed his promotion had been as much due to his aptitude with people as his skill as a chemist: his role here was to attempt to bridge the cultural divide. He began to see that as well as having his work cut out, he might have some fun too in this wintry wasteland.

"Then why do you do all this?" He asked, opening his arms expansively to include everything.

She looked at him then, really looked at him, her hard black eyes full of something that could have been fury, but could also have been frustration, or even passion. For a moment he thought he was going to get a revelation, but then she sagged, and looked away.

"Have you any idea," she said, her voice choked and heavy, "how incredibly *boring* life is here?"

It was an answer that was no answer at all. Other bored young women found different ways to make mischief than blowing up barns and dabbling in the cutting edge of science. However Ramsey let it go. If this girl needed her secrets she could have them, for now. So when, on their way out of the barn, he saw an envelope addressed to Eviytuk, West Greenland, he kept quiet – although it set his mind racing. He would have to check, but surely the only thing that came from such a god-forsaken place was cryolite? With a quickening of excitement he realised this might be the answer. It was certainly the clincher that made up his mind and stopped him in the middle of the yard, oblivious now of the cold that had so chilled him before.

"You may be wondering," he announced, "what brought me here today?"

She exploded. "To watch me fail?" she snapped. "To confirm that I am, after all, a mere girl at play and no competition to a real man, a business man, a man of industry like yourself!"

"Whoa! If you thought that then why did you let me in here? You know what you're doing – and you knew I would recognise that. Why, if you had adequate equipment...." He trailed off and she glanced up at him, unsure but hopeful.

"Don't patronise me," she said, half a question, half plea. "I can assure you that I have had enough of that in this place to last me a lifetime."

"Which is why, I suppose, that only last night Monsieur Longrin told me that if you were a man you would be famous by now – that you were a most intelligent, thorough chemist."

"Did he?" Pénélope's eyes gleamed with happy surprise. "Oh, isn't he a dear. He's always believed in me – always. He's not like the rest of them, old-fashioned, boorish –"

"I came here today to see if that were true." Ramsey cut through what looked like being a longish tirade. "Because if it were, and I see that it is, then I could do with someone like you on my team. What do you reckon?"

"What?" She spoke as if he were mad.

"Would you like to work on my research team?"

"But I keep failing!"

"Good God woman," pig-headedness was not a quality Ramsey appreciated. "Of course you keep failing – your equipment isn't up to it. Most people wouldn't even have lasted ten minutes, let alone persisted. Don't you realise that you're on the right track, for God's sake?"

"I would stop shouting God so loudly, if I were you," she answered smiling broadly. "My father is not too keen on such blasphemies."

"Will you stop trying to change the subject!" Ramsey dismissed impatiently. "Do you want to work with me or don't you?"

"Yes." She stopped absolutely still, ignoring the cold that had made her shiver, and looked him in the eye. "Yes," she repeated. Then she sighed. "If my father will let me."

Ramsey left soon after, mission accomplished, and enough of a politician to leave her father well alone. Instead he suggested that Pénélope bring Dr Frenet to his office when they were ready – to see the facilities and discuss things further. Dr. Frenet himself, who'd decided to come up with a slight indisposition that would make goodbyes unnecessary, watched Pénélope see Ramsey out from the top of the stairs. If the spring in her step wasn't enough, her humming as she shut the door told him all was going well. He retreated out of sight. She would give him the details in her own good time – she always did.

The pulp and paper factory had been the talk of the community ever since old Tremblay had sold his prime saw mill and site to the Sheen brothers. It was one of the best sites around, located on a rapid stretch of the rivière Toulega, flat, and with plenty of room to spread out on. Tremblay's father had been one of the first on the scene and he'd bought expansively wherever he could, intending to have an expansive family to share it out to. Things hadn't worked out that way, and now these Toronto-based incomers had taken over, fronted by Ramsey their right-hand man.

Pénélope knew a lot from community gossip about how they had half-demolished, half-transformed Tremblay's site and mill into the factory now standing. Half the town had been involved in the construction work, the other half were now employed by the Sheen's and everyone was an expert on what had happened and what was yet to come. The Frenet's however, had not been directly involved and hearing about something second or third-hand was not the same thing at all, Pénélope discovered, as going there herself. She felt as if she was entering the unknown – a totally new industry, headed not just by a new type of person, but a completely new mentality. And if her father was right, this was only the beginning.

Her father, of course, had accepted the invitation never meaning to come. "I need to become elusive," he told her, "hard to pin down. It's your turn now." And with a final squeeze of her hand he stopped and left her to cross the street alone. It was the moment she had been waiting for – the chance, finally, to unfurl her butterfly's wings – but instead of a sense of excited anticipation, she was surprised to notice more of a gnawing nervousness that bordered on fear. It was hard not to look back as she left him and walked across the slush to the doorway in the high iron gates that opened forbiddingly to greet her.

"Bonjour Mademoiselle Frenet," the watchman greeted her. "Comment allez-vous?"

"Monsieur Michaud?" Pénélope peered closer to investigate the small portion of face showing through the layers of scarves and hat that enveloped the small, wizened man.

"Oui. Jean-Louis lui-même. À votre service!" The man laughed with a sort of triumph that seemed quite out of keeping with his position.

"Mais je ne savais pas que vous travaillez encore! C'est magnifique!"

Monsieur Michaud shook his shoulders with a modesty that was belied by the gleam in his eyes.

"Ce n'est pas grande chose – mais ça me fait sortir de la maison, au moins. Ce qu'est une bonne chose pour ma femme!"

Pénélope nodded, understanding his wife's need to get him out of the house as much of his own need to work. "Je suis ici pour voir Monsieur Ramsey. J'ai un rendezvous à 10 heures."

Michaud waved his stump of an arm across the courtyard towards the back of the factory where an ordinary-sized red door, too new for the paint to have faded, spoke of things on a more manageable scale. "Allez par là mam'zelle. Quelqu'un là-bas vous montrera le chemin."

Pénélope went as directed, buoyed up by contact with a friendly face. The door was unlocked and led straight to some dark, narrow stairs at the top of which was another door marked "Bureaux". She knocked.

"Entrez." She opened the door to a blast of heat that made her reach to undo her coat buttons even as she looked around. She was in a rectangular room that was both office, corridor and anteroom. In front of her on either side, demarcated from the aisle by a low wooden balustrade, were desks and drawing tables, mostly empty. Two men looked up with a casual curiosity from where they had been murmuring quietly in English, then bent back down to their work. A middle-aged woman who was seated at the far end, near the half-glazed door that led out to the other side, stood up and came forward to meet her.

"Mademoiselle Frenet?" she asked with a strong Montréal accent. "Please come this way. Monsieur Ramsey is expecting you."

She led Pénélope through the far door into a proper corridor that was windowless, with doors off each side, leading to more stairs, this time going down. If the noise and surge of heat coming up them were anything to go by they were another way into the factory itself. Knocking on the first door to the left the secretary waited for Ramsey's cheerful "Entrez," showed Pénélope in and left.

"I didn't know you'd hired Jean-Louis Michaud," Pénélope said as soon as the hello's were over. "Has he been here long?"

"Well, no." Ramsey seemed bemused but not put out. "But then no-one here has. I felt that we needed a watchman and someone – it may well have been your father – recommended him. Why? Is there anything wrong with him?"

The question was disingenuous and naïve though she was, Pénélope realised it.

"You know there isn't. He's the hardest, kindest of workers. Only … since he lost his hand – well – everyone took for granted that he'd never work again."

"And I have spoilt everyone's expectations?" Ramsey tutted. "How unsporting of me. Yet, Monsieur Michaud, I think, is quite happy with the situation." He was smiling now, openly playing with her, and Pénélope took offence.

"How much do you pay him?" She asked angrily. "Or are you taking advantage of him because he can't do anything else? Abusing the cheap labour we Québécois are so good for?"

"On the contrary." Ramsey wasn't smiling now. "I hardly think, however, that M. Michaud would want me to discuss his salary with someone who, when all is said and done, has no concern whatsoever in his affairs. I'm afraid you'll have to ask him yourself."

"I'm sorry." Pénélope meant it. It would be a useful skill, she reflected not for the first time, to be able to work out when she was going too far before the event, rather than to merely recognize the fact afterwards. "It's just…, I know how much he missed work, and nobody except father – and Madame Michaud of course – seemed to understand. They all thought he'd be glad to retire. I was actually pleased to see him there – only it came out all wrong."

"Then it's as well I asked you here for your scientific abilities and not your diplomatic skills." Ramsey gestured to a chair and his words, though factual, had a kindness in them that put her slightly at her ease. "Shall we start again?"

"Thank you." She nodded her head gratefully, paused as if remembering her lines, then said, "My father sends his regrets. Unfortunately he has had an unexpected birth to attend to. He hopes that he can take you up on your kind offer some other time."

"Does he even know you're here?"

"Yes." She was surprised at the question. "Why?"

"Because I don't want to go behind his back."

"Oh." She looked almost disappointed, then feisty. "Why not?"

Ramsey looked back at her, meeting her gaze. The answer was, his eyes seemed to say, too obvious to need speaking. Pénélope's mood changed again and she giggled.

"He thinks you must have a – " she searched for the right word, "a tendresse for me. He thinks this offer of work is a novel kind of flirtation, a move to tempt me into your company so that you can spend more time with me."

Ramsey laughed, a short bark of dismissal. "Of course. He would. Well," and he started to look through some of the papers ready on his desk, "what he thinks doesn't effect us – unless, of course, you think the same thing?" He looked up suddenly.

"It had crossed my mind," she admitted with a smile. "It certainly seems the most probable theory."

"Oh?" Ramsey opened his eyes wide. They were less piggy, Pénélope noticed, and less pale when in action. "You have a better opinion of your charms than your scientific abilities?"

"Not really, no. But they would have boasted at the dinner party about how beautiful I am. I am intelligent and wilful," she explained at his surprise, "not qualities held in high esteem for a woman, so I must be held to be beautiful instead. It is a kind of compensation. And while it's not particularly true, it has to be said there is not a lot of competition around. Then too, you would want to please my father. He is one of the most important men in town and having a tendresse for his daughter would flatter him nicely. So I thought that, although you certainly don't appear to be attracted to me, perhaps the offer of work was, after all, more or less a game."

"Ah ha." James stood up. He was used to plain speaking about things rather than emotions, but he was nothing if not a quick learner.

"And what if I was genuinely attracted to you?"

"After one meeting over a scientific experiment?" She shrugged her shoulders graphically. "You are not the kind of man who falls in love just like that." She clicked her fingers. "Especially not with a mere girl. Why, you must be almost ten years older than me. An ambitious man like you will fall in love with the right person – perhaps an older woman.... Yes," she nodded her head, her imagination expanding as she spoke, "a rich older woman with marvellous social skills – and technique – as well as beauty. Am I right?"

"Well, it's hard to say, not having fallen in love with anyone yet." Ramsey wasn't sure whether to laugh or blush. "But if it does happen to be a beautiful older woman with – er – all that you say, I'll be sure to let you know."

"Good." Pénélope was more at ease now, gaining confidence along with the upper hand. "So, is it a false tendresse, or – " she leaned forward and her voice took on an urgency, "do you seriously mean to offer me proper work."

"I seriously mean to offer you a proper work." Ramsey held her gaze, then returned to his papers. "It won't be easy of course. There'll be resistance from more than your father. But," he smiled at her, his eyes twinkling, "I imagine you like a good fight. And if you can hold your end up once you get here, I can certainly do my bit to get you in. Would you like a tour of the factory?"

"Yes I would." Pénélope got up to follow him, but hesitated at the door. "I still don't understand though. Why me? Are you inviting others from the town to become chemists here too?"

Ramsey looked up and down the corridor to check no-one was nearby, then shut the door again and lowered his voice.

"There is no doubt," he said, "that if I come across others in this area who I think could do the job – or any other important job here – I would invite them to apply, man or woman." She seemed almost disappointed, he noted, as if she would rather he had a tendresse for her after all. "Look." He moved away from the door to the board above his desk. "This is a list of all the managers and senior technicians who work in the factory. What do you notice about them?"

Pénélope studied the list for a while, then shrugged. "It's like any other list of managers. I don't see anything different."

"Exactly." Ramsey's voice rose now as he warmed to his theme. "All English. Like everywhere else. Now that's no problem yet – but to succeed in business you have to stay ahead of the game and the time will come, soon, when we need to be able to offer something more than we have at present – to make a difference.... And to do that, I have to include the Québécois – and I mean *include*. Not befriend, not manipulate, not patronise, not use and abuse. Include. It's the way of the future and it's the only way forward. I need contacts here in this town, I need people on my staff – managers – who know what's going on. I need people on my side who live here and belong here – who know their employees and who will be able to motivate them to give us their loyalty, not just their time for a measly weekly wage. In short, I need friends – not political friends," he added, correctly reading the narrowing of her eyes, "not friends of convenience to be used when useful and cast off when necessary, but a genuine network of people on my side because they believe in what I believe in. You are Québécoise, you speak French, you are known by the whole community as Dr. Frenet's daughter – all these are assets – sincerely good reasons to have you on my staff. But if you were no good at the job I would merely be shooting myself in the foot. After the initial communal response to such a "compliment" you would be nothing but trouble for me. The real reason I want you, in addition to all your other assets, is because –" he hesitated, suddenly aware of his torrent of enthusiasm and finishing his sentence in a tame manner that, if anything, gave more weight to his words, "is because I strongly suspect you're a scientific genius."

He waked back to the door as she flushed with delight and this time opened it wide. "Shall we?"

Pénélope followed him through.

She returned home late that afternoon, exhausted, bemused, almost drunk on Ramsey's enthusiastic, anarchic outpourings – yet with an underlying core of contentment that she didn't need to analyse or question. To be with someone intelligent who understood what she was talking about – to bounce ideas off him, absorb new thoughts from him, argue and debate with him, to be treated as a serious equal – it was something she had never known before and it was a heady mix.

Ramsey was quite unlike her. Her intelligence worked in corridors, searching like a lighthouse beam for the answers she needed. She didn't deviate, she didn't give up – she certainly didn't socialise. Her social graces, if such they could be called, were clumsy and direct. She knew it and didn't care. Ramsey, on the other hand, or so it seemed to her, did nothing but socialise. On their tour he introduced her to everyone they met, stopped and chatted, exchanged ideas, asked questions, made mental notes and then continued his conversation with her wherever they had laid off. The factory itself frightened, almost horrified her. Everywhere she looked was violence and noise along with a heat that was already oppressive at this time of year. Heaven only knew what it would be like in summer. He gave her a full tour from the wood yard through to the rolls at the end of the Fourdrinier machines, raising his voice to describe how the grindstone softened the lignin, lowering it to hint at chemical breakthroughs to come. He seemed to be able to hold everything in his head at the same time, from a foreman's extra day off, to problems with the boiler – and he saw all the people who came before him, not as reefs on which to shipwreck his concentration, but as islands of plenty from which to restock his ideas. Pénélope couldn't help but be impressed. She was also reassured. Her father had been right: he was a nice man. Still a business man, of course, and English, but nice for all that. And she had the sense to realise how lucky she was that the prison her father was choosing for her should also be the doorway to so much freedom – so much potential power.

After she'd had time to calm down a little she went to find her father at his surgery, where he usually worked until supper time. She walked quickly through the cold streets impervious to the icy, irregular snow beneath her boots, welcoming the freezing air on her cheeks that cut through the whirr of her thoughts even as it added to her feverish flush.

Frenet was alone, sitting with a text book in the large, swivel leather-backed chair that was almost more of a home to him than the house where they lived.

"He's offered me work and I have accepted," Pénélope told him bluntly. "But he says he has no tendresse for me – not even a fake one."

"Ah ha." Frenet gestured her to take the wide-backed armchair on the other side of his expensive, yet practical wooden desk. Unlike some, he ensured that his patients too had somewhere comfortable to sit. "So you two have been conspiring against me?"

"On the contrary. He is most concerned not to go behind your back. He will tell you everything to your face – when you are ready." She grinned mischievously. "Including the fact that I am a genius."

"A genius, hmm?" Frenet rubbed his fingertips gently together, meeting the challenging look she sent him with a smile. "He certainly knows how to choose the compliments that will be best accepted."

"Oh Papa." Her face fell in frustration. "Is a compliment – a word of praise even – so very terrible? Just because something is flattering, that doesn't have to make it false. Is it so impossible that I am a genius? Why? Because I am a girl? Surely you of all people understand things better than that?"

The doctor met her gaze with a searching look then, to her surprise, dropped his eyes first.

"It is true that I have been hard on you," he said. "I have been hard on you all. You are all, except perhaps Benoît and Michel, capable of rising to the demands I make on you. To be less demanding would therefore be, in some way, to fail you – to allow you to fail yourselves. With Benoît, I admit, I have made mistakes. He was the eldest, and with your mother gone –"

"Benoît!" Pénélope interrupted scornfully. "I am not talking about Benoît, Papa. I am not talking about us, your children. I am talking about *me*, Pénélope, your daughter. Couldn't you for once talk about me too – and admit from your stingy supply of praise, just once, that I am all right – that you are maybe, even, proud of me?"

He got up then, walked around the desk to her, and took one of her hands in his.

"You are so very like your mother," he said after a long pause. "Sometimes I am almost afraid of loving you too much – of trying to carve you in her image. Fortunately," he continued as she tried to interrupt, "you won't let me. Since you are also so very much yourself. And yes, you are 'all right'. You are more than 'all right'. You are –" he stopped and searched carefully for his words. "You are a brilliant, stubborn, brave, moody, committed, hard-working, loyal, opinionated little rebel," he said. "You are the best daughter a man could have hoped for – and I *am* proud of you. And now," he squeezed her hand and turned away, "I think you should go and see about supper."

For the next few days Pénélope forgot she was the pivot of a complicated plot. Far from feeling a noble victim to be sacrificed for the greater good of the people of Québec, she felt that life had never been so full of potential. Ramsey had told her not to get her hopes up – that there would be bosses to check with and investors to soothe over before he could go ahead with such a radical step – but those were just words and she knew it. He was as determined as she was that she should help him with his research, and already she could see that a determined Ramsey was a force to be reckoned with.

None of which prevented her from fretting. He'd gone to Montréal and Toronto for business, including that of pleading her cause, and had promised to send a telegram as soon as he had news. It would almost have been better if he'd made her wait for his return, she reflected, her mind fluttering nervously around the all-consuming subject. At least that way she'd have been able to forget it for a while. Instead she watched for news daily, sometimes hourly, trying to seem cool and unconcerned but fooling no-one and knowing it. So when the news finally came, it was little sacrifice to her dignity to dance the telegram into the dining room where her father and two brothers lingered, shrieking her joy as she thrust the message before her father's face.

"Il est arrivé, il est arrivé, il est arrivé!" she sang. "Je suis une vrai chimiste! Oh Papa – je suis tellement contente."

Her father returned her kiss calmly but said nothing. Instead it was Benoît who spoke.

"You should be ashamed of yourself," he said in the tone of one who regularly said such things. "Going to work for that English bunch – selling your soul for their profit."

"But it's not like that," Pénélope returned, exasperated, "is it Papa? Michel? Benoît, you're so extreme."

Benoît shrugged. "I should hope so. Extreme circumstances call for extreme measures, eh Père? You have said so yourself, many times."

"I have," Frenet nodded. "And it is true. Just as subtle, complex circumstances require subtle, complex measures."

Michel laughed. "You won't get him there. Notre père is an expert fence-walker – eh Papa?"

"Let us say practised," Frenet amended. "But I think it is safe to assume that all our skills are going to be needed in the near future."

"Papa, you exaggerate," Pénélope said fondly, from the supreme confidence of being at the centre of the world. "After all, it's only a job."

Frenet looked at her a while, knowing that she had still not understood, that he would have to cause her pain and wishing it were not so. "It is. It is also, of course, out of the question."

The three of them stared at him in astonishment. Michel put down his coffee cup, opened his mouth to speak, changed his mind, stood up so abruptly that his chair fell over onto the floor, then changed his mind again.

"I knew you were hard," he said, his voice trembling with rage. "But I didn't know you were cruel. You – you –" Words failed him. He turned, left the room, and slammed the door behind him.

"Papa," It was Benoît, strangely, who came more efficiently to his sister's defence. "Like she said, it's only a job." His voice was calm, reasonable. "It is highly unusual, it is true, but you have hardly adhered to all the conventions yourself. What do you mean it's out of the question?"

"Pénélope knows what I mean."

Benoît looked at his sister. She had turned white, her robust strength suddenly frail. It was as if she had been kicked in the heart. But she nodded, bravely. Benoît went up to her, sat her down gently at the table, then looked from her to her father and understood.

"You have been plotting."

"Yes." Frenet let Pénélope speak. She swallowed, staring down at the table. "I am to marry him."

"Ah-ha." Benoît let out a long breath, shot a quick enquiring glance at his father then turned back to Pénélope. "You are sure? You want to go through with it? You *can* go through with it?"

Water welled up in Pénélope's eyes, gathered at their corners, swelled into fat drops that hesitated, then spilled over onto her white cheeks and down to the corners of her mouth in two salty trails. When she replied it was to her father.

"I had understood that we were to grow fond of each other while we worked together. I thought – you let me think – that this was how it would be."

"You have a great many strengths, Pénélope," he answered. "Acting is not one of them. I have to use means best suited to the people involved."

She nodded, took a deep breath, then looked up at Benoît without flinching.

"I will do it," she said fiercely. "I *will* do it. I swear this on our mother's grave."

"Good." Benoît smiled, and wiped away the remains of her tears. "Then I will help you." He turned to his father. "What is the plan?"

"Firstly, Michel is to know nothing." Benoît nodded, that was obvious. "Secondly, her traditional, conservative father will refuse permission. She is only eighteen – she has no choice but to obey him. She cannot work for Ramsey."

"Unless?"

"Unless he marries her and frees her from my grasp."

Benoît analysed the plan, saying nothing.

"It is risky," he said at last.

The doctor inclined his head. "If it doesn't work we will adapt, take the pressure off, see sense, reel out the line."

"And if it does work?" Benoît chewed his lip, still considering. "It is not enough for them to marry. He must trust her, need her – depend on her...."

Pénélope looked at him anxiously. She hadn't considered the work after marriage at all. For her, marriage had been the all, the end in sight, not a beginning. She began to have an inkling of what she was taking on.

"Oh he will," Frenet smiled. "He will." And then, as he registered Pénélope's increasing alarm added, "who could not fall in love with a girl like her." He raised his coffee in a superficial salute. Pénélope said nothing. She knew her father. That hadn't been what he meant at all.

As Frenet had foreseen, when the time came to face Ramsey her genuine sorrow negated the need for much acting.

"I can't do it," she told him, her face convincingly tense and pale from sleepless nights. "My father won't let me."

"What do you mean, won't let you!" She hadn't seen Ramsey thwarted before – had thought his easy-going charm an essential part of his nature, like Michel's. Suddenly he seemed almost frightening, and she was surprised to note a quickening of interest as a result. "What has he been playing with us for, letting you get this far, if he never intended to let you do it? I've told the whole board how wonderful you are! Does he mean to make me look a fool?"

"He didn't think you were serious," she retorted. "As I said, he thought it was your way of – flirting? That's how he thinks young men are with women. It wasn't his fault!" and Ramsey, remembering Michel's similar words, wondered what it was about this man that inspired such passionate loyalty in his children even as he destroyed their lives.

"Well if it isn't his fault, I don't know whose it is. *Francine*! You'd think a doctor of all men would understand about individual responsibility."

"Yes?" His secretary poked her head round the door.

"Ah, Francine. Hello." He made an effort to calm down. "Could you tell me if I have any important appointments this afternoon?"

"Certainly," there was a pause while she went back to her diary and flicked pages. "You have a sales representative at 2:30pm, sir, Monsieur Simard with the samples you asked for – and the project meeting at 4:00pm, as usual."

"Damn. I'll be back for the project meeting – tell them to get started without me if I'm late. Postpone Monsieur Simard please Francine and set another date. Give him my apologies and tell him it's not a fob off – I'm genuinely interested – but something urgent's come up."

"Certainly sir."

"Come on," Ramsey stood up and reached for his coat. "Let's go."

"Go. Where?" For a moment she was genuinely confused.

"To your father of course." Ramsey set his chin bullishly. "The time has come for us to take off the gloves."

Pénélope left them to it. Any joy she might have felt at being championed so vigorously was counter-weighted by the knowledge of her father's game. She would have liked to overhear Ramsey's enthusiastic, spontaneous words of anger, his defence of her and his attack on her father. But it wouldn't be a fair fight – and she didn't want to see him drawn into the spider's web her father would weave around him, capturing Ramsey's straightforward sentiments in a sticky network of futures already planned and chosen.

Instead she went in to see her father after Ramsey had left. He looked up at her with what she thought of as his "cat got the cream" expression and immediately some of her concerns fell away. Whatever he'd done, he'd done it well.

"Your Ramsey," he said, by way of greeting, "is a remarkable young man."

Pénélope felt a flush of pride. "Not so young," she scoffed to hide it. "And?"

"And he'll go far."

Dr Frenet picked up his newspaper as if that were all.

"Papa!" She walked to him and pushed it down, placing her face close to his in its place. "Aren't you going to tell me what happened?"

"Well." Frenet smiled with enjoyment and shook his head in memory. "Quite a man," he repeated.

"Papa –"

"I swear that if I'd been wearing my shirt collar he would have grabbed me by it. He told me that as a man of medicine I should know better than to stand in the way of science. That I was foolish and cowardly man, afraid to take risks who, for reasons best known to myself seemed bent on destroying my daughter's life."

"And?"

"Well, naturally I told him that, since they were my reasons and my daughter, I was at a loss to understand his interest in the matter."

"And?"

"He told me that as a *responsible* – with great emphasis on the word responsible – man of the world, it was his interest to nurture remarkable talent wherever he saw it, and not to stand by and see it extinguished merely because of a few misplaced social conventions."

"Goodness."

"Indeed."

"And?"

"I asked him if he didn't think he was perhaps exaggerating a little."

"And?"

"And he calmed down somewhat and said that while he had perhaps been a little disrespectful that didn't change the essence of his point."

"And?" They were both smiling now, playing. Pénélope extracting a story he was happy to tell.

"Well, I'm afraid I got rather foolish and conventional. I told him that if he was attracted to my daughter then he should come out and say so like a man, instead of pretending high-minded ideals like a neutered boffin."

"My."

"My indeed."

"And?"

"And while he was for once silent, still reeling from the shock, I told him that in any case it made no difference. I pointed out that while I considered myself far from prejudiced – indeed no-one in town is more well-intentioned to himself and his fellow English than I – the fact remains that my daughter will naturally marry one of our own kind. It is only right."

"Papa!"

"I know."

"You're wicked."

"I know."

"And?"

"And he became extremely stiff and formal and said that he had been guilty of completely misunderstanding me – that he had thought I was a man of sense and wisdom with an eye to the future. Then he apologised for troubling me – and left."

"Oh."

"Don't you worry, my dear." Frenet chuckled at her disappointment. "He hasn't given up on you. This was just round one – which he lost because he rushed in unprepared. A professional like him won't make the same mistakes twice. He will do much better in round two – you wait and see."

Two weeks later Ramsey and Pénélope went cross-country skiing together. Michel had urged her to come with them, then dropped out at the last minute complaining about the poor conditions. Pénélope wasn't sure who had enlisted his aid, Ramsey or Frenet, although she supposed it all came down to her father in the end, but whatever the case he'd been right about the snow: the late winter weather had turned it into a treacherous mixture of ice and slush beneath their skis and the going was hard.

When they had left habitation behind them Ramsey stopped to catch his breath, turned to her, and began.

"I have a proposal," he said.

"What kind of proposal," she laughed, never suspecting a move so soon.

"Business – and – more than business too."

She grew serious.

"Listen," he said awkwardly. "What do you think about marrying me?" Then, before she could reply, continued. "It would be a risk, I realise, for both of us. But it's a risk that might pay off. I want you to consider it."

Pénélope said nothing, not trusting herself, but her eyes signalled him to carry on.

"The pulp and paper industry is on the verge of a revolution," he told her. "Methods will change, become more efficient, make more money – and whoever patents these methods –" he stared hard at her to make sure she understood, "will be very well-placed."

"But what's that got to do –"

"That is one thing. It's an area I've been working on and I'm close to a breakthrough. We need to find a substitute for the soda ash – it's too expensive and I thought that if I could find something cheaper…. Anyhow – time enough for the details – but achieving that breakthrough is my overt reason for having you on my team."

"But I don't know anything about –"

"Let me finish. Then there is the other thing. There is your work on aluminium – a metal so valuable that Napoleon used it in place of gold. If your work succeeds – if you achieve a practical electrolysis – what do you plan to do with it then?"

"Well – I don't know – I hadn't thought…. Even if I could get it to work, the heat required would make it too expensive to be … I mean, the amount of energy would be…."

"What do we have here, on our door step?"

"Um – "

"Energy – land – property – mills – everything I use for pulp and paper could be used for aluminium. If your method works, we could do more than patent it – we could use it! Water is already being used to create electricity. A hydroelectric power station was opened in Northern Ireland only last year. And whatever *they* have in lakes, rivers and waterfalls, we have tenfold. Prices will come down dramatically and with cheap power all the usual limits go out of the window. With that – and your help – I could establish here – in Québec – the world's first aluminium smelter."

"But that's impossible –"

"Impossible? Nothing's impossible – impossible is just a word – a word ignorant people throw at a brilliant girl who does experiments at home. Do you believe them? No – of course not, because you know better. But you are a chemist and you don't think beyond your science. I am a business man, and it is my job to use the talent I have around me to make business. I don't really need you on my pulp and paper team – I know what I'm doing – I'm nearly there. But this aluminium business – if you were on my team when you made your breakthrough – if you made your breakthrough *because* you were on my team – with all the help, support and equipment I could get you – well then, forget about the Sheen brothers – Ramsey Incorporé would become powerful and rich beyond your dreams.

"Ramsey Incorporé," she was piqued. "What about Frenet?"

"That is my proposal. Marry me – take my name – and together we can take on all the world. Of course," he grew diffident and looked down. "If you don't join me – if you make your breakthrough on your own – or with others – with Québécois – well then, obviously the patent would be yours – or belong to whomever you worked for. You may prefer that. Your father certainly would."

Pénélope looked at him for some time, thinking. "So," she said at last. "You are playing all your cards."

He smiled ruefully. "Yes. Your father has left me no choice."

"And if I decide to go with someone else – a Québécois as my father wishes – now I know how valuable my discovery would be. You would lose all that."

He nodded. "Yes. I would lose it." Then he looked up, his pale eyes glittering. "But you would not necessarily win."

"Oh no?"

"Perhaps you haven't read the journals, but you are not the only one on the trail of accessible aluminium. The race is on. There is a man, Hall, in the States who is close to getting somewhere and another, Héroult, in France. Who in Québec is going to suddenly help you when they have turned their backs on you for so long? By the time you have found someone with the money and goodwill to get you what you need, someone else will have made the discovery and it will be too late."

He stopped and looked away over the snowy tree-bound hills that spread out before them. Pénélope too studied them, her heart thumping with adrenaline, her head a whirr of information and attempted analysis. What had her father known, what had he guessed? Was this future, in all its enormity, what he had planned all along? And how come saying "yes" to this man, and doing what her father wanted, felt so much like a step towards her own happiness and freedom?

"If you marry me," Ramsey said slowly, still not looking at her, "you can come and work for me. In law I will be your master instead of your father and in practice I will be your boss and own the work you do." He paused, then turned to look at her before continuing. "I put it like this to be clear. You may come to reproach me for many things in the future, but I don't want you ever to be able to say that I mislead you."

Pénélope felt a little constriction in her heart. Until now she had been so concerned with her role of martyr it hadn't occurred to her to think of Ramsey's position. Surely if anyone were to talk of misleading....

"Are you truly a Catholic?" she asked playing for time. The question wasn't important – and yet it was. It would bring some level of certitude to these shifting sands. "They're saying – some of them are saying – that it's just another trick to gain our confidence – the cunning move of an English devil." She smiled to rob her words of offence.

"Some of them would say anything rather than believe the English," he retorted. "I am not a deeply religious person, I admit, and I'm not above going to church more for the appearance of the thing than for the sermons – especially those of Père Martin." They shared a smile. "But I *am* a Catholic. It was my mother's religion, and since my father died young.... I hadn't planned to marry yet," he returned to the subject in hand, "nor to someone so young – and I don't pretend to love you. But," he reached his hand out and made her look at him. "I wouldn't suggest this if I didn't think it might work – you and me, as a team. I respect you. I admire your professional skill, I trust your judgement and I enjoy your company. It's a risk I'm prepared to take. If it doesn't work a divorce would be difficult, I admit – perhaps impossible. Neither one of us wishes to lose our good name. But I think an annulment could probably be arranged, if we are careful." He raised his eyebrows. "It could be a disaster of course," he admitted with a grin, his familiar enthusiasm spilling back over his cautious words – "but it could be a success. It could be an enormous success. What do you say?"

Naturally she said yes.

She didn't tell Benoît and her father what Ramsey had said about the patents, the potential power, wealth and glory. She was scared that Benoît in particular would put pressure on her to change plans. He surely would want her to sell her skills to a Québec company – to empower themselves in a way that would help liberate them entirely from the accursed English stronghold, not become part of it. The possibility was a complication that she shied away from, without examining her motives too closely. In any case she was sure her father would have already considered such options. Why bother to mention something he had probably foreseen before the whole plan was started? He, she didn't doubt, was playing a far deeper game for much greater odds than even the power and fame Ramsey thought might come their way.

In truth, English or not, and for all his lack of good looks, Ramsey was becoming valuable company to Pénélope, able to give her something her brothers could not. Apart from Michel, who was good-natured and stupid, her brothers were all intense and smouldering, serious and passionate like Pénélope herself. Ramsey had the ability to bring her out of herself and make her laugh, like Michel, but at the same time he could meet her on an intellectual plain. It was a fresh, heady mix – and while it was obviously impossible to fall in love with such a man, the life she'd agreed to share with him seemed infinitely more agreeable than any other realistic options she could imagine. So it was with a much lighter heart than she had ever imagined that she began to prepare for her wedding day.

"How's it going?"

"Oh!" Pénélope jerked up in surprise. "I didn't hear you come in." She finished washing her hands in the large lab sink. "Badly. Have you been braving Papa?"

"I have." Ramsey looked tired, almost grim. "We've been discussing the financial side of things."

"Ah." She hesitated, unsure how much interest she was supposed to show. "And... ?"

"It went well." His face, in contrast to his words, grew even grimmer. "Very well."

"You don't look very pleased."

"No. I think I am supposed to look humiliated."

"Well you don't look that either." She smiled, feeling a sudden sympathy for him. "Has Papa been giving you a hard time?"

"He has managed to show a great deal of generosity while simultaneously conveying the fact that it is purely because he has so little faith in me. Obviously none of this would have been necessary if you had been marrying a reliable Québécois. All without a word out of place of course, so I can't retaliate. It's most annoying."

"Good practice though."

"I beg your pardon?"

It was a thought often on Pénélope's mind these days – how her behaviour and comments would have to change and grow more subtle and nuanced as the stakes grew higher. She intended to use Ramsey as her role model.

"Well, if things go as planned – if we have the success we'd like – I should think you'll have to deal with a great many people who say one thing while meaning another. If you can keep your cool with my father – well...."

Ramsey smiled, casting off his grim expression as if it had never been. "Yes," he agreed, remembering his own words of not so very long ago. "You're absolutely right. Which brings me to my point."

"Yes?" Pénélope sat down on a lab stool and gestured to him to do likewise. "Shall we discuss it here? It's so much more comfortable than in the house."

Ramsey looked at the hard wooden seat offered and his lips quivered. He did however know exactly what she meant.

"It's certainly hotter." Sweat broke out on his forehead as he spoke. It was worse than a summer heat wave.

"I'm trying to dissolve the aluminium oxide in fluorspar." It was less an explanation than the start of a discourse. "Of course it's possible the aluminium fluoride didn't work because of my equipment, but I don't think so. Water-free fused salts *have* to be the next step. A man – I forget his name – Gretel, Pretzel –"

"Graetzel?"

"That's right, yes. He got magnesium – metal mind, not powder – by electrolysing fused magnesium chloride. It has to be the way forward." She paused as she took on board what he'd just said. "You know of this then?"

"I've been following it. I believe his furnace was capable of slightly greater temperatures than yours however."

"Tell me about it!" She had been picking up some of his idioms. "The fluorspar isn't even thinking of melting." She glared at it moodily as if mere willpower could change its state, then sighed. "It will have to wait until after the wedding. The furnace in your lab must be able to reach double – three times the temperature of this old thing.... Oh, I can't wait!"

Ramsey's lips twitched again. "Which brings me neatly to why I came."

"Yes." She shook her head slightly, both to clear it and acknowledging her preoccupation. "I'm sorry. You had something to say."

"Well, more of a question although I think I have the answer: do you want a honeymoon?"

"A honeymoon! I hadn't thought …. Well – no. There's not much point is there?"

"Perhaps not for us, but for the town gossips…?"

Pénélope grimaced. "To risk losing the patent for the sake of what people think. That would be rather stupid, wouldn't it?"

Ramsey was silent for a moment, approving yet perplexed. "And for yourself," he asked. "Have you no desires for yourself? To see Toronto, New York – Europe even?"

"Europe?" Her eyes lit up for a moment. Do you have so much money," she asked simply, "that we could go to Europe?"

"I think I could manage it. If that's what you want."

"No." The dreamy expression on her face switched off and she stared back at him with her more familiar directness. "What I want is to discover how to create aluminium, in vast, cheap quantities as soon as possible. Besides," she added awkwardly, "I'd feel a hypocrite going on a honeymoon. It's not –" she faltered and looked away. "It's not as if I would have earned it."

Ramsey reached out and took her hand. "I have a suggestion," he said.

"Yes?" Pénélope glanced at his face and was reassured.

"Let's work now and play later. If we achieve what we want we'll have all the money we need to go to Europe or anywhere else you fancy." He waited for her to agree but didn't let her hand go, instead fidgeting with the engagement ring on her finger. "I have another suggestion too."

"Yes?"

"Michel tells me you often work through the night."

"Yes, I do. I mean when I'm stuck into something – well – who could sleep anyway? And sometimes – sometimes it seems harder to think during the day – all those people with all those words and thoughts flying around. Whereas at night, especially during winter when the only sounds you can hear are the owls – or sometimes, far off, the howl of a wolf – well, I feel as if I were the only human left alive – me with my little lab – and then...." She trailed off, seeing him lift an eyebrow in astonishment.

"And you like that?"

"Oh, I love it."

"Hmm," he shrugged. "I'm more of a daylight person myself. But I think I can give you what you want. While I was in Toronto I started trying to raise support – in principle, without giving anything away – for this new sulfate process I want to try. I'll need to go back soon, perhaps even to New York, but before I do I have to prove it will work on a commercial basis and we're not quite there. Which means I'll need the labs."

"But – ?"

"So what I suggest is that you let my technicians and I use the lab during the day, and you can have it throughout the night. If you're agreeable."

"Of course. But...?"

"It's a working arrangement that has several advantages," he continued, answering her surprised expression. "Not only will it let us get on with our ostensible work, but it will also help keep the nature of your own work more private. And finally – well – you know how servants gossip .... Your working at night provides an excuse – rather an unconventional one perhaps, but an excuse all the same – for – um – for – well, why we don't share the same bed, conjugally speaking. Assuming, that is, that you'd still rather not."

"Oh no, much rather," Pénélope agreed wholeheartedly. She had never seen him tongue-twisted before and didn't much like it. The confident, ebullient Ramsey was far more to her taste. On the other hand it was hard to imagine how a man could be more thoughtful. His reputation in the town was certainly likely to suffer because of it – unless of course she convinced them all what a happy, well-treated wife she was – which was, she suddenly realised, another part of her new responsibilities. She almost sighed – the list seemed to be endless – then caught herself in time. It occurred to her that she had perhaps been a little too enthusiastic. "That is, I think not," she amended. "Just in case – the annulment and all that."

"All right, all right." He appeared more amused than offended. "Although I'll have you know that other women have thrown themselves at me with abandon."

"Oh yes?" She found it hard to believe and it showed. "When was that?"

"Primary school. Maisie Dixon. She used to knock me flat. Of course that was before I learnt how to take care of myself. I got her the following winter in a snowball fight. She left me alone after that."

Pénélope smiled as expected and the moment lightened. If Ramsey's smile back was tinged with some other expression – perhaps affection, perhaps even faint regret, Pénélope didn't know to look for it, and didn't see it at all.

Of course people talked – but less than normal given that Pénélope was already considered eccentric and the English were renowned for their lack of morals. Everyone tch-tched at the haste, expected a baby in less than nine months, and poured bitter sympathy onto the respectable Dr Frenet – all but his closest friends, that was, who knew him better. For Frenet, keen to speed on a marriage he should appear to oppose, a secret pregnancy was the perfect opt-out and he pretended to believe the rumours in a stiff, unspoken way that gave Ramsey no opportunity to deny them and annoyed him considerably.

"We shall make friends again soon, don't worry," Frenet reassured Pénélope on her last day at home. "I shall soon admit to being an old fool who has seen the error of my ways. In the meantime it is vital you do not become pregnant for real."

"I hardly think that likely," Pénélope scoffed. "He has offered me the choice of annulment should things not work out – and I have every intention of keeping him to it."

"He what?" Frenet looked startled, even alarmed. "When did he say that? You never told me."

"When he proposed." Pénélope was puzzled at his strong reaction. "I didn't mean not to tell you. I thought it was obvious – I took it for granted…."

"God help me against the good intentions of honourable fools. Are you really so naive girl?" Even as he asked the question Frenet knew he was being unfair. Of course she was – he had kept her that way. It was a point to remember though, and Frenet made a mental note to inquisition her more and leave less to her arbitrary revelations: from now on her naivety could be dangerous. And what was Ramsey's motivation in all this? Was he genuinely the gentleman he appeared? Or was he more cunning than Frenet had thought, out-playing him at his own game?

He gazed at Pénélope who stared back at him, perplexed and waiting. She had put on one of her new dresses for their last day together; a silver-blue silk that had cost him a fortune and made her look worth it. But it wasn't the dress, nor the sleek black hair that she had had curled and arranged for tomorrow's wedding – it was her whole body. The tension that was always there had changed somehow. Instead of a coiled, defensive energy, waiting to spring, there was a balanced, light feel to her that was reflected in eyes that no longer glowered, but glowed. The tiger had become a dancer. She looked – happy, excited – exactly as a young woman should on the eve of her marriage. Frenet sighed. She was more like Michel than she knew: the eternal optimist, always rebounding from every blow – blindly seeing what was in front of her and no more. Anyone would think she was getting what she wanted, *sacristie*! Which was fine, ideal even, so long as she made sure he got what he needed along the way.

"Pénélope." He took her hand and she stiffened automatically, the gesture generally heralding bad news. "Have your brothers' wives ever talked to you about the – physical side of married life?"

She relaxed once more. Was that all? "About having babies, you mean?"

"That and other things."

"No." She said it easily, as if it didn't concern her. "Élise tried once, but I couldn't follow what she was talking about. Nothing but allusions and vague stories.… I didn't pay much attention. I think after that they all thought I probably didn't need to know – that I wasn't ready."

"And are you ready now?"

"But there's no need Papa! An annulment means that we would never have consummated our marriage – "

"*I know what an annulment means!*" Frenet never shouted, considered it an unpardonable loss of self-control, and for a moment it was hard to say who was the most shocked, Pénélope or himself. He stood up abruptly and turned his back to her until he'd calmed down, then continued.

"Annulment," he said firmly, "means that Ramsey has his own opt-out clause whenever he chooses to use it." He took a deep breath. "It is, I am afraid, out of the question."

For a moment Pénélope genuinely didn't understand the implications. She remained silent, looking at her father with the same puzzled expression, trust still not quite giving way to fear.

"We cannot give Ramsey the option of annulling this marriage," Frenet spelt out. "Of course he presented the idea as an honourable way out for you – perhaps he even meant it – but he is not stupid. If you do not consummate the marriage he will be able to leave you, his honour unstained, whenever he wants to. Indeed as a Catholic you will be publicly seen to have failed in your duty. I didn't go to all this bother to have him cast you off as soon as you've given him the discoveries he requires."

For a few seconds Pénélope continued to stare at him, her face slowly draining of colour, then she turned her gaze away towards the fire. Her voice, when at last she spoke, was strained and quiet, but clear.

"You must think me a fool. But I see now that I must – of course I must...." Her body revolted at the thought. He was a good man, yes. A kind man, like Michel, interesting like Benoît, steady like Georges. He was like a brother in fact, and she could no more think of being physical with this florid, acne-pitted, heavyset man, than with one of her own. Why, even to let him kiss her...." Keeping her eyes sightlessly on the flames she began to see vistas of sacrifices ahead of her that she had never dreamed possible.

"You must be a wife to him, in every sense," Frenet hammered home. *But you must not get pregnant.*"

"But Papa!" She stood up, fists unconsciously clenching, her repulsion turning to frustrated anger at his seeming inconsistencies. "What do you mean? How can I do one but not the other?"

"There are ways." Frenet smiled, glad to see the tiger flash once more in his daughter's eyes. "I will get Élise to talk to you – properly this time."

"But –" Comprehension finally dawned on her face along with incredulity. "But we are Catholics."

"We are," Frenet agreed. "Good ones too, when that is what's required. First and foremost, however, we are Québécois. The Church has not always been good to us," he reminded her. "I have nothing against Père Martin as an individual – other than he is dull and unimaginative – but the Church is no more our friend than the English, as you well know."

"But –" Pénélope was beginning to feel this was the only word she knew. As a child they had all been encouraged to discuss the church with their father – even, within the discrete walls of their house, to dispute its reign. But words were one thing, actions another, and until now the demands of her father and those of her church had never caused her any major conflict. It was a dilemma too big for the moment and she put it aside. Enough for now to concentrate on the more immediate details.

"But why mustn't I become pregnant? Not that I want to, of course, but – why?"

"Because women change with babies!" Frenet didn't quite shout this time, but he was more rattled than she had ever seen him. "They stop being focused, their values change. Why even your mother, after Benoît, became ...."

"Yes?" He had never talked about their mother and Pénélope couldn't hide the hunger in her voice.

"She became more interested in mothering than anything else," he finished flatly. "You cannot afford to be distracted from your work Pénélope. Pregnancy, along with the nausea and tiredness it can bring would be disastrous. Your work is everything – *everything*, do you understand? See that you succeed there for now and leave babies for later."

He left the room, the subject closed, the conversation over. It had not been exactly the tête-à-tête she had hoped for.

For a long time Pénélope sat there staring into space, numb. Then, when she felt her legs would support her, she went to the drinks cabinet and poured herself a cognac, holding the decanter firmly against the rim of the glass to stop her hand from shaking. She had begun to realise that, far from leaving her father, she was only just beginning to enter into the sphere of his machinations.

The wedding was an uncomfortable affair and the reception afterwards even more so. Lies and deceit had never come easily to Pénélope and she, eager only to start work, was hard put to smile, be gracious and answer all the platitudes with equal clichés. In the end though it was over, she and Ramsey had shut the door on the last guests, and she could finally relax. She could not, however, go to the lab. Keen though she was to get started, even Pénélope had to concede that appearances required them to spend the first night together. She had accepted the delay with more frustration than grace, but discovered she was so tired out by the day's nervous tension that sleeping instead of working wasn't so hard after all. And while she fully intended to obey her father's commands, she didn't demur when Ramsey took himself discreetly off to the spare room. She would do it, of course she would – but not yet. Not tonight. Not until she had to....

Ramsey left for work early the next morning, pressing ahead with his own discoveries, and Pénélope lay in till late, delighting in a luxury her father had always disapproved of. Alone and undisturbed she relaxed, reading, dozing, and generally conserving her energy for the night ahead. Once up and breakfasted however, the pleasures of her new home began to pall and the day dragged out before her. Moving restlessly from room to room, she didn't so much explore her new territory as search for distraction – but nothing could hold her interest for more than a few minutes and the clock ticked more slowly every time she looked. By the time Ramsey got home from the factory it was all she could do to not dash straight out the door.

His arrival at least sped up the clock however, and once they had eaten supper together the waiting was finally over. As the servant cleared the dishes into the kitchen, Pénélope went to change into her work clothes, abandoning Ramsey with a last brief nod of complicity and a smile nervous with anticipation. She was off.

A different watchman, an Englishman, let her in, locking the gate behind her and escorting her across the frozen yard to the red door, now also locked. Silhouettes against the bright, starlit sky showed where others stamped their feet and blew on their fingers against the cold, and at the far side, by the wood pile, a dog barked an answer to a distant howl. Guard duty was, it appeared, taken a lot more seriously at night. The watchman made to accompany her upstairs, but here some instinct of rebellion made her stop him.

"That's fine," she said. "I know the way. Give me the key to the lab and I'll lock up when I've finished."

"Don't worry ma'am, it's no problem." She could almost see the man's thought processes: the boss had told him what to do and he would do it. She however, had other ideas. The lab was her territory now, and should be a private affair. Biting back on the sharp retort that came immediately to mind, she thought instead of what Ramsey or her father would have said.

"Thank you for your concern," she said graciously. "I appreciate it. However, I don't want to trouble you any further. You may go." And she held her hand out for the key in a gesture that brooked no further discussion. It worked. And why shouldn't it? she asked herself as she climbed the now familiar stairs, her heart pounding with excitement. She was the boss's wife. Didn't that make her, in some way, a boss too?

The lab was off the corridor, kitty-corner to Ramsey's office where it could stretch out over the factory below. One lamp had been left dimly glowing for her, throwing the large space into shadowy relief. It was four times the size of her own workshop, divided into sections by benches and the larger equipment, some of which seemed almost industrial in capacity. Whatever Ramsey was working on, he obviously had his bosses' full confidence. Two sides were windowless, the third wall had a large internal window that looked over the factory floor and the fourth was lined with small windows that opened out onto the far side of the building. Automatically Pénélope walked over to one of them and pressed her face against it to check the view. Beneath her she sensed more than saw the frozen Toulega, while the cut-off constellations of stars revealed where the hills loomed beyond. She drew back, smiled to herself and went to light the rest of the lamps. She would like it here.

Quickly she set to work, checking the crucible for any cracks, preparing the anode and cathode. Tonight she intended to use Ramsey's superior equipment to retest the fluorspar she'd failed to melt in her lab – a failure she felt ambiguous about: she wasn't sure her makeshift equipment would have withstood the molten substance even if she'd been able to produce it. Calcium fluorite had a melting point of around 2480°F and, whatever she may have said to Ramsey, she did not want to replicate Davy's fame by loosing an eye. Here she would be able to do it properly and she was almost vibrating with eagerness. She felt like one of Benoît's hunting dogs, quivering in anticipation of the kill. Surely and deftly she got everything ready, then waited for the fluorspar to begin to melt.

She was so immersed in what she was doing that at first she didn't even hear the tap on the window. It came again, louder, and she jerked upright, heart-pounding, to stare out into the blackness beyond. She was on the second floor. The tap came again, and with it the flutter of white like a ghost or, she told herself firmly, a hand. Staring fixedly she walked forward to the window, took a deep breath – and opened it.

"T'as pris ton temps," a voice greeted her. "Bouge-toi. T'es dans mes jambes."

Pénélope stood back as a tall, flexible figure folded his way through the small opening then, as he was still straightening up, she said in English.

"What do you think you're doing?"

The man ignored her and leant back out of the window, his fingers fumbling at something out of sight. Then, with a quiet "ah-ha!" he began to pull in some thin string, tied to thick cord that was tied in turn, if his increased effort was anything to go by, to something heavy.

He stopped for a moment to flick his hair out of his eyes and said, in English as good as hers;

"Well don't just stand there – give me a hand, tabernac."

Instead Pénélope deliberately folded her arms and stood watching. A flicker of amusement sparked in his eyes and he said no more, returning to his load. When he had finally levered a small wooden crate onto the floor he closed the window, turned around, leant against the sill, and looked at her.

Pénélope looked back, taking in his working class clothes, unusual in that even the shirt was black, his long, lean body and the weathered face that spoke of a life lived mostly outdoors. He was young – only a few years older than her – and she wasn't scared so much as angry – an anger flamed by the small, arrogant smile that played around his lips as he met her gaze.

"Well," he said finally. "I'm sure you could stare at me for hours – and you're not bad-looking yourself – but don't you think we should get to work?"

"I **was** working," she retorted, "before you disturbed me. And as soon as you leave I shall be able to work again." She smiled coldly and indicated the window.

"Ah-ha!" The man nodded to himself. "They didn't tell you a thing, did they?"

"Didn't tell me what? Who are you, anyway?" The questions came fiercely but they were empty, an attempt to cover the sudden chill she felt at his words. So even the lab, her one retreat, was to become part of her father's domain.

"I've been sent to help." He bent down to open the box. "With this."

Pénélope gasped as he threw back the top.

"Magnesium." She moved closer. "This must have cost a small fortune!"

"Money is no object."

"With this amount I'll be able to experiment properly. But –" She remembered her dignity and continued more calmly. "But even if it works – it's far too expensive to be commercially viable." She echoed Ramsey's words consciously, revenging herself on this stranger for his unwanted intrusion. "Don't you know anything?"

"A little bit, yes." And he lifted up the top tray of the crate to reveal the contents below.

"Manganese, chromium, zinc, potassium, sodium, calcium, beryllium, bromine, copper – coke for the carbon, fluorite – and then the compounds …" He lifted another tray to reveal yet more treasures, all carefully separated with protective padding. "You name it, we have it, or can get it quickly. The magnesium may still prove useful in some way – but all this is ours to play with. Some cost a fortune, sure – but others are comparatively cheap. It is what your father said you needed."

"My father got me this …?" Pénélope was filled with a strange contradictory mix of fury and triumph that crowded itself into so many thoughts she didn't know what to latch onto. *He believed in her. He thought her worth a fortune. Yet he told her like this – sending a lackey to dog her heels as if even now, despite everything, he didn't trust her.* One sentiment at least was clear. "Le bâtard!"

The man raised his eyebrows but said nothing and Pénélope didn't even realise she'd spoken aloud. She was astonished at what was happening and yet, behind her astonishment, another more detached Pénélope was taking it more calmly. *Well you didn't think he'd tell you everything, did you?* she berated herself. *You're just a pawn like all the others, you always knew that. Why the surprise?* The first Pénélope, the emotional one wanted to answer: *because he loves me; because I'm his daughter; because this is important to me – because I wanted to win the discovery by myself, alone.* But she knew with what contempt her naivety would be met. She had forgotten what she was here for. Chemistry wasn't an end in itself, a pure activity to be done for the sheer joy of discovery – of combating her brains against the laws of nature and coming up trumps. Chemistry was a pawn in the hands of the politicians – a tool to be used for the good of the Québécois.

She swallowed hard, looked up into the man's face and said simply: "So. You are here to help me?"

"I am."

"As a delivery boy – or…?"

"We are to collaborate." And while he said it with a quiet air of finality, he also said it gently, as if he understood the loss this meant to her.

"And the results? The patent? In whose name will it go?"

"That is not our concern." He paused, then realising that she needed something more, added, "No doubt you will be told when the time comes. In the meantime you are to take credit of everything as your own work and tell no-one – naturally – about my visits."

"I see." She nodded, but her eyes were fixed elsewhere with an inward gaze. A sudden vulnerability softened the jut of her chin and took the elasticity from her body which seemed to slump without moving. She looked, for a second, like a caged animal that was wild no longer, accepting it's captivity. Then she sighed, stood tall, and looked at him with a hard intelligence in her eyes. "Well then," she said. "We'd better get started."

Since she had already got started there was little to do but wait and watch. The intruder checked her equipment – more with an air of curiosity than the will to criticise – then took off his jacket, unbuttoned his collar against the growing heat of the lab, and sat down quietly to wait. Pénélope chose a stool at the far end of the bench, angled it away from him, and did likewise. Her head was too full for talking and besides, angry at her father for this latest upset, she had no-one to take it out on but this arrogant stranger. She would treat him with polite disdain, she thought bitterly, and he'd soon see what she was made of.

Unfortunately, things didn't work out that way.

"It hasn't melted." Her voice was more astonished than frustrated. "I don't understand…."

Calmly the man got to his feet – almost floated to his feet indeed, so effortlessly did his muscles work, and came to look.

"It has a very little bit," he contradicted mildly, pointing to the softened edges. "See."

"Try telling that to a scientific journal." Now her voice grew gruff with disappointment. "I don't believe it," she continued more to herself. "With a furnace like this – I was so sure...."

"You were?" He flicked her a glance of surprise and she smarted under the implied criticism.

"But it should work! All the laws – why, even common sense – if only we can get it hot enough!"

"Or find something with a lower melting point." He turned away, picked up his coat and put it on. His clothes were loosely cut, she noticed, allowing his limbs easy movement – perfect for climbing up the sides of factories. "What else have you tried?"

She told him.

"Well, now you've got it why don't you try the magnesium fluoride? That should have a lower melting point. I'll be back tomorrow night to see how you're getting on." And he winked, hauled up the window and left.

Pénélope sat down and stared after him, seething, until enough cold night air came in to make her stir. To arrive like that, do nothing, pronounce, and leave. Who did he think he was? Except that he was right. And now, thanks to all those new materials she could experiment to her heart's content. Her heart however, was far from content. In fact it had rarely felt so dreary. She had so been looking forward to tonight. If she had succeeded, the patent would have been hers – he'd come too late to grasp any credit. Now, however, she had no choice.

Suddenly immensely tired, she went home to bed.

He came every night that week. Each time they would adapt the electrolyte – changing the solvent or refining the alumina – and each time it would fail. The magnesium fluoride would not fuse – nor would aluminium fluoride, another obvious choice. Potassium fluoride melted in the furnace at least, but dissolved only negligible amounts of aluminium oxide, as did the sodium fluoride. It was regular trial and error work that didn't in itself need a companion and Pénélope resented his presence even more for its apparent irrelevance. She maintained a hostile professionalism; collaborating fully without ever being friendly, and being wilfully incurious about his background, his wider role within her father's plans – even his name. She would probably be told to mind her own business anyway, she rationalised, and she certainly wasn't going to give him that satisfaction.

Superficially the stranger took it well. When no business needed to be spoken, he was quiet; when it did, he spoke it. This, however, only irritated Pénélope more. She quickly saw that the distance he maintained was not due to the well-mannered respect of a gentleman or of an inferior who knew his place. Rather he was ignoring her just as she ignored him – with a subtle but mocking deliberation.

For both of them however these were positions taken, not a natural stance, and such positions were hard to maintain when grappling together with some problem in the dead of night. Where the stranger did come in useful, whether Pénélope liked it or not, was after something had gone wrong. Whatever else he might be he knew his chemistry, and his ideas when discussing what might work better and why, were astute and daring. His intelligence too was more in step with hers than Ramsey's: like her he thought linearly, progressing from start to finish in a logical fashion – a process that left her less giddy with excitement than Ramsey's melting pot of ideas, but which she was familiar and at home with. It was a situation she could not fail to respond to, and as their minds met their behaviour became less calculated, more spontaneous, until a genuine rapport became unavoidable. Slowly the relationship gelled, found a rhythm, then consolidated despite themselves.

By the sixth night she felt relaxed enough to admit defeat.

"It's no good." She turned away from the paltry deposit, her body slack with failure. "We're on the wrong track."

"No." The word came out vehemently and she looked up surprised. "We're on the *right* track," he contradicted. "I can feel it in my bones. It's only the details that are wrong." He stood up quickly to walk over to where they stored their materials, then swayed as a wave of fatigue hit him. Reaching out to the work bench to steady himself, he waited until the moment had passed, then changed direction and walked over to the wall instead, sliding down it to where he could half-sit, half-lie against it's solid support.

"You need a break," she said. "You're worn out. Me too, come to that."

He nodded. His tanned skin had a pale sheen of exhaustion that emphasised the dark patches under his eyes, and intensified the deep blue of them. They were, she noticed for the first time, almost the exact colour of hydrated copper sulphate. "We'll take a couple of days," he was saying. "In any case, there's no point in doing more experiments until we know where to go next. I'll go back to the city and consult a few colleagues. It may be we could use a fresh brain or two here."

Pénélope agreed. If she'd been working at home at her own pace she'd have stopped trying so hard long ago. Instead she'd have let her brain wonder off down seemingly irrelevant corridors until somehow, given the space it needed, it found the solution on its own. Commanding it to search through brute intelligence and will-power was alien to her, both stressful and distressing. She had a feeling it wasn't her partner's natural method either, though he never complained. Indeed he seemed a perfect example of party loyalty and self-sacrifice to the greater need – one of his more annoying characteristics.

You should take a few notes, the new, more cynical Pénélope told herself. *He's a perfect role model.*

She poured water for them both, took one over to him, then sat on a high lab stool to wait and see what came next. He sat up slightly to take it, his jaw cracking on a yawn.

"Tonight, I admit, I could do with something stronger."

Pénélope stared at him. It was the first time he'd said anything chatty. Normally he got straight down to business then left in a hurry before the dawn shift crept up on them. But now it was only 3:00am and they'd given up.

He was, she allowed herself to admit, handsome, with the kind of looks she imagined D'Artagnan to have. His fine black hair, so different from Ramsey's stiff curls, was brushed straight back from his forehead, but needed a cut, so that he was constantly pushing it out of his eyes as he leant over their work in a manner that was both frustrating and endearing. His body moved like his mind; flexible, direct, with no wasted movement – a little like her father's hands, she thought, when they deftly touched a patient, and very unlike Ramsey's expansive gestures. They couldn't have been more different if they'd tried. She imagined Ramsey climbing up a sheer wall with just a rope to help him, and while the idea wasn't quite ridiculous, it clearly wasn't plausible. For the first time she let curiosity raise its head.

"How did you learn to climb like that?" she asked. "Or is it an obligatory part of the training?"

"The circus," he said surprisingly. Then, at her look of disbelief: "My parents were circus folks – he was a trapeze artist, she did the horses. I grew up learning all that as a matter of course."

"And you gave that up for this?"

"I know." He grinned, a real grin that, robbed of its mocking edge made his face boyish and engaging. "I was a great disappointment to them. Circus boy goes to school and makes good. It was almost unheard of."

"I know the feeling," Pénélope sighed. "It's so selfish, isn't it, to have desires and ambitions that don't fit in with what's been planned for you." She'd meant to say it lightly, but the bitterness edged in regardless. He put down his water and looked at her, considering.

"Having a father like Dr Frenet," he said eventually, "a great man... an anchor of the resistance.... It can't always be easy."

"It is heaven and it is hell," she answered simply, surprising herself. "He is the most wonderful man – so calm and wise and brilliant – that you feel you would do anything for him. So then you do – anything – everything – for him. And then... and then...." She stopped, not sure of what she had been going to say and instead swallowed a sudden lump in her throat. "No, it isn't always easy."

"So.... Ramsey...." He was hesitant now, feeling his way on uninvited territory. "He wasn't your choice?"

She was silent for so long he must have thought he'd offended her. He said no more and instead got up, rinsed out his glass carefully so no-one would know he'd been there, and was reaching for his jacket when she said:

"Do you know what my name means?"

"Pénélope?"

"Yes."

He looked bewildered. "Why?"

"Because it describes my fate. It was a conceit of my father's, chosen as soon as I was born. He used to tell me stories about my namesake when I was little. Then he would invent new ones, describing how I too had a destiny to fill – how I would follow in her footsteps."

She stood up and threw her water violently down the lab sink. "I never had any choice," she said tightly. "I am no freer than the people of ancient Greece – those playthings of the gods. Ramsey is my Odysseus, chosen for me because he will be the winner of the game. I will be faithful to him because that is my part in this play – this *future* – we are creating for Québec. It is my fate."

She stared at him aggressively; her pride challenging him to feel sorry for her. Instead he grinned again and said:

"Just as well then, that he didn't call you Hélène."

She laughed with surprise, disarmed. "My father always maintained that no-one would understand the underlying meaning – that no-one cared about the classics anymore."

"Well," his eyes gleamed. "It's a pleasure to prove him wrong. People don't often do that to your father. So," he changed the subject. "When can you start again?"

"Hmm." She poured herself more water and sipped it, thinking. While keenly aware that every second counted, she had to consider how she worked – and to work efficiently her brain needed a rest. That would get her answers more quickly than all this puritan work ethic, and she knew it. She sighed.

"If only the cryolite would arrive. I'm sure that would make a difference."

"Cryolite!" He stopped buttoning his jacket and walked towards her, looking perplexed. "You have ordered cryolite?"

"Yes. Only it still hasn't come. I got Ram – James to chase it up last week. He says he has – he knows it's important, but –"

He interrupted, gripping her arm so tightly it hurt. "Why didn't you tell me about this before?"

"I did! Didn't I? I thought I did. I don't know...." Pénélope trailed off. Hadn't she told him? Why hadn't she told him? The problem with playing so many parts, of having different reactions – different Pénélopes even – required for different situations, was that it became hard to untangle who did what and why? Had she wanted to keep it to herself? Or had she simply taken it for granted that he would know it from her father, who seemingly knew everything. But who obviously didn't after all....

"Never mind." He was back to his old efficient self now, all friendly informality forgotten. "The important thing is to waste no time. Do you really think it might work? What are it's components?"

"Sodium aluminium fluoride. Of course it's still expensive, coming from Greenland – but we could probably synthesise it later and yes, I really think –"

"Sodium aluminium fluoride...." He wasn't listening to her. "Yes. It might – it could.... When did you order it?"

"What? Oh – I don't know.... I sent a letter to ask about it before I even met James, only I didn't see the hurry then because I didn't have the equipment to use it properly anyway – I was just curious. But then James told me to go ahead and get some – that must have been, well, a little before we got married – I remember because he was showing me the lab and I said –"

He stopped her with a brusque movement of his arm. He was calculating urgently inside his head. "It could be normal delays," he said slowly. "At this time of year.... On the other hand – Does anyone else know about this? Is it in the journals? Have I missed it?"

"I don't think so." She was unsure of everything now, too flustered to think straight. "Just my letter."

"Your letter?"

"I wrote a letter to la Société Chimique de France suggesting it might work. Ages ago – before I knew anything about this." She gestured all-inclusively "But nothing ever happened – it was never published. I must have been mad to think they might take anything submitted by an unqualified girl."

"And you never told your father?"

"Of course not! Why would he want to know? Until James came along my father never took me seriously. I suppose I thought – if it was published – then I could show him ... prove myself to him – *make* him take me seriously." She shrugged.

"But it never was – and I suppose I forgot – or tried to forget all about it."

"This is serious." He buttoned his coat and opened the window, letting in the cold air. Pénélope followed him to stand by it, welcoming the chill that cleared her head and calmed her emotions. She felt like a naughty puppy, scolded for something she didn't understand and that no-one had told her was wrong. "There may be normal reasons for the delay – but given the stakes – and your letter – I wouldn't count on it." He swung himself onto the windowsill in his now familiar fashion, then paused, and softened at her stricken face. "Get some rest," he told her. "I'll sort it out, don't worry."

"Wait," she called urgently, as he threw down the rope. Then, as he waited, realised she didn't have anything to say. It was only that she felt so confused – so alone. At least he, in some small way, understood. For the first time she didn't want him to go. She became conscious that she was leaving him silhouetted against the light while she stood there, dumb.

"Your name," she asked. "I must call you something. What is your name?"

"Ah-ha. At last…." He transferred his weight over to the rope, thinking, and then his face lit up with amusement at an inner joke. "Why not call me Paris," he suggested. "Just to see what happens."

And he was gone.

Pénélope went home with a sense of trepidation. To date she had done virtually nothing but sleep in the elegant new house Ramsey had rented for them, and she wasn't yet sure of her role there. More importantly, she still hadn't conveyed to Ramsey the purport of her last conversation with her father. Nor had she let her father know that she was still a virgin. It had been less than a week after all, she told herself – hardly any time at all to get started on *that*. But now she would be spending time with him, including a weekend, and her ability to do things properly would be put to the test.

She awoke late as usual, opened the curtains and went back to the warm covers of her bed. It was a beautiful afternoon. Sunbeams angling through the window caught the dust the servant had missed, and shone on the hothouse flowers that had survived her wedding. The house was still and she felt that curious peace that came to her only when she knew she was alone. No lab today. And despite the urgent excitement of their work and her worries about being at home with Ramsey, her tired heart rejoiced. Reaching for her latest novel recently arrived from France, she began to read.

She was still in bed, engrossed in *Germinal* – no father to make her read in English now, ha! – when Ramsey came home. She heard the bustle of him in the entranceway, stamping snow off his boots, handing over his hat and coat, then the murmur of voices, and she stiffened in panic. Normally she would be up by now, dressed so that they could have an early dinner together before she in turn went off to work. If he came up he would see her awake in bed, in her night clothes, vulnerable.... She heard his footsteps coming quickly, almost running up the stairs and along the landing to their room. A knock came at the door. Resigning herself to the inevitable she clutched her book for comfort and tried to appear calm.

"Entrez," she said.

"Hello," he came in easily and shut the door behind him. "Suzette told me you were still in bed. Not ill I hope?"

"Oh no." She smiled. His concern seemed genuinely for her and not at all for the work that lay waiting. "Tired. I've reached a kind of sticking point," she continued feeling sure he'd come for some kind of explanation but was too polite to ask. "And I've got so that I can't think straight anymore. I thought a day or two off would be more productive."

"Good." Again he sounded sincere, not disappointed or frustrated at all. She had been expecting to have to defend herself, to field detailed questions about her work. Instead he walked over to the easy chair, brought it near the bed and sat down.

"Well?" he asked.

So he *did* want explanations.

"Well...." She was uncertain where to begin.

"Aren't you going to ask me why I'm home so early?"

"Oh! I didn't know you were. I thought…." She looked at him properly and suddenly realised this wasn't about her at all. It was about him.

"You've done it!" she exclaimed. "You've got your proof."

"Not only that…."

"Not only that?" She sat back and watched him, relaxed now they had fallen into their familiar role of colleagues.

"We appear to have stumbled on an extra discovery…. My main concern, as you know was to reduce the cost, and I thought we could do that by using saltcake in the recovery furnace instead of soda ash. But I now think we can also make our pulp stronger – significantly stronger. The furnace reduces the sulphate to sulphide, as you'd expect, but what had never occurred to me is that the additional sulphide speeds up the delignification process. With pulp like this we can make all sorts of new papers! Shopping bags will never split again, pack lunches can leak relish to their hearts' delight, books will last ten times longer…. I need to do more work on it of course –"

"Of course."

"Ha! Always more work, eh?" He grimaced sheepishly. "Always something more to discover or test – the next step always beckoning from afar. Tell me, do you think it's in the nature of the discoveries, or the discoverers never to be finished?"

"I should say both." She smiled back at him, absorbing his good cheer. "But if that is the case, why have you stopped?"

"I gave the team the rest of the day off. It's too late to start something from scratch in any case, and they deserve a chance to celebrate. They've worked hard for me these last few weeks."

Who wouldn't, Penelope thought. The man was a natural leader. Of course it was shrewd to give them time off, motivating their good will at no real loss to productivity, but it was more than that. Ramsey was straightforward, that was what was so confounding. He genuinely appreciated the hard work they'd done for him and discounted completely the hard work he did himself. Although to be honest he probably didn't see his efforts as work so much as simply being alive.

"We'd better celebrate too," Pénélope suggested, rising to the occasion. "Could we get some champagne, do you think?"

"We certainly could. There is some left over from the wedding, laid by for important events…. And I have asked Suzette if she could cook us up something a little special. You don't mind if we eat later than usual, do you?"

"No."

"What a pity we're not in Québec or Montréal. I could take you to a restaurant, then a show afterwards – celebrate properly."

"You miss that don't you – all that socialising and public life." She suddenly saw her small town through Ramsey's eyes and understood how much it must be found wanting.

"I do." He nodded a moment, remembering. "But not in any important way. I get my dose when I go back for business, and there's no shortage of socialising here – it's just different."

"I should say." Pénélope barked a short laugh. "You will have to learn how to dance to the fiddle and drink Caribou."

"Never." He pulled a face. "Well, not the Caribou. There are limits. But dance, yes – I should love to. Will you teach me?"

"Oh." She hadn't expected a serious response to such a flippant remark. "I could try, but I am not very good. We shall have to ask my brother Georges and his wife – Manon loves dancing. They could show you everything you need to know."

"And the fiddler?"

"Oh Benoît, obviously."

She had spoken unthinkingly. Benoît was the best player in the region and a natural choice, but as soon as the words were out she wondered at her insensitivity. Ramsey however, didn't flinch.

"Very well. We'll arrange it – a celebratory dancing lesson for when you've discovered the secrets of aluminium. We could invite all your family – all the factory, why not – have a real party."

"You have a taste for very public lessons."

"Oh – I shall learn in a discreet corner – if Manon will let me."

"Hardly. She will be right out there in the middle of things. It was always me who kept to the corners."

"Then *you* will have to teach me!" He looked at her triumphantly as if he had won a point and she shook her head, not in denial, but amusement. She felt herself actually *wanting* to dance with him, for goodness sake. The feeling of intimacy led to a small revelation.

"Don't mind Benoît," she said. "He is a very bitter man. He doesn't dislike you personally – he doesn't even know you – you're just a convenient target to pick on. He's a different man when he plays."

"What happened to him?"

"Eh?"

"To make him so bitter?"

"Oh." Pénélope thought. *Being the eldest of an exacting father; being expected to carry a political fire in his loins when all his passion is for music; being unable to go his own way yet unable to respect himself for going the way of another; being caught*, she suddenly realised, *in a mesh of their father's making that he wore as if he'd made it himself…*. She felt a sudden sympathy and fellow feeling with her brother that she'd never understood before. "Oh I don't know," she shrugged the subject away. "I guess some people just are."

The evening passed far more pleasurably than she had anticipated. They spent most of it talking chemistry and when the conversation finally veered onto wider topics, including Québec, she was so relaxed she forgot she had a position to take and talked quite naturally.

Ramsey was the first to start yawning. He was an early riser, whereas she was a natural owl with her body clock switched to nights. When after the third yawn he had still made no move to leave she decided to encourage him.

"You're tired," she said.

"Yes."

"What are your plans for tomorrow? Will you start on the next stage?"

"Oh yes. If I can prove it quickly we'll get financing much more easily. It doubles the reason for change – and at the same cost!"

"Well … I think I'll stay up a bit – read my book." It was the most subtle hint she could think of. She would like him to go – she was tired of talking and could do with some time alone – but was unsure of a married couple's etiquette. Did he need her permission to retire? Real married couples, she thought with a sudden blush, would surely retire together for the first few weeks or months: theirs was an unusual problem.

"Right." He got up. "You've been working flat out, Pénélope. It's nice to see you've got the sense to know when to stop. Not that I'm much help, smothering you in talk of chemistry all evening."

"You have no idea," she said with feeling, "how delightful it is to be able to talk chemistry all evening." And suddenly she thought of the stranger – Paris, for lack of a better name – and blushed again at the thought of her secret. The knowledge blurted her into a different kind of honesty, as compensation.

"But I have had enough of talking now, I admit. At home I could disappear when Papa, Michel and the others got going.... Here, things will be different."

"They will." Ramsey hesitated, then came up to her. "There's something I've been meaning to say, Pénélope."

"Yes?" Her stomach lurched.

"Yes." He cleared his throat. "I don't quite know how to put it, but it goes something like this." He hesitated again, then started in self-conscious tones. "In going ahead with our marriage we have chosen to live some kind of lie. Some of the consequences of that lie are obvious, and we have accepted them – others we have yet to deal with. In public particularly we will have many roles to play, some quite out of keeping with our natural selves – particularly yours." He meant it as a joke, to lighten his words, but Pénélope missed it completely. She could hardly look at him. This was the first time he'd spoken of them as a couple since the wedding and she was afraid of what might come. If he mentioned marital obligations she would be duty to bound to seize the opportunity. Yet, whatever her duty, this sexual aspect of things was something to which she still felt quite unequal.

"One of the dangers of the life we've chosen," he continued, "is that in living the lie in public, we ourselves will forget what the truth is and how to share it with each other. One of the things I value about you, Pénélope, is your honesty. And I want you to feel that you can tell me anything – *anything*. Because...." He paused and she glanced up at him, apprehensive now with a different fear. What did he know to be talking to her like this?

"Because," she prompted, needing to know the worst.

"Because...." He was searching for the right words. "Because what we have going for us is a mutual respect – or so I think – and a degree of friendship. Tell me if I'm wrong." He looked at her keenly, waiting for her answer. She shook her head. He nodded. "We are a team then. And if we forget that – if we start pretending to each other what we pretend in public – that we are in love, that being a couple is more important to us than our work – then, well – it's no way to live. You *name* things, Pénélope – you look things in the face and speak the truth. That's what gave me the courage to take this risk with you." He shook his head with a small smile, frustrated at the way his words were coming out. "What I'm trying to say is don't change. Certainly there will be pressure to change, but not from me – never when you're alone with me. I hope we can always be relaxed and honest with each other."

Impulsively she reached out and took his hand. He was such a good man. Such a sensible, strong, clear-headed, good man.

"Thank you," she said.

He squeezed her hand. "Good friends eh, however the future turns out."

"Good friends," she agreed. "It's a deal."

After he had left she spent a long time sitting by the cooling fire, her book forgotten. He *was* a friend, that was the problem. He treated her like a friend – in fact he treated her better than anyone ever had before: looking out for her, forestalling her needs, using his better knowledge of the world to make her transition into it as smooth as possible. It was, she supposed, how a gentleman treated a lady. It was certainly very different from her brothers and Paris, who demanded her maximum and gave nothing to ease the way – no doubt following her dear father's example.

She stopped. Such thoughts were disloyal. And while she had no doubts about where her loyalty lay, she was deeply disturbed to discover that doing her duty could at times feel so treacherous. Loyalty, surely, was black and white. Yet Ramsey's behaviour was beginning to make it seem an altogether murkier thing, laced with elements that felt almost like the grey seeds of betrayal.

On Saturday they went skiing together. The day dawned perfectly suited to their plans, winter having sent in a final flurry before ceding to spring. A fresh fall of snow, dry and soft, made the going easy, while the sky shone a deep blue that intensified the scenery around them, making the snow gleam whiter and framing the dark green of the trees. Ramsey had had a picnic packed and he took her out onto one of the routes Michel had shown him, across the river and through the woods beyond up to the summit of the local 'mountain'. It was one of the shorter, easier trails, but by the time they reached the top Pénélope was almost doubled over in exhaustion.

"We should have stopped," Ramsey reproached himself, clearing some snow off a fallen tree and putting down an oilskin for her to sit down on. "I'd forgotten this trail was so demanding."

"It's not demanding and you know it," she retorted when she'd got her breath back. "What you mean is you hadn't realised how unfit I am."

He smiled acknowledgement. "It's true. But that doesn't change the fact that we should have gone back. Your father won't thank me for making you ill."

"Ha!" Now she was offended. "You couldn't have stopped me if you'd tried. All this time Michel has gone skiing and it has taken until now for me to understand...." She looked out at the view that stretched out below them. "It is beautiful."

It certainly was. As a doctor's daughter Pénélope had by-passed much of the physical work that befell most women in the area, and as an intellectual she had by-passed much of the physical enjoyment too. She had blown up barns while her friends skated, and read books while they went out walking and courting.

"Isn't it." Ramsey followed her gaze out down the wooded slopes, across the river to his factory that cut off the huddle of streets and houses behind. "I thought you'd like it. So much space, and silence."

"Is that why you like it?" she asked doubtfully. He was such a man of company and noise it seemed unlikely.

"I like the skiing. Given the choice I prefer team sports, but I don't think this place is quite ready yet to have the boss on the hockey team. I was a pretty good player you know," he continued at her look of surprise. "Now *that* was fun...." He trailed off. "But it helps me to think, moving. In Toronto I used to walk the streets. I must have mapped out the whole city with my boot soles at one time or another. Now I've exchanged the traffic for bird call and cracking wood." He shrugged. "Not quite my thing, but all right so long as I keep moving. And Michel's good company – I'm lucky to have him. Most of the men here work too hard to want to come skiing for mere pleasure."

Again she marvelled at his capacity for expanding and including. It had taken this man from the city to show her her own countryside – something her brother had been exploring, and she'd been ignoring for years. She felt almost ashamed at her single-mindedness, which seemed quite inadequate in comparison. Her father, she acknowledged for the umpteenth time, certainly knew what he was doing. She only hoped she could live up to his expectations.

"Your father," Ramsey said uncannily, making her start. "I've invited him to dinner tomorrow. Is that all right?"

"Why ask," she said, sudden anger flaring. "If you've already done it."

"Oh." He turned away, but not before Pénélope had caught the hint of a smile. "I suppose it wasn't a real question – more information." He looked back at her. "Do you really not want him to come?"

It was an impossible question. Of course she didn't want him to come. With everything that was gong on in the lab – the arrival of Paris and their discoveries – she would be worried about slipping up and giving something away. Not to mention the fact that she and James still weren't sharing a bed. If her father should find *that* out....

"I'm surprised he'd want to," she evaded, and then, knowing it an unworthy answer to an honest question added: "I'm afraid it'll be awkward. He's been very prickly with you, to say the least, and I don't want to have to be – well – pig in the middle." It was all true. She threw the ball back in his court. "Do you really want him to come?"

"I think it essential," he answered simply. "Firstly because he loves you and I respect that; second because I am sure he is incapable of making the first step – whereas I, a mere English invader, have no pride or standing to lose. Believe me, I don't want Frenet as an enemy any more than I suspect he actually wants to be mine." He smiled. "Keep your dignity and allow others to keep their pride," he confided, "and you can't go far wrong."

"I shall write that in a book." Pénélope was impressed. "The wise sayings of James Ramsey, pioneering homme d'affaires and diplomat of the late 19th century. I shall learn them by heart and act on them in public when we are rich and famous."

"Yes," he agreed. "I think you'd better. It will certainly be an improvement on your current style."

A snowball seemed the only adequate response and the rest of the day passed quickly and enjoyably.

She was nervous before her father came, but yet again it was an emotion that could be explained away by words so close to the truth that she had a twisted sense of transparency. This, Pénélope began to understand, was the art of lying. That last element, the one percent that made the difference between honesty and deceit – that in chemistry would make all the difference between success and failure – well, in the sloppy dealings of mankind it got lost between assumptions and forgotten by all. By all except the liars, she amended, or maybe even by them too. Deceit was so uncomfortable a feeling perhaps you had to pretend, even to yourself, that you were honest. Perhaps *she* did, rather. Her father, convinced of the integrity of a righteous cause, saw deceit as a necessary weapon he'd been driven to use. And of course he was right – in general. The fact that Ramsey happened to be a decent man made no difference whatsoever to the general state of affairs.

Michel came too, of course, and his company was a balm to Pénélope's stretched nerves. Talkative, good-natured, on easy terms with Ramsey and apparently impervious to atmosphere, he asked her questions, let her tease him, and laughed as animatedly as he always had.

As the meal progressed however, and conversations came and went, it slowly dawned on Pénélope that while Michel's diversions were fun, they weren't actually necessary. With Ramsey, Frenet was acting as expected – a slight thawing allowed to seep through his perfect manners – but to herself he was more than well-behaved. He was – well – she was hard put to find a word for it, but finally she pinned one down. He was being kind. It's effect on her was as powerful as a slap on the face, and as soon as she felt its impact she wondered why she had been so afraid. Her father was a hard taskmaster to be sure, but then she was a hard worker – and after all she had done nothing wrong. Her confused, guilty feelings were just that – a fear of failing when so much was new, so many unwritten rules to learn…. But she would learn them and he knew it. It occurred to her that giving up her life to this greater cause involved sacrifices for her father as well as herself. Probably he would have wished nothing better than for her to fall in love with a Québécois: someone passionate and clever like he was – someone with whom he could talk the night away, and with whom she could have children whose pure heritage would make him proud. Someone strong and committed to a cause – someone like Paris…. She stopped. Where on earth had that come from?

She realised she was forgetting to eat and looked down at her plate to let the moment pass. When she looked back up she met her father's eyes and he nodded discretely, in approval and pride: she was doing all right. It was all she needed. Everything seemed clear and simple once more, as if she need never worry over her choices again.

By Monday she was itching to get back to the lab. Whether Paris were back or not, there was still work to get on with – work that was calming and restful in its all-consuming nature and far more straight-forward than the complications of everyday life. And if Paris were back – well then, there was not a moment to be wasted. She decided to take a flask of whisky to keep there for him. He would appreciate that. They worked well together, she reflected as she filled it: he too was calming and restful, all-consuming and straight-forward…. She felt a slight sense of shame. These were very different thoughts to those she had had – was it just a week ago? It occurred to her, with a small internal blush, that work wasn't the only thing she was looking forward to.

His tap on the window came on her first night back. It seemed to Pénélope to have an extra rap to it, and as he folded himself through the small gap she could almost see the extra energy vibrating through his limbs.

"Well," she asked smiling in anticipation. "Did you find it?"

He untied a packet from around his waist and held it out to her.

"You found it!" And before she knew what she intended, she had given him a kiss on his cheek. His eyes widened in surprise.

"My. That's a slightly different welcome to last time." There was again that mocking edge to his voice, a suspicion of her motives that instantly put her back up.

"It's for the cryolite, not for you," she retorted then looked away, aware of the blush creeping across her face and powerless to stop it. She felt a hand on her arm – hesitant and gentle.

"I'm sorry," he said. "It's nice to see you too." He shut the window and walked to the bench, taking his jacket off for work in his familiar way. "We were right," he continued, as if she had been in on all his thoughts. "It arrived two weeks ago. For some mysterious reason it had been side-lined into one of the storage dépôts 'to await collection'."

"But –" she was shocked, perplexed. "Who would do such a thing? *Why* would they do such a thing…?" She trailed off realising how naive she must sound.

"Business is a dirty business," Paris shrugged. "Napoleon used aluminium instead of gold, n'est pas? And no-one can make gold. We're talking about no less than modern alchemy here, Pénélope – and there aren't many people around, honourable or not, who could withstand that sort of temptation."

"Who was it?"

"Eh?" Paris was tinkering with the equipment, his mind already moving on.

"Who did it? Diverted the package?"

He looked up at her with his eyes narrowed, then smiled dismissively. "No-one you know."

"But –"

"Come on," he interrupted. "We've wasted enough time. Let's get down to work."

It struck her again that whereas a week ago she had resented his appearance, felt robbed of her solo, honest glory, he now felt an intrinsic part of the team. She must be very fickle, she decided, to change her mind so quickly and suddenly, and yet fickle was something she had never thought herself. She had always been determined, persistent, loyal....

"It's like a war," she said suddenly. "The intensity, the camaraderie. I begin to understand what they mean."

"It is a war," he said, his tone dropping back into seriousness. "And a war we must win."

The cryolite melted satisfactorily at around 1800°F – that much they'd suspected. Whether or not it was a good solvent for the aluminium oxide or not was the next test and Pénélope found she was literally holding her breath as they merged the two. It was. Even Paris couldn't resist a tight smile of triumph, echoed by a flash in his eyes. His words though, were more circumspect.

"Doesn't mean it will electrolyse."

"Doesn't mean it won't," Pénélope retorted, her face naked with hope. "This is the closest we've ever been and you know it."

Paris said nothing. It was as good as agreement. Carefully he poured some of the solution into the clay crucible and Pénélope dipped in the electrodes. Then they stood back to watch. After a short period of almost unbearable tension, a gas started to form around the anode.

"Look." Pénélope's voice came out in an awed whisper. "Look," she repeated.

Paris nodded, but brusquely, merely noting the observation. If ever there was a man not to sell his bearskins before killing them, Pénélope thought, then he was it. She herself was filled with the same resilient certitude that had kept her going through so many set backs: this time they'd done it.

Only they hadn't.

"That's not aluminium!" Pénélope's voice was accusing, as if the experiment itself were at fault. "That's not aluminium at all."

"Nope." Paris felt in a pocket for his cigarette case, took one out, and went over to light it from the Bunsen burner. Pénélope looked at him in surprise.

"Do you think you should?" she asked. "If they smell smoke in the morning, I can hardly say it's me."

"Let's take the risk." Cynicism had crept into his voice, belying his earlier composure. "I'm sure we can think of some smelly chemical reaction to out-stink my cigarettes before I go." He sounded so discouraged that Pénélope gave in. Whereas she had come back to work refreshed and well-slept from her break, Paris, now that the vigour of brief success had worn off, seemed tireder than ever. Perhaps he'd run out of steam. She took the flask of whisky she'd secreted in her coat pocket and offered it to him. Once more his eyes widened, and she felt a sudden surge of pleasure at having anticipated his needs.

"You don't want them to think you a secret smoker, but alcohol you don't mind?"

She shrugged. "Do you want it or not?"

Paris took a swig then sat down on the floor and slumped against the wall, flicking his cigarette ash carelessly into a beaker. She threw him his coat to use as a cushion and for a while they sat in silence. Pénélope's mind turned back to the problem in hand. If she could only work out what that new grey deposit was.... Suddenly she started.

"Of course. We're going the wrong way about it. Paris, listen –" It was the first time she had said his false name aloud and it sounded strange on her lips. She stopped and looked over at him. His head was tilted to one side and he was breathing deeply, asleep, cigarette still burning. She stood up quietly and went over to take it from him, then lingered to study his unprotected face. Asleep he looked approachable, almost delicate – very unlike Ramsey's solid, fleshy form – and very ... desirable. As she looked she felt a jerk, like an electric spark, pull around her groin, up from her vagina to her lower stomach, followed by a dull ache that she had never felt before. So this was what Élise had meant.... She had a bizarre longing to put her hands on his chest, on his forehead, through his hair, down his long, muscular legs..... He stirred and she turned away, hot with embarrassment. The cigarette was still in her fingers and she took a long drag on it to calm her, then coughed in astonishment and pain at its effect. The spell was broken. Stubbing it out, she threw away the ashes and washed the beaker out carefully before returning to work. What had she been thinking of before she got distracted? Concentrate woman. Of course, that was it. Methodically, with an effort of will, she pulled herself back into the work that, before, had been all engrossing.

She woke him around the time he usually left.

"I'm sorry," he said, when she'd finally managed to rouse him. "I must have drifted off."

"Died and gone to heaven, more like. But don't worry, the time hasn't been wasted. I think I've found a way forward."

"You have!" Paris shook off his sleep in an instant and looked at her keenly. "How? What?"

"I haven't got the solution," she cautioned. "But it occurred to me that we were going the wrong way about it."

"Well I knew that –"

"Just wait before you get all sarcastic, Mr Cynical." She was unperturbed, sure of herself. "Don't you see – it's not the experiment that isn't working – it's the equipment."

She paused while Paris thought it through. "You mean the deposit. If the experiment's working correctly, then what's causing that deposit?"

She nodded but said nothing, watching him retread the paths she'd explored while he slept.

"It's not shiny. It *is* greyish. It's not aluminium. It *is* ...." For a moment she thought he had it – a night's work in thirty seconds, but then he shook his head in defeat. "It *is* something else," he finished lamely with a grin. "But what, that's the question."

"It's a metalloid," she told him, unable to hold back any longer. "In fact, I think it's silicon."

"Silicon!" He held his hand up, preventing her from saying any more. "If that's the case," he continued, thinking aloud, "then where do the silicates come from?" He met her gaze and a spark of comprehension jumped between them. "The crucible – the clay crucible. You think it's polluting the solution!"

"I knew you weren't a *deux de pique*!" she exclaimed, laughing. "No matter what you look like. Now – the only problem left is how to modify it."

Paris flowed to his feet and pulled on his coat. "I must go," he said, excitement gleaming from his eyes. "But I have an idea."

"Yes?"

"If we made a liner out of graphite…. It works for the electrodes after all."

"Graphite." She said it reflectively, trying the idea out for size. Then: "Yes, of course. I wonder if we have enough? But James would have some, I'm sure – I could start work on it straight away. No – I'll never have time before they want the lab. I'll have to start early tonight instead. *Ciel!* Half a night wasted…."

"Oh not wasted." He was mocking again, but this time it was directed at himself. "I haven't slept so well for months…."

"You needed it," she said, surprised at her herself. It was true, but since when had she wanted to put him at his ease? "Lord knows what you get up to when you're not here, but even Übermensch need a break sometimes. Especially when they've just saved cryolite from a fate worse than death…." She broke off, suddenly fearful he would think she was fishing for information.

"Well then, let's hope my brain shows the benefit tonight." He glanced outside. "It's late. They'll move away from their brazier soon – pretend they've been working all night for the morning shift's arrival." He opened the window quietly and checked below before letting down the rope. Then he hesitated, made as if to say something, and changed his mind.

"À ce soir," he said instead.

"À ce soir." It felt like a pact.

She went home excited, her mind pulsating and not just with their new discovery. A small treacherous portion, almost unconscious, was also wondering what he had been going to say, and whether she'd have liked what it was. She found herself undressing with a new consciousness; looking at her body with slightly different eyes, weighing the strength in her limbs and remembering her exhaustion when skiing. Paris, she was sure, could ski across the whole of Québec if called to – if someone needed him. For some reason the person she pictured as needing him was her.

She decided to skip dinner and returned to the lab much earlier than usual, arriving as Ramsey was about to leave. It was a mistake. Her eagerness buzzed around her like a trail of black flies and Ramsey, sensing her excitement, felt the coming of a great event. Until now he had refrained from questioning her closely, contenting himself with her reports and being careful to let her keep control of her progress. This however was too much for him. Instead of leaving her to it he lingered; watching, asking questions, making suggestions, offering help, until Pénélope could bear it no more.

"Please go!" she exploded. Then, worried she might sound not only ungracious but secretive, continued by way of explanation: "I can't think properly while you're here – I want too much to impress you. Let me plod on as usual through the night – alone. Whatever happens, you'll still know by the time the patent office opens in the morning."

"Very well." He hid his disappointment well, as Pénélope had learnt to expect, but he lingered at the door and as Pénélope leant over her work she felt her back tense in her desire to freeze him out. Why couldn't he just go? "Pénélope?"

"Yes!" She spat the word out and whirled round in frustration, her whole body exclaiming: *what now*?

"I'm sorry. I was going to say – bonne chance." To her astonishment he looked hurt and her frustration broke instantly into remorse.

"No. I'm sorry. I am. I'm horrible sometimes – when I've got an idea, when I'm working…. Benoît calls me La Princesse – and believe me, it is not a compliment." She walked towards him, her work forgotten for a moment, and held out her hand. He took it, and she stretched up to kiss his cheek with genuine compunction. It was going to be hard, she realised with a sinking feeling, not to take advantage of this gentleman in far more ways than her father had ever dreamed of.

The sense of oppression lasted until he had closed the door. Turning back to the graphite she felt a sense of quickening excitement that overruled mere human considerations. After all, everything she had told him was true – and if her style had been rather abrupt – well, he would get used to her ways. None of which explained how her heart lifted at the thought of Paris's arrival and why she waited, even more than for his ideas and suggestions, just for him.

By the time he arrived the experiment was ready to run once more, a crude but acceptable graphite crucible lining the original clay. Paris examined it intently, a smile at its amateur appearance competing with respect at it being there at all, then with a nod of confirmation he helped her put it to the test.
It worked.
No more hiccups, no last minute snags, no new problems. It just worked. Pénélope was now so prepared for further defeat she could hardly believe it, but this time Paris was not so restrained. He picked her up and swirled her around the room laughing quietly until it sunk in. They had done it – the beginning the middle and the end of it. They had won. When he put her down it seemed only natural for them to kiss – a kiss of joy, of celebration – of victory. And when that kiss turned in to another, altogether different kiss, that seemed natural too.
After a moment Paris drew back.
"What's the matter," she asked. "Don't you want to?"
"Oh I want to. If you only knew…." He was almost trembling with desire, his hands holding her face with a tenderness that yearned, yet still held back. But Pénélope wouldn't let him. It occurred to her that this was her only chance. If she was going to have to sleep with James – and of course she *was* going to have to sleep with James – then God knew she would do it first for pleasure. Let her have one time, this first time, as it should be.
"What?" she asked. "If I knew what? Show me…." She raised her mouth to his again, and this time he didn't break away. After that, it was only a matter of removing their clothes – a passionately slow, tentative, exploratory matter – but then they had the rest of the night to do it in and exploring together was what they did best.

"What," she asked him sleepily afterwards, lying in his arms, "do I say about the cryolite?"

"Tell Ramsey that your father gave it to you. When did you last see him?"

"Sunday. Michel and he came for dinner."

"Well, he gave it to you then. A friend of his from Québec had offered to bring it back with him, but not realising it's importance he stopped off at Roberval en route – hence the delay. You hadn't wanted to tell Ramsey until you knew it worked."

"And your involvement? In all this?"

He kissed her forehead. "That will be our secret."

She wriggled around to look at him. "But that isn't fair. The fame, the prestige – the money from the patent. It'll be mine. You won't get anything…."

"If I had wanted fame I'd have stayed in the circus. Besides…."

She felt him stiffen and stiffened herself in anticipation. Something bad was coming. He got up and pulled out an envelope from his coat pocket then opened it to produce three sheets of paper, thick, crisp and formal. "You must sign these."

She read them. It was a declaration plus copies of his involvement and a statement that the discovery had been a joint effort. While the truth of it was undoubted, the morality of it worried her.

"But – if it is to be our secret …" She shook her head. "How will my father use this?"

Paris sighed. "He might not. But as you know he is a man who always likes to keep an ace up his sleeve. It's his safety insurance, to be played only if we can't win by other means."

Pénélope was silent, trying to work out exactly what that meant. Was it a mere precaution, in case Paris should be killed or she should die in some accident – or was it more complicated? Was it even a huge insult to herself, an insurance against her ever turning against her own people?

"You needn't worry that I'll use it to steal your glory," Paris added with his old formality, misinterpreting her hesitation. "It won't be in my hands, you should know that."

"I do, I do." Pénélope picked up his pen to sign, anxious to reassure him. "It's only...."

"Only what?" His voice was harsh, suspicious.

"You think you know what you're getting into." Pénélope's voice was trembling now. "You think you're doing it with your eyes open. And then you get there, committed, and you find that you hadn't got a clue. All these wheels within wheels. These plans, and counterplans and aces up sleeves.... I thought –" She stopped. Another word and she would cry. It occurred to her that it was over. They had achieved what they needed to achieve, and as a consequence she would never see this man again. She couldn't understand how she had been so naive as to not see it coming. And now that it had come, unforeseen, thrust upon her, she suddenly felt as if she couldn't bear it – while knowing that of course she must.

So she stopped talking and instead signed and dated the paper and its copies. They dressed in silence.

"I shall miss you," she said almost calmly, when he was ready to go.

"Yes." For a moment she thought he would say something more, but again he hesitated and the word stood alone, leaving an empty space to follow it. Pénélope was too proud to beg, but she couldn't keep the yearning from her eyes as she looked at him one last time, and suddenly he took her in his arms and crushed her to him in a fury of need and despair.

"Ah Pénélope," he said. "Ma brave Pénélope, tenace et courageuse. Si seulement la vie était autrement. Si seulement...."

It was the declaration she needed. If she could know that for all his strong demeanor and loyal words, he too was a victim of the greater plan – that he would have, if only he could have – then that knowledge would give her the strength to carry on. She kissed him one last time, then pushed him gently towards the window.

"You'll be back," she said as if she meant it.

"Of course," he played along. "Who knows what future discoveries are to be made. Future inventions...."

"Yes," and unconsciously she put her hand over her womb. "Future creations...." Paris blanched, for a second showing a quiver of fear: fear on the face of a man who had never before even shown anxiety. She recoiled in pain at such naked rejection.

"You'd better hope not," he said, as if it were something that she, and she alone could control. "For both our sakes."

And he went, leaving her utterly alone.

Later that morning she showed Ramsey their achievements. That evening, after the celebrations were over and tanked up on champagne, she slept with him – combining a wholly calculated desire to protect herself with wild abandon. Paris was gone, gone with brutal last words. Ramsey was here to stay. She may as well make the most of it. He was willing. He was also, to her surprise, for all his brotherly mien and punctilious sense of honour, sensual and experienced. It wasn't the same, not at all, but it wasn't horrid. Prepared to be self-sacrificial, to find it distasteful and even more painful than before, Pénélope found instead, in his slow, generous love-making, that if she couldn't have love, solace was not to be scoffed at.

The next few months were a whirl of new experiences. Pénélope was wined, dined and fêted, keeping a level head only by dint of her own, serious-minded personality, her father's discreet backing and – most of all – Ramsey's practical common sense. She had never before been with someone who managed to combine ambition with fun. Ramsey, sure-footed as a chamois in their ascent, seemed to leap from one responsibility to another for the sheer joy of it, with hardly a glance at the potential pitfalls – even though she quickly learnt that he, like her father, keenly calculated every possible risk. His enjoyment was contagious. People wanted to be with him. Pénélope wanted to be with him. He wasn't her first love, it was true, but her first love had, in the nature of such things, ended badly. She told herself it was for the best. Paris was good at chemistry but useless with people: with him she would never have been steered by such a sure hand onto the peaks she was now beginning to climb. With him she could never have done, outside of the lab, what she was doing now for Québec. It was a pragmatic, sensible way of thinking; it was probably true. She tried to live as if she believed it important. So as the couple's prestige grew she put aside thoughts of the past and instead observed, analysed, joined in and slowly began to steer events – at first according to her father's counsel, then increasingly according to her own. Everything was falling into place. Everything that was, except one small detail.

Her pregnancy was a development that filled her with a strange mix of terror and wonder, mostly at the same time. The wonder was natural. She, an ordinary woman, was creating in her body something more marvellous, by a process more mysterious, than a chemist could ever dream of. The terror however was only partly natural, and gained an edge as the weeks passed by. What woman isn't scared at the birth of her first child, at the unknown future that unfolds before her in a way quite beyond her control? That, she could live with. What kept her awake at night and sent her prowling, restless around the house was the thought of her father's reaction. He had told her not to have a child. If she kept up her current success after the child was born she could probably buy his indulgence. What though, if on top of her flagrant disobedience to him the child turned out not to be Ramsey's? Fear of Frenet's reaction drowned out all other emotions, including any consideration of what she had done to her husband, and at how she might be repaying his openness and trust.

It would all hang on what the child looked like. If only the child was Ramsey's, or even; if only everyone thought the child was Ramsey's, the rest she could deal with. She thanked her stars that Paris had similar colouring to herself and then, since there was nothing else she could do, concentrated her arguments on convincing her father why a child wasn't such a bad idea.

"It's normal," she told him, when she couldn't put off breaking the news any longer. "People have been talking since our marriage – imagine how much worse the gossip will get if I produce no baby. I need to be seen to be happy – in love. Rightly or wrongly, people measure these things by children. I won't let it affect my work – I promise you – and how else, tell me honestly – could this be a bad thing?"

"Ramsey?" Frenet asked, playing for time. "How is he taking it?"

"James is a born father and you know it." Pénélope flinched internally at the shame the words engendered. It was so true. If only the child *were* his and all else could be forgotten. "He can't wait for the child – he wants more – a host of children to play with and teach and draw into his enthusiasm for the world. He...." She hesitated, sensing a truth that would persuade her father but not sure how to voice it. "He – I don't think he quite saw me as a woman before.... Of course he *did*, but he never bought that line about my beauty and all that. I don't think I was his type – anymore than he was mine. But since this pregnancy he seems to have become more than kind ... almost tender. I think that his tendresse for me is almost becoming a true thing. I honestly believe that if I asked him now for the moon he would try and get it for me – in reasonable, practical steps, of course."

Frenet burst out laughing and Pénélope joined in with relief. "Of course," he agreed. "Far be it for our James Ramsey to take a false step out of mere blind passion. However – it's true what you say. I too have noticed the change – and in you too...." He paused to let her absorb the full implications of what that meant. "If you are right," he continued. "If you can have the baby without it affecting your work – all your work – in any way at all, then it is true that the changes it has brought about in Ramsey are to our advantage." He paused again for so long that she thought he'd finished, and was about to kiss him in relief and delight when he continued, bringing her up short. "However, you cannot know how complicated the emotions of a mother become, in relationship to both her baby – and to the *father* of that baby." He looked her in the eyes then and she felt the blood drain from her face. Did he know? Had he guessed? But no, he just meant Ramsey. "Just as he has fallen a little in love with the mother of his child, so you must be careful not to fall too much in love with him. A little fondness is necessary – is right even – you must live intimately with the man after all. Respect is essential. But love – no. You must never forget whose side you are really on."

They never talked about it again after that and Pénélope's fears reduced considerably. So long as the baby turned out all right, she felt, the real danger was over. And how, when she thought about it, could it fail to? At best it would look like Ramsey; at worst it would be dark and nondescript and people would say it looked like her. One wrinkled ugly baby looked much like another, didn't it?

She was right and she was wrong.

The birth itself was long and tiring and Pénélope was so exhausted, so glad it was over, that she forgot to worry when Ramsey came in to take her hand and gaze at his firstborn child.

"My daughter," he said, gazing at the crumpled red face that peered out from its flannelette covers. "My beautiful daughter." He turned to Pénélope, where she lay drenched in sweat and equally ugly. "She looks like you."

It was the view of the midwife also, so when her father came later to check up on things and examine his latest grandchild, Pénélope felt reasonably safe as to his reaction. He took the baby in his arms without asking permission, an old man more used to newborn babies than many women, and held her close to him, examining her with more intensity than wonder.

"She looks like you," he said, and Pénélope smiled, almost complacently. "Except –" she glanced up quickly. "Except her eyes. So vivid, so blue…. Your own went black like mine, very soon after you were born." He paused. "They must be from your mother."

Relief made her daring. "I had assumed they were from James," she said. "Not knowing anything of Maman."

"Oh no. Ramsey's eyes are pale – far paler than these will ever be. They're not his – not his at all." He stared back down at the newborn with a scrutiny that almost stopped Pénélope's heart. Then he smiled, a tight, distant smile, and she understood that it wasn't enquiry that held his look, but nostalgia. When at last he looked up there was something new in his gaze that she didn't recognise. "They are your mother's eyes," he said firmly, and Pénélope breathed again.

She saw little of her father for the next few days and, having tried to keep him at a distance throughout her pregnancy, was now perversely piqued by his absence. She felt that a test had been passed, and that his comments about the child had been typical of the man. Of course it would be important to her father to deny the influence of any English blood in favour of some other explanation. She was even hopeful that his linking her daughter with his wife might open the way for her to finally question him about her mother. It was he who had raised the subject, after all. Yet his acceptance, while emphatic and territorial, had not been given in a manner guaranteed to completely reassure an uneasy mind. She would have liked to have seen more of him, to take advantage of his nostalgia, and confirm by his easy presence his total approval.

"You'd have thought he'd have wanted to see his granddaughter," she complained to Ramsey, "My first child."

"*Our* first child," Ramsey pointed out reasonably, "but his tenth grandchild. Or is it eleventh? Lets face it, our daughter is hardly a novelty for Dr Frenet, however marvellous she is to us. Besides, it was you who didn't even want him at the birth, taking over everything. Perhaps he's trying to be tactful?"

"Pah." Pénélope had rarely been on the receiving end of her father's tact.

Ramsey walked over to where Pénélope sat with the baby in her arms and stood over them for a while, absorbing his daughter's tiny, perfect features.

"What do you think about Patience for a name?" he asked, careful to pronounce it the French way. "She'll need it with us two as her parents."

Pénélope wrinkled up her nose, considering. "I like it," she agreed, "but it's too didactic. What if she doesn't want to be patient? I never did – nor you, if I'm any judge of character."

"Elizabeth?"

"No family hand-me-downs, I told you. Pronouncing Elizabeth the French way doesn't make it any less your grandmother's name."

"And you're sure you don't want to name her for your mother?"

"No." Pénélope was silent a moment, thinking of the mother she'd never known. "It would be like naming her for a ghost – giving her some kind of burden to carry with her – some impossible legend to live up to. God knows I should be the last person to want that."

"All right." Ramsey moved on to more neutral territory. "Something classical perhaps. What about Hélène?"

"No!" Pénélope got up abruptly and walked away from him. "What is it with you? Names, names, names. What does it matter? She's only a few days old – she's got her whole life ahead of her. Why won't you leave things be for once!"

"But …." Ramsey was hesitant, unsure of what he had done. Perhaps it was true then that new mothers were volatile, going off at any moment for the smallest reason – and to be sure Pénélope had never been exactly reasonable. He tried once more. "We'll need a name for the baptism, Pén, you know we will. I'm only trying – "

"Well stop it," she snapped. "Stop trying." The baby whimpered in her arms, picking up her tension, and she made an effort to calm down. "I'm sorry," she came back and kissed his cheek. "I *am* sorry. You're right. I don't know what got into me. I'll put her to bed. And I'll think about it – I will. It's just …." She shrugged, unsure how to explain herself. "Nothing seems right."

Ramsey watched her go with bemused eyes. It was hard to understand the problem when he himself didn't care what the child was called, so long as she stayed healthy. Why so much fuss over a mere name?

She was alone with the still nameless child at the end of the week when her father finally called. Ramsey was at the factory, and normally her father would have been working too, so it was with surprise that she heard Suzette usher him in.

"Papa?" she went to the door to greet him, too pleased to wait. "Venez vous en. Comment ça va?"

"English." He said automatically, lowering his face for a kiss. "I have to go to Québec."

"Ah oui?" She was puzzled. Her father had grown to dislike travelling of late – one of his few concessions to the onset of age – and for him to go during winter implied something urgent. "Is something wrong? Can I help?"

He watched her for a moment as if making up his mind, and she had time to regret such a rash offer.

"No," he said at last. "But I have some rather tiresome business to conduct there. The sooner I go, the sooner it will be finished. I called to see if you wanted me to get you anything while I'm there."

"Some books?" It was only half a question. "I've nearly finished my last batch. Now I'm not working in the lab…. When she sleeps I have nothing else to do."

"I believe the mother is supposed to sleep also – to rebuild her strength." But he looked indulgent, almost proud. No danger, it seemed, of his Pénélope going the maternal way. "Some books then," he acquiesced. "I think I know what sort by now. Anything else?"

"Papa…." she hesitated, wanting to take advantage of his good humour but fearful of ending it.

"Something for the baby perhaps…?"

"No. I mean yes, if you think so, but nothing in particular. It would seem we have all we need. Élise and Jacques have been very kind…. It was something else." She steeled herself. "Do you have a photograph of Maman? Or a painting, a drawing – anything I could see…? What you said the other day," she rushed on, forestalling any *no*, "about her eyes. It made me realise…. You will be able to see things in my daughter – things from my mother – that I will never know. And I thought – if only I could *see* her – find out about her…. Do you understand?"

"I do." He said it gently, answering the need in her voice but nothing more. Instead he stood up to go. "I have no portrait of your mother of any kind. I'm sorry. And now I must go or I will miss my train."

He came to kiss her and she let him distractedly, trying not to cry. She had let herself hope more than she knew. She should have had more sense. He touched her on the cheek.

"Look at me Pénélope." When she met his gaze she found in his eyes a sadness that almost echoed her own. "I cannot speak of your mother," he confided. "I cannot. You must ask your brothers."

"The only one who'll talk about her is Michel," she burst out angrily. "And he was eight when she died. The others are as useless as –" she stopped.

"As me?" He took her hand. "I have many faults, Pénélope. I know it. But you must remember this," and here he unconsciously clenched her fingers. "Whatever I have done, and whatever I do, I sincerely believe it to be my duty. I have always tried to do my best, for Québec, *and* for my children. Do you believe me?"

Her eyes opened wide in surprise. Her father was making an appeal? To her?

"Yes," she said automatically, because he needed her to, and then, her instinct for honesty winning over, added; "No. I don't know." She shook her head. "I believe that you believe you have always tried to do your best for us – as you see fit."

"Hmm!" It was his turn to be surprised. "My little girl has become a Sophist?"

"No Papa. It's just … do you really believe that what's best for Québec is always best for us, and that there is no room for compromise, for – for – shades of grey? Could your children not have their own melody to play," she added, thinking of Benoît. "One that carries a different rhythm to your own?"

"To play a great piece of music," he answered, continuing the metaphor, "it is normal for different parts of the orchestra to play different parts of the tune – at times even to play their own melody, seemingly independent of the rest. But no great player ever forgets that he is part of a whole, that the rhythm he plays belongs to something far greater than he alone."

"And who decides?" she asked. "Who decides what that great rhythm is to be?"

"The composer, of course." It was obvious. "Who in this case, is me." They met each others gaze levelly for a moment, then, as one, realised he was hurting her. He let her hands go and rubbed her fingers gently.

"Believe me," he said, but quietly now, with no sense of oratory. "Whatever I do for Québec, I do for you. You *are* my Québec. You are the future. And no matter how hard it may be for you, no matter how hard *I* may be on you, I have your long-term interests at heart. Because I love you."

He seemed strained. For the first time ever it seemed important that she believe him and, contradictorily, whereas she had always believed him before, his sudden need made her suspicious. But it also made her tender. For the first time she saw him as an old man, getting older still, with little time left to achieve his dreams. And that knowledge made her respond to him with a kindness that had never occurred to her before, because he'd never needed it.

"I love you too, Papa," she told him.

She watched him go to the door then, feeling that her grave echo of his words had not been enough, comparing her life with that of the mere ordinary mortals around her and reproaching herself with ingratitude, she suddenly called out –

"Papa!" He stopped, turned. "Vous êtes le meilleur papa que j'aurais pu avoir. Le meilleur. Comprenez-vous ?"

"Oui, Pénélope." And now he smiled. "Je comprends. Je comprends tout."

It was only after he'd gone she realised that he'd replied in French.

A week later, Pénélope received an altogether different visit.

Ramsey was at work, Suzette out shopping, the baby asleep. Pénélope had tried to doze but was feeling restless, like the weather. Winter, kept at bay for the short summer months had the region firmly back in its grip and the skies were dark, the wind buffeting from the north, building up snow drifts and rattling the windows. Finally she got up and went to check her daughter was warm enough. When she saw a man standing over the cradle, silhouetted against the grey clouds, she gave a short scream of fear. Her daughter stirred, moved, slept again. The man turned round and came towards her.

"Paris!" And before she knew it she had run into his arms.

He winced, then returned her embrace gingerly, and as her first rush of euphoria died down she realised something was wrong.

"You're hurt!" She let go immediately and led him to the sofa on the far side of the room. "Sit down. Wait. Let me get a proper look at you." The weather had made the room prematurely dark and she went to light a lamp.

"Close the curtains first," he said quickly. She did as she was told. "How long do we have?"

"An hour at least. Suzette will call in on her family while shopping. She thinks I don't know, but I don't care. There." She turned up the lamp and brought it over. "Mon Dieu, Paris. What happened?"

"It's not as bad as it seems."

"Just as well." She spoke lightly for his sake, but she was badly shaken. His nose had been broken, leaving puffed, swollen eyes, and there was a ragged welt down one cheek that would almost certainly scar. He moved awkwardly too, holding himself in a stiff manner that was far from his usual grace. "Where else does it hurt? Let me see."

He shook his head, not in answer to her questions, but to their relevance. "No time for that."

"But you need help." She protested. "You should see a doctor. Wait here and I'll get my father. He'll help you."

To her discomfort Paris broke out laughing – a painful, short-lived affair that ended with a cough. "I don't think so."

"But – but...." Pénélope fell silent with sudden understanding. The dread of discovery she had carried with her for so many months evaporated into a great calm of certainty. She took a deep breath. "You'd better tell me what happened."

"I've been looking at the baby," he said instead. "Trying to see what was so obvious – how he could be so sure. She's a pretty little mite, eh? Our daughter."

"My daughter." For Pénélope that was still the one solid fact. "I don't know who the father is."

"Well Frenet certainly does. He came to me in Québec last week – sent me a note to meet him on the Plains d'Abraham. I have never seen him so angry. He accused me straight away."

"And what did you say?"

"I told him that he was blackening the name of his daughter; that it was you he should be asking. I asked what he thought of you, to come running to me with such questions."

"So you didn't deny it."

"I refused to answer either way."

Pénélope nodded. She would have done much the same. "So...?"

"So he attacked me. Began to hit me with that ivory tipped cane of his, ranting on about some man called Mendel."

"He did that to you! Alone? But you could have stopped him easily – you could have stopped five of them, let alone one frail old man...." She trailed off.

"Well, perhaps not five," he amended with a trace of his old humour. "Although your confidence in me is touching." He took her hand. "But he was not alone. And he had chosen the spot well." He shrugged, the action turning into another wince. "I didn't talk," he told her, "I promise you I said nothing. But it made no difference. As far as he was concerned he already knew the truth."

"But if he thought he knew – if he wouldn't listen, then why did he...?"

"Discipline." He answered the question she was afraid to finish. "Let one rotten apple go unpunished and we all know what happens to the cart."

"No." She couldn't believe it. Her father abhorred meaningless violence. She'd never seen him lift his hand against anyone her whole life. "He must have just been beside himself – seen red with rage – he was never a man to be thwarted...." She leant forward to reassure him and noticed a slash wound beneath his collar, rising from his sternum. She drew her breath in sharply. "Sacrament. You're lucky they didn't kill you."

"Lucky," his smile was bitter. "Oh no, there was no luck involved. I had my insurance...."

"What do you mean?" Her eyes opened wide at the innuendo, the little colour she had draining from her cheeks. They were talking about her *father*.

"Nothing." He shook his head, dismissing it as irrelevant. "The bottom line is that your father is convinced it was me, whatever I say or don't say. It would appear that my blue eyes and Ramsey's blue eyes are two altogether different blues. And you know what he's like once he's made up his mind. Besides, we have to admit that, baby or not, he is right about one thing – that his suspicions are true."

She nodded, not knowing what to say. For a while they remained silent, looking not at each other, but at the crib silhouetted in the darkness beyond the lamp's faint glow. Then, as Pénélope began to absorb the wider import of Paris's words, she turned back towards him.

"So why are you here?" she asked, fear beginning to flutter in her stomach. "You didn't come to show me your wounds. Does Papa know you're here?"

Suddenly everything hinged on his answer. Either he was for her or against her – and for a moment her heart soared. Perhaps he had come here against her father's wishes, without his knowledge, to help her escape. They would run away together with her daughter and be free of this Québec that had begun to weigh her down like a rock around her neck; they would live happily ever after, chemists together with their own little lab…. But the time she took to invent this little fantasy was more than enough time for him to answer, and his silence admitted the other option: he had come here as her father's minion.

"You – *snake*!" She pushed him away from her and stood up, shaking. No words were strong enough, bad enough. "Get out," she said instead. And when he didn't move, she turned back on him and began to pummel him with her hands. "Get out, get out, *get out*!"

He didn't resist her, although she clearly hurt his already bruised and battered body, and she had a sudden image of her father doing the same thing. She stopped immediately. Only then did he begin to speak.

"Pénélope," he said in a tone of explanation. "I had two choices. Either I let someone else come and see you – perhaps a stranger, perhaps Benoît, perhaps even your father – or I came to tell you myself. It seemed to me that you would rather hear it from me." He paused, and then as she still said nothing. "Perhaps I was wrong?"

"Of course you were wrong!" she exclaimed. But her anger now was laced with affectionate frustration, as with a dumb child. He hadn't seen the other option. He genuinely hadn't seen it. God, what creatures of little vision men could be! "We can go away," she told him. "You and me and the baby. Leave Québec…." She spoke rapidly, expanding her plans as she spoke. "You must have friends, a network who could help get us out of here. Once we're gone there's nothing he can do. What would be the point? The scandal would ruin everything for him! It would be too late to force me back. He could publish the papers we signed instead, and make sure Ramsey didn't get sole rights to the patent. Québec would still be all right...."

"And Ramsey...?" He said it so quietly that for a moment she wasn't sure she'd heard.

"Ramsey...." For a moment she faltered. Ramsey would have been badly served indeed. "Ramsey lands on his feet," she rallied firmly. "He always has done and he always will. Besides, he would probably be on our side. He has offered me an annulment if things don't work out, it was part of our deal right from the beginning. He's a decent man who won't go back on his word...."

"Whereas I am a low-down piece of circus life who'd run off with a man's wife just for the asking, is that it?" Paris's voice was harsh and bitter.

"No! It's not like that – you know it's not. We love each other!" There was a pause when he didn't respond, a pause that finally stopped her torrent of words. Her voice dropped to a whisper. "Don't we?"

"Love," he replied at last. "What have pawns to do with love?"

"But we don't have to be pawns, that's what I'm saying. We can be our own people, decide our own future – to hell with others' plans!"

"Like the Greeks?"

She stopped and stared at him. What did he mean?

"Pénélope." He stood up, awkward with the pain, and held out his arms to her. "Come here." She didn't move. He gestured, insisting. "We don't have much time. You've had your say and now I must have mine. You ask me if we love each other, if I love you. Well, I don't have many words for that kind of thing, but let me hold you now, as I speak, and show you how I feel."

It was an appeal she couldn't refuse. She went to him, felt his safe, treacherous arms around her, laid her head on his chest and bit back her tears.

"I don't know," he began, "how much of what you have done you have done for your father, and how much you have done for

Québec. With such a father it would be natural to confuse the two. I though, however much I respect your father, have done this for Québec. Not him, not you, but for the hope of some better land where people can live freely as equals." He moved a hand to her head and began to lace his fingers through her hair where it escaped from her plait. "Just because there has come this complication – this young, tough, brave, intelligent woman whom I care about, and want to be with – is that a reason to give up my fight?"

She made to speak, but he moved a finger down onto her lips to stop her. "If I do as you want," he continued. "Many people will lose. Possibly everyone. Ramsey will become a laughing stock: first his wife cuckolds and leaves him, then his father-in-law publishes documents to show he was seriously duped. English businesses will not invest in a discovery they do not control and he will be financially and politically ruined. Instead of us having a rising star sympathetic to our cause, guided by an astute, level-headed wife, someone else will fill the vacuum. There will be a backlash. People will note what happens when you trust those treacherous French, and we will be lucky not to have another Lord Gosford ruling over our lives. I will not only have abandoned my people to their fate – I will have helped cause it. Perhaps you don't care? Perhaps this is nothing to your conscience?"

Again she tried to speak, to deny his words, and again he silenced her. Gently he traced his fingers down her cheek to her chin and held it for a moment between his finger and thumb, looking at her, before he sighed and carried on.

"What then, about us? Do we ride off into the sunset with our daughter? And then? Perhaps you think we can work as chemists – after all, we have made a major breakthrough – people would be happy to employ us, wouldn't they? Let's look at it from their point of view. A slip of a girl has betrayed her husband at her father's instigation, and then betrayed her father when tempted by her lover. Who is to know, from their point of view, who she will betray next? In any case she is only a girl. Probably all the real work was done by the man, this lover. This lover, yes, and what do they know of him? Well, that shouldn't be too hard to find out now he's lost his friends. Chemical experience – ah-ha, the majority gained in making bombs. Work experience – ah-ha again, when he hasn't been in prison he's been fighting for the rebels – giving a hand to that pathetic Louis Riel. Hmm, not quite a Ramsey, eh? Not quite a gentleman. Not quite the sort of person they'd like to do business with, don't you think?"

He kissed her then with great tenderness, the act contrasting strangely with the harshness of his words. "What then, ma chère Pénélope, do you think we should do?" This time he let her speak.

"We could go to the Métis," she said urgently, "or others who'll accept us. We could find another cause to fight for –"

"We *have* a cause to fight for," he interrupted. "And you don't like it. What is to say you'll like another better? Will you still love me after a year on the run? Will you still love me when I'm in prison, or with a noose around my neck? Will you still love me when we're living in poverty, your daughter crying with hunger? Will you be happy then with the life you have chosen? Think." He gave her a little shake. "Here you have comfort, money, leisure, the work you love, influence – and Ramsey. He may not be your love, but he is your husband, chosen with your eyes open, and believe me you could have done worse. Most importantly, here you have the good of Québec, real power, held in your fingers to keep or throw away. You have our future Pénélope – our *future* – held in the palm of your hand."

He'd finished. A final long trembling sigh ran through his body and then he pulled her even closer to him, nestling his good cheek against her head as if it were he, not her, who needed comfort.

"You want me to stay?" She said it almost in wonder.

"You must do as your conscience sees fit, just as I must follow mine. I can't regret what I've done, whatever the consequences …. But look at me Pénélope – look at who I am. Could I abandon this cause and go and fight for another like some mercenary on a whim? Could you respect me if I did?" He shook his head. "No, Pénélope. I had only two choices – and out of those I chose to tell you myself." He let her go then and stared at her, his eyes flicking over every detail of her face. In the dim light he could almost have been an apparition, some kind of battered dream.

"So you have told me," she said, her voice congealing as the pain set in. "And now all that is left is to say goodbye."

"If only." He shook his head. "Do you really think your father would leave things to such chance?"

She felt a stab of dread and her heart started pounding. What had they been talking about if the worst was yet to come?

"What then?" she asked, grabbing his arm. "What has he done? What else must I sacrifice to your *sacré* cause?"

Something stirred in Paris's face. He took her by an elbow and steered her back to the sofa, away from the crib, sat her down then sat next to her. He took her hand and she let him, leaving her fingers lifelessly in his. Something awful was going to happen.

"Your father saw any child at this point as a hindrance," he started. "As you know. But the child of another man.... Ramsey the cuckold, with his wife's bastard as a legacy – it could ruin everything."

Pénélope was silent for a moment, then, in a low voice wrestling for control asked: "What does he want from me?"

"Your daughter."

"No!"

"You are to tell Ramsey that she is too much for you. That she keeps you from your work, from him – "

"No."

"That you cannot give her what she needs. Your brother Georges and his wife are childless. They will look after her well."

"No." She sank back into the sofa, her body curling over itself, her hands clenching into fists.

"Ramsey will understand. Especially if his instincts tell him it is wiser so. He would do it for you if you are convincing. He would do it for a girl."

"No. Please –"

"It's the kindest option, Pénélope, don't you understand?" He shook her shoulders. "Imagine if your firstborn had been a boy? Don't you realise how lucky we are?"

"*Lucky.*" She pulled away. "If this is your luck then I want none of it. This is not luck – this is the fate we were born to, sealed in our names. Oh mon Dieu, if only my father had dared to christen me Athéna or Aphrodite –" She broke off, the words choked by sobs.

"Then call your daughter such a name and let her make a new fate for herself – away from all this. What your father thinks best doesn't have to be so bad for you." Reaching out, he turned her back to face him, almost pleading. "If she lived here, with you positioned as you are, it would be impossible to teach her the wrongs done our people. With Georges and Manon she will at least be brought up a Québécoise – and if she does turn out to look like me… if she does turn out to be mine…" he faltered, "then the damage done will be minimal."

"*No.*" Pénélope could barely see through her tears. "You can't let him do this to me. You can't." Her voice rose in despair, disturbing the baby who whimpered in her sleep. Stuffing her hands to her mouth she tried to stifle her groans.

Paris took her hands and held them in his. "You have no choice," he said quietly. "We have no choice."

"This is your fault, your doing." A thought struck her. "It's because you want the baby isn't it? At my brother's you'd be able to see her all the time – you'd be her father at my expense. You told Papa on purpose. You –"

"Pénélope." Something in his voice made her stop. "Do you think I want to do this? Do you think I care to see you suffer so? Do you think I don't suffer, knowing the fault is mine? Why do you think he let me come here, rather than send anyone else?" He pushed his face close to hers. "We will be punished for this until the end of our days. Your pain is to be separated from your daughter, mine is to cause that separation – and yet how could I let you hear this from another? Le maudit Docteur understands all that, you can be sure."

Pénélope listened. And as she listened her heart hardened, her tears dried and a plan to began to form at the back of her mind – unclear and desperate, but a chance for all that.

"You must give me time," she told him. "Tell him that. For me to convince James I must have time to seem fed up. Right now I seem so – I *am* so – in love with her…. He would never believe me."

"You have three weeks." So even that had been decided. "Your father says that if you have not handed the baby over yourself by then, then someone will come and take her. Of course it will be me. How could I let another touch her, hold her – perhaps harm her…. He says to think of Québec – of our plans and the future. He says to remember the orchestra, whatever that means; he says to remind you of the last time he saw you, and that everything he said then still holds true. He asks you to not be selfish."

"Selfish!" She spat out the word with more venom than she knew she could feel. She stared at Paris, beginning to hate him already for his pathetic repetition of her father's will. "And you? What do you say?"

"Me?" Paris gave her a long steady look then got up and went to the crib. Pénélope followed him anxiously, as if he were going to snatch her daughter from her there and then, but he only looked down at the baby then reached out one of his long graceful fingers and placed it gently into her tiny fist. He smiled – a slow, remembering smile – and when he turned back to her the look on his face was the same as that night a lifetime ago, when they had made love. "I should be sorry," he said quietly. "I should be sorry for what I've caused. But I can't be. I can't be at all."

After he'd gone Pénélope went over to her daughter, picked her up and held her close, clutching her so tightly that she woke and screamed in protest. It was a sound Pénélope echoed in her heart.

The next day she tried to see Michel. She didn't dare go to her father's home so instead she waited for him on his favourite skiing route. The day was bleak and windy once more, the snow icy and uneven – not great for skiing – not great for being outdoors at all, and after she had waited for over an hour she began to fear he wouldn't come. Her alarm had brought her out earlier than Michel's usual hours however, and when she could no longer feel her limbs and her eye lashes were white with frost, he finally arrived.

She told him everything. Of all her brothers Michel was the most protective, the kindest, and – thanks to the dull wits that

ensured that he alone was not enmeshed in her father's plans –
her only hope. For the first time it occurred to Pénélope how
lucky Michel was to be stupid. How clever, even. She began to
wonder if it was to some degree an act, a doubt fortified by his
reaction: Michel listened well without interrupting, and with little
surprise.

"I knew something was up," he said stamping his feet
against the cold. "I heard them talking. But I never dreamt ...."
He looked worriedly up at the sky as though a solution might be
there, then after a long pause when it evidently wasn't said:
"What do you want me to do?"

Pénélope had thought it all out.

"Get something on our father – something compromising –
something written down that we can use if we need to. Also, get
back the declarations I signed." She described them in detail,
along with Paris's role. "Try to find out his true name. There
must be a dossier on him somewhere. He's been around a lot,
that man." She paused, hesitating before her final betrayal, then
took the plunge. "He's been to prison, and before he came here
he fought with Louis Riel.... He makes bombs. Probably he's
wanted by the police – I could hold that against him." She shut
her eyes. She couldn't afford to cry – the tears would freeze in
this biting cold. "And get me a gun."

Michel laughed in astonishment. "All that in three weeks?
You don't want much, do you?"

"I know. I'm sorry. But what choice do I have? Papa has
driven me to it."

"Yes. This time he has gone too far." Michel put his arms
around her to ease the trembling that was half-cold, half-
emotion, and rubbed her briskly as a cure for both. "Well," he
released her with a nervous smile that was far from inspiring.
"You can rely on me. God help us, I shall do what I can."

Pénélope watched him go with an uneasy heart. He was her
only hope, but what a risky only hope to have.

More than two weeks went by and even that hope began to
fade. Perhaps she'd overestimated him. Perhaps he was merely
stupid after all. Afraid of her father's spies and almost powerless
to do anything herself, it became no acting matter for Pénélope

to appear bad-tempered and difficult. If any of Ramsey's staff were reporting back to her father she would seem to be doing exactly as required.

Finally, as the end of the third week approached, Michel came round uninvited as he sometimes did to have a drink or two with Ramsey.

"You look terrible," Michel told her in his usual amiable way.

"She does, doesn't she," Ramsey agreed. "She's been acting pretty cranky too. I've been telling her to get out more – have some exercise or get back to work. Sitting at home with the baby doesn't suit her."

"Why don't you come skiing with me?" It was the perfect cue. "Tomorrow. Not far. I'll curtail my route, just for you."

Pénélope tried not to let the eagerness show on her face. "All right," she said ungraciously. "No harm in trying." And she left the room abruptly before relief gave her away.

"Here you are." Michel showed her a well-wrapped package. "Two of your declarations – the third I couldn't find. I couldn't get a gun either, I'm sorry." He didn't sound sorry and Pénélope guessed that he hadn't even tried, but there were more important details to talk about.

"And on Papa?"

"Ah yes. Something on Papa." Michel hung his head. "That wasn't easy."

"I can imagine!" Pénélope thought he meant practical difficulties, but as he started to speak again, seemingly quite off the subject, she saw that wasn't what he'd meant at all.

"When I was little, after mother had died – when you were a baby – I went into their bedroom."

Pénélope gasped. "How did you dare?"

"I was only eight. At the time I didn't think it so serious. I hadn't realised …. I missed Maman terribly – I'd always been her favourite – and Papa didn't seem to care. Of course I understand now that he was wrapped up in his own grief, but at the time all I could see was my pain and how he couldn't help me – couldn't help any of us.

"Then one day he went out and forgot to lock the door to their room. I was angry with him for keeping Maman all to himself and when I saw the door ajar – well, I went in. I wanted to find something of hers, some old clothes or an ornament, a hairbrush – anything I could hold and use as a keepsake. I remembered she had a grey silk dress that she often wore to go out in the evenings … she was so beautiful in it … and I wanted to touch it, to run my fingers along it like I had sometimes when she came to say goodnight. So I went to the wardrobe and there was her dress, just as I remembered it, and behind it, hidden amongst all her clothes, was a row of rifles."

"What did you do?"

"I heard Papa."

"What!"

"I was in there, touching Maman's dress, looking at all these weapons and starting to understand the real reason why we weren't allowed in her room – not because of Maman's memory at all but because he was using her, using her for his own selfish aims – when I heard his footsteps running up the stairs."

"What did you do?"

"I nearly wet myself. Somehow I knew that if he caught me, having seen what I'd seen...."

"So what happened?"

"I shut the door of the wardrobe, just in time, and looked out through the keyhole. I could see the foot of the bed and Maman's dressing table. He came in quickly, threw something on the bed, and opened one of the drawers. I couldn't see what he was doing because it was blocked by his body, but he was in a hurry and not suspicious. He found whatever he wanted and left again quickly."

"I bet you did too."

"No. I waited until I heard the front door slam. Then went to the window and watched him go. After that – why hurry?"

"But weren't you terrified?"

"Yes. But I was also angry. How *dare* he do that? I knew I couldn't risk coming back again, so I decided to take a bit of mother with me – a bit of her dress. Papa wouldn't notice. It was quite obvious to me at that moment that he didn't care about her at all – that he was merely using her to his own ends, that he'd never touch her dress again. So I went to the dressing table to get her old scissors. And while I was there I noticed that he hadn't shut the drawer properly, and that some papers were sticking out. Well I could read well at eight, I was quite bright then, you know." He gave her a knowing smile. "And now I was hungry for information, for more proof of Papa's betrayal.

"There were many things – too many to read. But the first was a letter from Papineau, dated 1837 and clearly implicating both him and my father directly in the Patriote's revolt – when Pierre's uncle was killed."

"Pierre?"

"Yes. He was my best friend at the time. Somehow I couldn't look him in the eye after that."

"Oh Michel."

"It named Papa, Pénélope. It named him, and he was proud of it. Of course, now I realise he was keeping it as a security against Papineau, but at the time I thought it was some kind of trophy. God how I hated him."

"What did you do?"

"I became stupid." He smiled at her look of understanding. "It wasn't hard. At first I *was* quite stupid, numbed and confused by these new discoveries. People said it was grief and to leave me alone, and that was fine with Papa. We'd never been close and once I was no longer even bright.... I began to see it was the perfect defence. It's served me well too. No-one, except sometimes I think perhaps Ramsey, has seen through it till now."

His story told, he handed over the package to Pénélope's frozen, clumsy hands. "The letter is in there. I am not a lawyer, but as I understand it there is enough evidence to put Papa on trial for murder." Pénélope looked up from where she'd been stowing it in her pocket, sobered.

"Then it has come to this," she said. "Him or me."

"Him or us," Michel corrected. "I trust you Pénélope. But please, I beg you, don't use it unless you have no choice. Because for all his faults...." He broke off.

Pénélope cleared her throat and said hastily, "And Paris? What do you have on him?"

"Ah yes, your lover."

"Don't call him that."

Michel shrugged. "Papa should not leave all his important papers in one place. His name is Félix Lachance. He designs and makes most of their bombs, along with other duties. He did a year for burglary four years ago, and met members of the resistance while in prison. His father was in the circus apparently – a trapeze artist until a bad beating from the Montréal police damaged one of his legs. He was an easy convert."

"Thank you." Pénélope kissed her brother gently on his lips. "You have saved me."

Michel smiled, a deeply sad smile that sat strangely on his usually happy face.

"Be very careful," he said. "It could be that Papa will play your game and agree to compromise rather than lose all –"

"Yes," she cut in, "that's what I –"

"But he is old," Michel continued firmly. "And compromise is a concept he has almost forgotten. His other solution might be to … cut his losses."

"He won't kill me." Pénélope uttered the words with a certain relish. She was facing all the facts now. "And not because he loves me – don't worry, I'm not such a fool as that. But because I've written my will, given a sealed copy to James, and put the original in a safety deposit box, where these letters will also go." She indicated the package. "If I die the whole world will know about him, and my daughter will be safe in James's hands. He is her legal father after all, whatever Papa may think."

Michel looked at her with respect. "You are your father's daughter," he said in a tone that was not wholly admiration. "You have thought of everything. Or at least I hope so," he added, readying his ski poles, "for both our sakes. Come on, let's get out of here before we freeze to death."

But Pénélope had one last question.

"Michel?" she asked.

He looked back. "Yes?"

She hesitated. The question was easy, it was the answer that would be difficult. Did she really want to know? She closed her eyes. Of course she did.

"My mother. *Our* mother. What colour were her eyes?"

"Don't you know? I thought the whole region remembered that – she was famous for them. Papa had his own pet name for her – Ma Reine aux Eméraulds, he called her – because they were such a piercing green."

Two nights later, at the end of the third week, Pénélope sat up in her daughter's room. Paris arrived in the early hours of the morning, opening the window easily and climbing in. He had a papoose with him to carry off the baby. Pénélope didn't move.

"I have come," he said quietly.

"When you called yourself Paris," Pénélope asked him, "did you realise what a bloody war you would set off amongst our family."

He didn't answer. Instead he moved towards the baby.

"Stop," she ordered. He didn't, then did as he heard the click of a gun. "That's better," she said, "Félix."

She felt more than saw him stiffen in the darkened room. "I have a feeling," she said, that if I screamed now, and my *husband* called the police, things would get very uncomfortable for you Monsieur Félix Lachance – ex-prisoner, rebel and bomb-maker that you are."

"It's true," he admitted. "But how would that improve things for you?"

She smiled in the darkness. "I think perhaps that you have something I need. I think perhaps that Papa only gave you two copies of that document for us to sign – that the third was your idea – your own little ace to keep up your sleeve."

She felt as much as saw him nod. "In this game," he explained without shame, "a man can always know too much or outlive his usefulness. Those without some kind of security don't last long."

"Give it to me."

He turned at that and took a pace towards her.

"I warn you," she said quickly. "I *will* shoot." Her tone carried conviction. "I don't think people will question me much once you are dead, do you? The body of a convicted burglar in my own house, patently doing wrong. And while I am not used to my husband's gun, my father taught me to be a passable shot."

"I believe you." He paused. "But do you think shooting me will solve your problems?"

"Do you think I will let you take my daughter away, just because it is you?" she countered.

"Do you think anyone else would have waited until you were ready?" he retorted. "Would anyone else have walked into your little trap and let you have your way? Come on now."

"But…?" It was true, she recognised it as he spoke. He was a circus artist, a professional burglar. He could have taken her daughter at any time – certainly not on the precise date specified, when she knew exactly what to expect. She began to feel uneasy. What plan could he and her father have concocted now that would let her get this far, but no further?

"Just give me the document," she said harshly. "Give me that and I'll let you go."

"So you think I carry it with me? To be taken by the first person who wants it?" His old mocking tone was back. "That wouldn't be much of an insurance now, would it?"

Pénélope sat back in the sofa, took one hand off the gun and used it to rub her temples. Everything was going wrong.

"Besides, what good would it do you?" he continued. "There are still the two others."

"There *were* the two others."

"Ah-ha." He seemed impressed but not surprised, and once again she had the impression that everything was slipping from her grasp, though where to she couldn't say. There was nothing for Paris to win from this game, surely, so why was he here? Did he actually think he was doing her a favour? That betrayal at his own hands would be less brutal than at those of another?

"Benoît thought Michel was up to something," Paris said casually, as if changing the subject. "But I have convinced him he is wrong. Michel's too stupid to be up to anything, eh, other than keeping Ramsey sweet? Your *stupid* old Michel." His emphasis was unmistakeable.

"Does Benoît know …?" She trailed off, the "about us" sticking in her throat.

"Benoît knows nothing. Nobody knows anything but you, me and your father. Lucky for me I have friends in high places, n'est-ce pas, and documents as security. Because with me out of the picture there'd be nobody troublesome to know anything at all." He turned towards her slowly. "It may even be that there is nothing to know. I've looked into this Mendel your father was raving on about. Nobody knows anything about him. According to Georges he's some monk, a pet of your father's whose theories fit in with his own. It could be that for all Frenet's certainty, he's wrong."

"All the more reason then to keep my daughter."

"Pénélope." He took another step towards her and she put her second hand hurriedly back on the gun. He stopped. "Why can't you just play the game? It's only a baby – she doesn't even have a name yet. Georges and Manon will look after her well – you know they will. You can have another baby, a boy, Ramsey's true inheritor…. It may not even be for long. Once your father's calmed down – or died – who else will care about her eyes and their shade of blue?"

She stood up, too angry to stay sitting, and gripped the gun hard. "You have no idea, do you?" she accused. "No idea."

"No." His shoulders slumped. "I have no other option. What else can I do but try to convince you? You give me no choice."

"I give *you* no choice!"

He came to her then, mindless of the gun. "One of us must lose," he spelt out. "Isn't that how it happened for the Greeks? All those terrible sacrifices? All that wasted life? Because of some throw of the dice, some cruel joke of the gods on a couple with the hubris to think they controlled their lives…. We are on different sides now, Pénélope. You can't give up your baby and I can't give up my cause. It is over. So what have I come for, you ask? I suppose I have come to say goodbye." He reached out a hand and touched her gently on her cheek, his eyes shining in the dark. "Adieu," he said, so softly she could hardly hear him. "Adieu, ma Pénélope – et – bonne chance."

She didn't move, thrown by his seeming capitulation, knowing she hadn't won, yet not quite understanding what he was doing either. Was he really backing off? For her? Was he refusing this act that made her suffer so? What then? What would happen next?

He sensed her uncertainty and his words seemed to want to reassure her. "Let me say goodbye to the baby too," he asked, confirming his departure. "Perhaps we'll never know, not with the certainty of your father, but I'd like to think that she was mine."

Pénélope nodded, uncertainly. Her instincts didn't like it, but what could she do? He was conceding honourably, and to deny such a last request …. She watched him turn away from her and walk to the cradle. Something in his step changed as he did so, something slow and sad changed into something slow and stealthy, some heaviness in his shoulders mutated into something of his old cat-like grace. If he got hold of the baby Pénélope wouldn't be able to risk shooting him, if he got away with the baby she couldn't risk blackmailing her father – the possibilities of his revenge would be too awful, if he got hold of the baby ….

And Paris was planning to get the baby.

"No!" she shouted, and at the same time he leapt towards the cradle. She fired instinctively. There was a moment of still time where he was frozen in his leap, and then he fell, a sprawled heap on the floor. Quickly she ran to the gas lamp and brought it over to where he lay, her hands shaking so much the light nearly went out. She had to check his pockets before Ramsey came. She'd aimed well and the bullet had gone solidly into his upper body, blood spattering out the far side onto the baby and its crib. He wasn't quite dead. His fingers fluttered weakly to where she fumbled at his clothing and his lips moved.

"It's at Benoît's house," he murmured. "In his old violin. He doesn't know. No-one will suspect you going there…." He swallowed. "I wanted to give you a fighting chance – ha! More fool me. You Frenet's are all the same…."

He stopped and his lips twisted in pain, a parody of his old sardonic grin. Pénélope leant forward and kissed them one final time.

"Merci," she whispered. "Merci, mon amour."

Footsteps banged in the corridor, racing towards her. Quickly she stood and went to her daughter, picking her up and smoothing the blood from the baby's face. She was just in time.

The door burst open and Ramsey ran in, then stopped in shock.

"My God." Then, "What happened?"

"He was after my baby," Pénélope said, clutching the screaming infant to her. "He was going to take her." Then, illogically. "I have thought of a name."

She was obviously in shock. Ramsey went to her and put his arm round her stiff, trembling body. It would be best to humour her.

"Yes?"

"I shall call her Artémis." She kissed the child's forehead then held her out, not so much to Ramsey as to the night, even, impossibly, to the twisted corpse on the floor. "She will be Artémis, the huntress. And she will be nobody's prey."

Ella

My father christened me Ella because he was a jazz fiend and our surname was Fitzgerald. I had been going to be Louis, after Armstrong, right up until my birth when, inconveniently, they discovered that I was the wrong sex. My mother, in the kind of doomed-to-failure compromise that was her trademark, suggested adding an 'E' to make Louise. My father treated her suggestion with the contempt it deserved and said that just showed what a fat lot she knew about jazz.

So I was stuck with Ella, and while this was no problem while my mother was alive – in fact I rather liked it – it played right into the hands of my wicked stepmother and cruel stepsisters once she was gone.

Dad, of course, denied that they were cruel, wicked, or anything other than a good influence. He said I was just playing up. He said that of course I missed my mother, he did too, terribly, but being bitchy to my new sisters wasn't going to bring her back, and why, for once, couldn't I make the best of things instead of trying to tear down everything that he so painfully built up for me.

We didn't understand each other. He'd have liked me to be a sweet, feminine, silent type like my mother: long-suffering with just enough on show for him to feel he was worth suffering for, but not enough to make him feel guilty. I don't say this was deliberate; just his natural ego. If he had ever believed for real that they were genuinely cruel to me, I'm sure he would have reacted strongly. Inadequately, but strongly. As it was, it suited him to see my moans as the whinging of a discontented adolescent so that he could get on with his music.

"It's always me who does the washing up" I told him. "Always. Monday to Sunday, week in, week out, it's always me. How do you explain that – huh?"

"Well, your stepmother can't do it," he replied. "She has her hands to think of."

"Mother did it. And she played the piano a million times better than that old hag ever will."

"It's not the piano," he explained, so happy to have a winning argument he overlooked my 'old hag'. "It seems they want to use her hands for washing-up liquid commercials. You know –

the older woman who still has beautiful hands. She can't soak them in water everyday, it'll ruin them."

There were several answers to that, all of which seemed futile. If my father couldn't see them then I was on a losing battle.

"What about the Disgusting Duo?" I changed tack. "What's their excuse?"

"Been there, done that, apparently," my father quoted, his voice devoid of all flippancy. "Colleen says that when they were your age they had to do the dishes, just like you do now. She says it was very good for them to have to learn what kind of work goes into running a kitchen, and that it wouldn't be fair on them – or you – to deprive you of the same experience. She said they hadn't liked it either at the time, but that they appreciate it now and that if she were to let you forgo your turn they'd see it as favouritism."

For a minute I didn't say anything. I was stunned by the monster's degree of deceit and manipulation. Then I grasped at a straw of hope: she'd needed to justify herself; my father had queried her actions of his own accord.

"And you believe that?"

"Hm?" My father, taking my silence for acquiescence, had already plunged back into his work.

"I said, 'and you believe that?' I mean, Jesus Christ, you just have to look at them to see they've never done a day's work in their life. Honestly, dad, you can't seriously believe her."

I had made a wrong move. Dad was now supposed to say 'are you calling Colleen a liar?' to which I would say 'yes' and the showdown could commence. However we'd been there before. There's nothing craftier than a father who doesn't want to look things in the face.

"I have tried to do my best for you," he said instead, gathering up his dignity and injecting sorrow into his voice. "Lord knows I'm not perfect and neither is your stepmother. But she has made many sacrifices to come and live here with us and it isn't easy for her either. I can't make you like her – I can't even make you understand if you don't want to. But please, please, try and be patient. It'll all work out in time, you'll see."

Then he gave that sudden smile of his – the rare one that lit up his face and crinkled his eyes, and he chucked me under the chin and kissed me. And I realised why my mother had stayed in love with him all that time. My rebellion melted even though I knew that I was right and he was wrong, and I agreed to be patient, because it would, of course, all work out in the long run.

Big mistake.

What in fact happened, in the not so very long run either, was that my father died. The doctors said it was a stroke: I said it was my stepmother's constant nagging, which set the tone of our relationship to follow. My mother had always given him a quiet life. Colleen on the other hand, while seeming all soft and tractable in the courting phase, had actually made sure that the only way he got a quiet life was to give her – and by extension her daughters – what they wanted first. And Colleen wanted. Underneath that glossy exterior with its phoney smile and calculating eyes there lay a heart of greed. Why else would she want my father? I'd warned him of course, but he was far too unworldly to see it. He'd put my predictions down to jealously and general adolescence like everything else.

Well he paid the price for it, and while I surprised myself at how bloody awful and grief-stricken I felt at his loss, I also reserved a lot of sympathy for myself. Life from now on, I could tell, was going to be a bitch.

I was given a week after the funeral. My father was famous in a mild sort of way, and it wouldn't have done for the papers to get a sniff of his poor little daughter being maltreated once he'd gone. So, for a week I was allowed to mope in my room, play heavy metal as loud as I wanted, get a new black outfit for the funeral and not even do the dishes. A week may be a long time in politics, but it's desperately short in the life of a grieving child.

I wasn't very wise I suppose. If I'd been less suspicious and bloody-minded, I could have kept the war down to sniping level instead of gearing it up to a full-frontal attack. But misery and rage made me reckless. I had no cause to trust my stepfamily, so I threw caution to the winds and tried to get them before they got me.

Note: three against one are not good odds.

It was Mimi who struck the first blow.

"Look at poor little Ella," she mocked, a week after my father had died. "Crying on the rug in front of the fire. You'd think she was Cinderella, wouldn't you, and we the Ugly Sisters."

Lily clapped her hand to her mouth and the two burst into peels of giggles at the idea. They were both considered very pretty and I suppose they were – if you liked the over-made-up, doll-like, artificial look.

"Well, she won't be going to the ball then, that's for certain," Lily continued.

"Shouldn't think she'd want to," Mimi took up. "She is grieving, after all." I stood up to go. Tears were pricking at my eyes and I didn't want to give them the satisfaction.

"Goodnight," I said roughly, to prove that I could talk and that they didn't bother *me*.

"Night night Cinderella," said Lily,

"Goodnight Cinders," said Mimi at the same time, which set them off laughing again.

Needless to say, it stuck.

The important thing to remember about life is that no matter how bad it seems, it can always get worse. Before my father's death I had been a victim of my stepfamily's countless injustices; picked on, unloved and generally used and abused, but all within a containable way. My stepmother never let her daughters overstep a certain line and never herself went beyond what she felt she could justify to my father who, although distracted, wasn't *completely* stupid. I didn't know how lucky I'd been.

I was now on one of those downhill slides where it's hard to tell how or when you precisely got from there to here. One thing led, vaguely but remorselessly, to another. When a visitor came to stay I was asked to give up my room for him. When he left, somehow I never moved back in from the box room. Doing the dishes came back again, naturally, to be joined by the odd meal 'to help out', which slowly but inevitably became all meals, and soon all the housework, until I was a full-time unpaid servant. And while I objected to each specific new thing they introduced, it was never so obvious that I could rebel against the whole thing.

Then there was the ball. Mimi had been right about my not going to that. Before dad died I'd pushed my 'staying out' boundaries to the limit, going out whenever I could and stopping out as late as I could get away with. I'd dance to loud music, drink as much as I could afford, take the usual drugs and tell anyone and everyone who cared to listen what a bitch my stepmother was, what utter twats my stepsisters were, and how miserable they made my life. And people did care to listen. My friends felt sorry for me, genuinely cared about me and were mostly at the same stage of rebellion as I was. At least I had something real to rebel about. We'd discuss my situation and dream up fantasy solutions to our hearts' content.

After dad died all that changed. Somehow it seemed too important to bitch about, too humiliating to talk about – too complicated and messy to deal with. Besides which, I was knackered. Full-time servant to a lazy family of three in a semi-mansion is no easy number and I challenge anyone to prove otherwise. In a strange kind of way I almost welcomed the tiredness. They were mean to me; that was clear and straightforward. I was too tired to think; that was a relief. Why not just go to bed when I could, and stay there as long as possible. Sometimes I would even get up early or in the middle of the night and do my work then, to avoid seeing anyone. It was a solution that suited everyone and my stepfamily conspired in my isolation. When my friends phoned up to ask me out or to come round, my stepmother would explain, oh so gently, oh so convincingly, that I needed to be alone right now. I didn't argue. After a while friends stopped calling. I was alone, truly alone, like I felt in my heart. It was easier that way, and christ knows I wanted life to be easy.

The invitation to the ball though, was addressed to me – me *and* them. That is, me first, and them as a polite addendum because they were connected to me. It touched my pride.

Lily rubbed it in: "Royalty" she swanked. "We're invited to a ball by real royalty. Oh, I can hardly wait!"

"What a shame Ella doesn't go out any more." Colleen was sure of her ground. "She'll be missed."

"She will, will she?" I retorted, stung. "Well, I wouldn't be so sure about that. Besides, if I don't go you can't go – and where would that leave your precious daughters?"

Her precious daughters looked at each other and laughed. I think they practised that laugh in private, tinkling in unison in the mistaken belief it upped their sex appeal.

"We *can't go*," echoed Mimi. "How delightfully old-fashioned. But Cinders, dear, don't be absurd. Of course we can go. Our names are on the invitation. We just need to explain that you don't go out anymore."

"The idea that we'd stay in because of that," continued Lily with a sniff. "Honestly, Cinderella, dear, for a modern girl you have some delightfully old-world notions."

I looked at them all with their triumphant faces and felt my ground slipping away from me.

"Well, maybe I will go" I said, too loudly. "Maybe I will go after all. I haven't been out for a long time. It'll do me good."

"Of course dear," Colleen agreed in her most oozing tones. "Of course you shall go if you want to. We'll have to see what we can find you to wear."

I knew at that moment that I'd lost.

When I went to my old wardrobe to look through my going-out clothes, I wasn't surprised to find they'd disappeared.

"We needed the space," Colleen murmured, sounding apologetic, "and, well, to be honest dear, the money too. Some of them fetched a good price at the seconds shop and you weren't wearing them any more."

"You could have asked," I protested, but without hope. "Oh, I did," she assured me. "Of course I did, didn't I girls?" Pause for the chorus of assent. "But you just weren't *there*, Ella dear. You just shrugged and said 'whatever'. So I waited as long as I could...."

"As long as you could," I shouted. "As long as you *could*. Since when did you wait for anything longer than instant gratification? We've got a whole great big house of space here – I should bloody well know, I clean it. There was no need to get rid of them and you fucking well know it."

My stepmother gave one of those victimised sighs she's so good at and looked to her daughters for support. Mimi put her arm around her.

"Maybe we've got something you could wear," she offered on cue. "Anything you want, Cinders. I'd be only too happy to help out."

"Me too," echoed Lily.

I got up and left. A wise woman knows when she is beaten. Mimi and Lily's clothes were fine if you wanted to look like a real live Barbie; but if you're into Marilyn Manson and Manic Street Preachers.... Well, do me a favour.

I got my revenge though. I waited until they were out one afternoon then took a selection of their favourite clothes. I slashed them and stitched them, cut bits in half, swapped them around and tagged them together with safety pins. Then I put on the result and waited for them to come back in.

"Da-daah!" I sang, leaping into the hallway from behind one of the pillars. "What do you think?" Lily put her hand to her mouth. For once it wasn't studied.

"Oh my god," she whispered, "my Armani. You've ruined it!"

Mimi said nothing. She went pale.

"Don't you like it?" I asked, gliding around, model-like, to give them a better view. "I have to admit I'm not sure myself. I really appreciate your kind offers – 'anything you want' – and all that – and believe me I've worked really hard at trying to create something suitable – it was so kind of you both. But, well, I don't know.... It's not really *me*, is it?"

Mimi found her words. "You little bitch," she said, stepping forward. "You fucking cow. Just wait till I get my hands on you...."

I waited. It was the first time I'd seen her lose control like this and it felt great. If she wanted a fight, she could have one.

Colleen, however, was on the ball.

"Mimi," she said coldly. "Please take the shopping upstairs." Mimi looked surprised. She wasn't used to her mother speaking to her like that.

"But-" she protested.

"Now, Mimi," she cut in. "Right now." Then she smiled. "I'll come and find you in a minute." Years of implicit collaboration

117

paid off. Mimi went, now. I could feel my heart beating with adrenaline and frustration. She was going to make me lose this one, too. Then Lily started crying, which made it all worth while.

"Lily," her mother snapped. "Go to your room."

"My Armani!" Lily cried, one hand to her mouth and the other pointing at what was left of it, safety-pinned to my shoulder. "She's ruined it. She's – *ruined* it." She brought up her other hand to her mouth and cried into her knuckles. "Oh mummy, she's ruined it!"

"Go to your room!" Mummy snapped. Then, at Lily's look of surprise and anguish she softened. "Don't you worry blossom, everything will be all right, but just now I'd like you to go to your room and freshen up. You're smudging your makeup."

It was a comment aimed straight at Lily's heart. She went.

"Right, young lady," Colleen started, advancing on me. "This time you have gone too far."

"You don't like it?" I asked, skipping out of her way under the pretext of a model's pirouette. "I have to admit I agree with you. It was so generous of the Duo to offer me anything in their wardrobe, but let's face it – they just aren't me. No matter how I tried to alter them...."

I stopped. She was getting close now and her face looked dangerous. She'd never hit me before, but that didn't mean she never would. I felt uncomfortably like the time had come.

She stopped a foot in front of me, glowering into my body space, and brought her face down close to mine. I could smell the garlic on her breath, see the mole underneath her foundation.

I looked straight back. I was scared, but I wasn't going to let her know it. We were at some kind of crisis and I wasn't going down without a fight.

She opened her mouth and I waited for a torrent of words. Weak words, faulty words, words showing up her sins and failures, words I could attack in response. I was good with words.

But she was too clever for that. I could almost see her counting to ten. She held my gaze and I could feel her stealing the initiative. Silence and the currents of the unsaid were her best weapons and she knew it.

"That's the way you want it," she hissed suddenly. "That's the way you get it." And she turned abruptly to leave me standing there alone, victor of an empty space.

Why hadn't she tried to send *me* to my room instead of her daughters? Why hadn't she let us have a fight? Why wasn't she punishing me right now? Because she was too clever by half, that was why, and she'd won again. Slowly I took my clothes off and dropped them in the bin. I'd have liked to burn them, but despite my nickname this house was strictly central heating only. I pulled on my jeans and sweatshirt. I felt heavy and empty at the same time; mocked by my hollow victory and oppressed by a sense of dread. Something bad was going to happen.

Then I thought of Mimi and Lily's faces. I'd got them, whatever their mother might say. I'd got them good. I nursed the feeling. It was all I had.

Of course they had new dresses for the ball. They'd probably have got them anyway but I'd made sure of that. I was spared the humiliation of having to help them get ready because they were too scared of sabotage, but they made sure I suffered in other ways: showing off their new clothes in front of me, practising their dance steps with each other, prancing around with the invitation, pretending it was the prince.

"Me?" They would say to each other in mock surprise. "Dance? Oh, I'd looooove to." and they'd flutter their eyelashes and smile in their sappy Barbie way, and off they'd go until they collapsed in giggles.

"You have no idea," I said scornfully, after one performance too many, "how boring and stuffy these things are. First, you'll be lucky if you even get to talk to the prince; second, it'll be so crowded that getting a drink will take half an hour and third, even if you do get to dance it's not exactly a disco. Waltzes, pah! You're not meant to enjoy yourself, for god's sake."

"Oh listen to her," Mimi mocked. "Doesn't she know it all."

"A hell of a lot more than you, dearest," I smiled. "But then you nouveau riche get so excited and tawdry about these things."

I'd hit home.

"Well, all I can say is you must be so glad you're not going," said Lily, coming to the defence. "You must be relieved to stay at home and miss such a boring occasion – not to mention the embarrassment of watching your *tawdry*," she spat the word out, "stepsisters."

"You bet," I smiled and walked out. I'd carried it off, but the fact was I minded like hell. Why are people so contrary? Two years ago, my parents would have dragged me kicking and screaming to a royal ball and I'd have sulked until I got drunk enough to forget I wasn't supposed to enjoy myself. Now I'd have given anything to go.

The week before the ball whittled down to the day before. Colleen had piled on extra work, of course, using the ball preparations as a pretext, but she still hadn't officially 'punished' me for the clothes episode. This was worrying because I knew she wouldn't let an opportunity like that pass her by. I understood she was hoping to make me stew; but just because I understood that, it didn't make me stew any less. Something fundamental had changed since that day when she had looked me in the face and kept her temper. Some kind of cold violence had been unleashed that scared me far more than if she had screamed and shouted and locked me in my room. I tried to tell myself I was being melodramatic, but that didn't stop the feeling I had to keep checking over my shoulder.

I still didn't expect what happened. The day before the ball I went down to the cellar to bring up some champagne they were planning to drink before leaving. While I was still down there I heard the door slam shut and the key turn in the lock. It was the kind of practical joke that made Mimi and Lily's day so I didn't even respond. I just sat down on the bottom step to wait, wishing I'd brought my book: it'd have been a good opportunity for a quiet read. They'd soon let me out when they wanted some work done.

Then the light went out. I sighed and climbed up the steps to put it back on again. There were switches both sides of the door and I supposed we were going to have some kind of a switch war. To my surprise though, nothing happened. They must have taken out the fuse. So I sat down where I was, a little less phlegmatic – I'm not that keen on the dark – but still not really worried.

What seemed like an hour later I was cold, bored, stiff and wondering how long they could keep it up. Another hour or so, and I was beginning to think it might not be too much of a loss of face to call out. Yet another hour, and I hammered on the door.

"OK" I shouted, "the joke's over. You can let me out now."

Silence. Not the silence of someone trying not to make a noise, but the silence of nobody there. No one.

I started to get scared. How long were they going to keep me down there?

It turned out to be 24 hours.

I drank a bottle of champagne to keep me company and started on one of the big round cheeses that had been there since my mother's time. Then I tried smashing a few bottles of wine to see if it would make me feel better, but it didn't. The wine splashed back over me, so I ended up wet and smelly as well as cold and miserable and then I had to worry about stepping on broken glass in the dark on top of everything else. I'd gone down in my socks. Besides, I'd begun to understand that whatever I did she would get me for it; that she would always win, and the more I upped the stakes the more I would lose. She'd killed my father, I told myself, feeling melodramatic in the cold dark. She would finish by killing me off too. Come to think of it, maybe I wasn't being so melodramatic after all.

When there was finally a knock on the door I was so tired and lethargic that my brain only just registered it. The knock came again.

"Yes," I said, as if someone were waiting to come in. "Who is it?"

"Ella," it was my stepmother's voice. "I want you to know you can come out now."

"Yes," I said, but I didn't stand up. There had to be more.

"I hope that this has given you time to reflect," she continued, "on what a bad, ungrateful girl you have been." There was a pause as though she were waiting for an answer. When I didn't reply she carried on.

"I hope that this will be a changing point. The start of a new relationship between us: of a new you, Ella. A helpful, cheery, pleasant Ella we would like to be with." There was another pause. I still didn't answer. When she spoke again her voice had an edge to it.

"I warn you, Ella," she warned me. "Any more behaviour like that you displayed last week and you will be severely punished. Do you understand me?"

"Yes" I said, because I did.

There was the sound of a key turning in the lock and the door opened.

I stood up. I felt shaky and as if nothing were quite real. I don't know if it was the champagne or hunger or cold or the sudden light, but I just couldn't seem to get a grip on the situation. I stepped clumsily up and over the doorjamb into the bright fluorescent strips of the kitchen. In my confused state it seemed as if the floor was littered with shreds of material.

"The girls have been rather naughty," Colleen told me indulgently. The 'girls' sniggered. "They have taken their revenge. I have told them that two wrongs don't make a right and they have assured me that they will never do such a thing again, isn't that right girls?"

"Yes, mama," they choroused. A smirk lit up their eyes and painted their lips. So it was material on the floor. I looked more closely; it was my clothes. It had been my clothes. Everything was chopped up into little pieces. Everything: tops, jeans, bras, knickers. I doubted I had a sock left bar what I was wearing. Even my shoes had been hacked apart. I had nothing but the wine splashed clothes I stood in.

"When?" It came out as a croak, although the word was clear enough in my head.

"What?" Colleen was surprised. This was not the reaction she'd expected.

"When?" I repeated. And then, as they still didn't seem to grasp it, I spelt it out. "When are you going to lock them in the cellar? As their punishment?"

"Oh." My stepmother smiled. The girls giggled. "Don't you worry about that. They've been punished all right. Haven't you girls?"

"Yes, mama," came the chorus. I gave up.

"We're going out now." Colleen changed the subject. "We're off for drinks before the ball. Please clear up this mess by the time we come back – oh – and have all the tea things ready for us. I expect we'll be glad of a cuppa after all that dancing."

She turned to go.

"Maybe you could stitch your rags into some trendy new clothes" Mimi hissed before following her, "*Cinder*ella."

I stood there until I heard the front door shut behind them, then I sank down into the rags. I was cold, very cold, and I didn't even have a jumper to put on. For a few minutes I crouched amongst the material getting even colder, like when you cower in a cooling bath to keep warm. Then I got a grip. A bath was a good idea.

I stood up, put the kettle on for a cup of tea, then went to run the water. I tried the wicked relations' doors but, unsurprisingly, they'd locked them. They hadn't thought about the towels though, and I wrapped a couple round me while I fetched the joints I'd kept hidden under my floor boards, waiting for some suitable occasion. I made a mug of tea, found some matches, grabbed the cordless phone, and headed off for a long soak.

When I'd started to warm up, I rang God. Hallelujah. He was in.

I was so relieved I almost cried and he had to wait until I could continue. Briefly I explained my situation, cutting short his exclamations.

"I don't need sympathy, I need clothes," I snapped, frightened of choking up again. "And the sooner the better."

"I'll be there in an hour darling," he cooed reassuringly. "45 minutes even. Get yourself a hot water bottle, go to bed, and hold on. God will fix all. Don't I always?"

I smiled despite myself. God – or Gordon O'Dare as his birth certificate puts it – very rarely fixed anything, but he always tried. If friends were the sum of their good intentions then Gordon was solid all the way. He was also one of the few people I felt I could bear to see me like this. I hoped to hell he brought a range of clothes with him. Gordon's tastes were not always conventional.

Instead of taking his advice I went down to the cellar and opened another bottle of champagne. Then I raided the fridge for niblets before heading up to the attic. It was warm up there.

It was also where I'd stashed the rest of my dope, along with a couple of tabs I'd been given ages ago and had never got around to using. Life had been weird enough lately without resorting to drugs. But now was different. Tonight was the first night of the rest of my life and I felt the need of a flexible reality.

He arrived an hour and a half later – predictably – but I wasn't counting. I'd been sipping steadily at the champagne, and was on my third spliff. Life wasn't necessarily looking good but it was certainly looking more vibrant. I floated downstairs to let him in.

"Christ," he said. "Darling." He put his arms around me and held me for a moment, tight and gentle. God never did that: he was shocked.

"Do I look that bad?" I asked. "I thought thin was all the rage these days."

"All the rage," he agreed with a false smile. "In which case, darling, you've got it made. Now," he took me in hand, "give me some of that delightful-looking cigarette there, and come and drink some strong black coffee."

"Coffee?" That did surprise me. "What do I want with coffee?"

"To sober up," He took a long, measuring look at me and then really smiled. "You, my dear Ella, are going to the ball."

When I'd got over the shock I had to admit it was a good idea. Then I got the giggles just thinking about it. I didn't sober up, but I did mellow out, which was even better. Meanwhile God got out his clothes and explained the plan.

"By the time I've finished with you, darling, they won't even recognise you," he said, fondling a pink, silk evening dress. "I mean – who in their right senses would expect to see *you* wearing something like *this*."

He was right. Gordon was into pretty dresses – all frills and flounces which he wore whenever he got the chance, and it was a selection of these that he'd brought with him. He was also the makeup queen of London and he dyed and curled my hair in the time it takes me to put on lipstick without smudging it.

He didn't let me look in a mirror until we had finished, and my first instinct was to look behind me for the pretty woman. I was beautiful. I still looked a bit gaunt, but that was so trendy it was hardly out of place and the dope was softening out my face nicely. I really did look like a gorgeous young girl out at her first ball. I sniggered. If only they knew.

"Right," said God, looking at his watch. "9:30pm. You'd better go if you're going. I'll get you a taxi."

I moved to follow him and realised something.

"Shoes," I said.

"What?"

"You've forgotten the shoes. Aren't I supposed to be wearing glass slippers or something?"

"Glass slippers!" He was shocked again. "You can't dance in glass slippers, my dear. They'd ruin your feet."

"Well, naked toes for people to tread on isn't exactly a winner either."

For a minute God looked worried, then he bounced his fingers off his forehead and up into the air as an idea hit him.

"Mine are no good to you, Sweetie," he said unnecessarily, looking down at his size twelves. "But I know where we can get you just the thing. Come with me."

He directed the taxi to Soho, and left me in it while he rushed down into the depths of a topless bar. I lay back in supreme confidence. I hadn't a clue what he was up to, but it obviously made perfect sense: God moved in mysterious ways.

Five minutes later he was back clutching a shopping bag. He gave the driver the address of the ball then sat back to show me his booty: shoes.

"I don't need three pairs," I said ungratefully.

"I wasn't sure about size," he explained. "You'll want them to fit as well as possible dear, if you're going to be on your feet all night."

They were stage shoes, made to look like stilettos but with a perspex see-through wedge between heel and toe to make them more stable. The toes were made of strong, soft leather and offered a lot more support than at first appeared.

"These are brilliant," I told him, having chosen my pair. "How on earth did you wrangle it?"

"It's just a loan," he told me hastily. "Please take good care of them. They're doing me a real favour here."

"Who are?" I asked. "Don't tell me you've got a string of secret girlfriends God, 'coz I just won't believe it."

"Not exactly," he suddenly looked shy. "But I do seem to have acquired a, um, a boyfriend."

"At last!" I took his hand. "Oh God, I'm so pleased for you."

"He's called Melissa," God confided. "Well, that's his stage name. And he does a wonderful act. Really creative, you know. Not just the usual curves and wiggles. Anyhow. His sister works there too – she and Tilly, her friend, offered to lend you their spare shoes. I explained a little bit of your predicament – nothing detailed, don't worry – and they were happy to help out. But they do need them back tomorrow. All right darling?"

"All right?" I leant forward and gave him a long kiss. "You are the best friend a girl could have. Thank you."

"Right." Gordon changed the subject, typical British male at heart for all his dress sense. "We're nearly there. I'll keep the shoes you don't need. Now here's some money. Don't forget to leave by midnight or you'll miss the tube."

"Midnight! It's after ten already. What's the point of going if I have to leave by midnight? I'll get a taxi."

God pulled a face. "I do feel you need to be back safe and sound before the – er – wicked relations," he explained. "If they got back to find you missing all hell would break loose – and – well, you know who'll suffer if it does...."

He didn't need to say any more. "Midnight," I told him firmly, and smiled. "They'll never know I've left the house."

The taxi stopped. I leapt out, tottered on my new stilettos and caught my balance. When I looked back to wave he'd already gone. Ahead a row of fairy-lit steps led up to the ball. I went on in.

I kept being asked to dance. Normally, the places I went, the only kind of bloke who asked me to dance was the kind who wanted to fumble. Actually, that's probably what they'd have liked to do here come to think of it, only it was too – well – light. Here, dance meant dance.

I'd had a couple of spins with an Honourable Henry and was just beginning to remember the steps again when the good old prince himself came up and tapped my partner on the shoulder.

"Don't hog all the pretty girls to yourself," he said by way of introduction. "Go and dance with somebody's mother and give the rest of us a chance."

Honourable Henry dutifully bogged off and left Prince Charming the field. I looked around for the wicked stepfamily. If they could see me now.

"I don't think we've met before," was his opening gambit. "I'm Richard, Ricky to my friends."

I had a moment of panic. If I gave my real name I'd blow it.

"Cinderella," I said. "And my friends do *not* call me Cindy."

He burst out laughing. "Oh you poor thing, saddled with a name like that." I agreed with him and conversation blossomed. Every time it got sticky I lied, which leant a spontaneity to our banter that fitted well with my reality-bent state. He seemed to think I was the best thing since sliced bread. When the dance was over he went off to get me a drink and when we'd finished our drinks he asked me to dance again. I hoped to god that the wickeds were watching it all, and accepted.

"Aren't you supposed to socialise?" I asked him. "There must be something on it in court etiquette, surely?"

"There probably is," he replied airily with a mischievous look in his eye, "and I'll probably get my ear bent tomorrow. But you're only young once, after all!"

'Young!' I said, but only to myself. Tact wasn't my strong point, but even I could see there were some jokes he wouldn't appreciate.

Deprivation can be a wonderful thing: I had a whale of a time – and when midnight struck it was a big surprise. I froze.

"What's the matter?" he asked.

"Midnight," I explained, then smiled when he looked as though I were odd.

"My namesake," I reminded him. "Don't forget that I turn into a pumpkin when the clock strikes 12." He laughed uproariously. Here was a man who liked to laugh. "On a more serious note," I added, "I need to use the bathroom. Would you excuse me a moment?"

As soon as I was out of sight I headed towards the exit. I had to move quickly now – it was a ten-minute walk to the underground and I was late. To make things worse, it was a conspicuous exit. I had to walk up circular stairs to a kind of balcony and then through a door at the back to other stairs that led down to the front door. As I got to the balcony Richard met me there, having shimmied up the opposite side.

"Thought so," he triumphed. "Running away? You can't go without giving me your number, at least. We've had such fun."

I looked at my watch. I had no time to mess around. I looked back at him with some false number ready on my lips, only to see the wickeds walking towards me. I panicked, pushed past him, and ran down the stairs taking them three at a time. I lost a shoe at the first landing and pulled off the other one to help me run more quickly. He shouted out behind me but only once – thank god the British hate a scene – and then I was out. One shoe down and one shoe in my hand I rushed for the underground and began my return to hell.

God was waiting for me at home.

"Just to see how it went, darling and check you're OK." He brushed aside my thanks. "Now, tell me all about it."

I did while he got me a cup of tea and washed the dye out of my hair.

"I'll take the one shoe back to Tilly," he decided, when I confessed about the other. "I'm seeing Melissa after his show anyway. Don't worry about it darling," he added, seeing that I was indeed worried at repaying her generosity in such a way. "I'll get her a new pair. I'll put it on your bill."

The next day the wicked stepfamily were full of the prince's mysterious new dancing partner, as were the tabloids. I enjoyed both versions: the wickeds full of my affront and bad manners; the tabloids full of titillation and sex. Hearing the commotion, some of the paparazzi waiting outside had got in through the main doors as I ran out. Seeing Richard pick up the shoe must have struck them as heaven sent and they would have been making up their stories even as they photographed the scene. The morning papers had a hey day.

Cinderella's Slipper Clue said The Times, while The Sun went for *Court It*. They all speculated on whether he'd try the 'slipper' on every foot in the land, and what he'd do if it fitted more than one person. The odds, the Mail calculated, based on a size 5, were that it would fit approximately a million women in the country. The Mirror used its photos to work out computer-generated dimensions and started up a competition: *'Guess its size and you could win a trip round Buckingham Palace'*. Whoop de doo.

Two days later, God called by. He waited until the wickeds had gone out then knocked on the back door.

"Tilly wants to take him her spare stiletto," he said as soon as I let him in. "She says that at the bottom line she'd at least get the other shoe back, and at best there'd be a reward. She says her only other option would be to sell her story to the newspapers." God was white with rage. "That little bitch looked me in the eye and told me she reckoned a story like that was worth at least £20,000 and what did I think? I ask you!"

Personally I was more scared than angry. Once you'd got the tabloids on your tail they kept at you until they dragged you down. And they'd surely drag Gordon down with me, which would be a fine way to repay his help.

"I'll go with her," I offered. It was all I could think of. "I'll explain as much as needs explaining and Tilly can come to make sure she gets her shoe." I sighed. "There won't be a reward of course and she'll feel short changed – and let's face it, the opportunist will probably go to the papers anyway. But we'll at least do whatever damage limitation we can." I made an effort to smile. He looked so stressed out and worried. "Don't you worry God," I reassured him, "I'll get us out of this or my name's not Cinderella."

"It isn't," he retorted, but not too loudly.

He leant me his coat to go over the one pair of jeans and T-shirt I now owned, and we got a taxi back to Soho. It was early afternoon and I had naively expected it to be closed, but the lights were flashing cheerfully as ever around the photos of what waited inside.

"Won't she be working?" I asked, once I saw it was open. "Will she be able to leave just like that?"

"Oh she'll think of something." Gordon gave in to rare cynicism. "This is a young lady who'll go far."

Sure enough, ten minutes later he came up the steps with a young, blond woman. They got into the taxi without a word. I'd already given the driver Honourable Henry's address; it seemed to me that the fewer details she knew, the better.

For a while she maintained a stubborn silence, looking defensive. I guessed God had already had a go at her and she was expecting me to do the same. I decided to try a different tack.

"I just want you to know, Tilly," I started, "that whatever happens, I think you were very kind to have leant me your spare shoes the other night – and I'm very sorry I lost one of them and landed us in all this trouble."

"I bet you are," she sneered. "Not at all what you were planning, was it?" I don't know what I'd expected, but her voice surprised me. Behind the sneer, she was well-spoken.

"I wasn't planning anything," I replied, keeping my cool. "Just reacting. But now I'm planning." Her hostility deepened into suspicion. "I'm planning how we can get you what you want, and us what we want – that is to be left in peace. You wouldn't feel the need to go to the papers if you were well done by, would you?"

She sniffed. "It depends what you mean by 'well done by', doesn't it?"

"It does," and I smiled. Not a sympathetic, 'trust me' smile, but one of pure joy. Inspiration had just kicked in. "And believe you me, whatever I mean by it, you'll get more out of this if you put a smile on your face and play along. All right?"

To my surprise she relaxed a little and nodded. "All right." She got out a packet of cigarettes. "So, what's the plan?"

It was the voice and blond hair that had done it. Her shading was so similar to the colour God had done mine, I suspected he'd borrowed her hair dye. She was thin too and nicely turned out – not too tacky. Physically she'd got what it took. The rest was down to personality. I crossed my fingers and coached her for the rest of the journey while Gordon looked on, his expression ranging from protest through hope to disbelief, and finally back to the po-faced British gentleman required for the following scene. We had arrived.

I didn't know how good a friend of Ricky's the Honourable Henry was, but I suspected from their comments, and the *Hello*-type gossip I remembered from my past, that they were close. We obviously couldn't go straight to Richard, carving a path through the paparazzi camped at his door, so we went to Henry and I crossed my fingers that his flunkies would let us in. Once face-to-face, I was fairly sure I could make it work.

They did. Both my name and Gordon's were up there with the lesser aristocracy and that, along with innate British good manners, was enough. An hour later we were drinking tea and waiting for Richard to turn up while Tilly was practising her charismatic charm, bubbling personality and spontaneous wit on Henry. He seemed to be responding nicely.

The prince, when he finally showed, was in a foul mood.

"This is all your fault," he yelled at Tilly as soon as he saw her. "All this rubbish about Cinderella and glass slippers and running away at midnight. Have you no sense of propriety at all? Mother's absolutely furious."

Tilly didn't blink. "Well, it depends what you mean by propriety," she retorted. "But within the context of my business I consider myself as honourable as the next girl."

"In the context of your business...." Ricky had now seen me and the shape of my face, combined with Tilly's unfamiliar tones were confusing him. He sat down.

"Look, what on earth is going on here?"

We told him. In fact, what with one thing leading to another, we ended up telling him pretty much everything (apart from God's penchant for pretty dresses), and as we did so I understood that this was going to make me free. Sod the media, sod Tilly, sod the money – if this plan worked the wicked stepfamily were going to be history. It was exhilarating.

"So that's it," I finished. "Believe me the last thing we wanted was to get the media involved." I shot a glance at Tilly.

"Well," she said, with a straight-forwardness that left me standing. "I *had* wanted to get them involved, because in my line of business just about all publicity is good publicity. But that was just thinking about me – I can appreciate that with you lot it's different."

"It certainly is." Richard sighed. He stood up and absently poured us all a glass of Henry's sherry. "The point is, what are we going to do about it?"

"Well," I coughed a little nervously and was glad to sip the sherry as all eyes turned to me. "I have a plan.

"It seems to me," I continued, "that Tilly looks quite similar to the media descriptions of me at the ball. It's also obvious that I don't normally look like those descriptions at all – my own stepmother didn't even recognise me. It also seems likely that none of the Royal Watchers in the press would ever have come across Tilly before, or know anything about her. Finally, nobody could deny that the shoes fit her perfectly – they're hers.

"What I suggest," I rushed on, as Richard looked unconvinced, "is that without ever actually saying so, we let the press conclude that Tilly is Ella Fitzgerald, a perfectly acceptable young woman who happens to fit the shoe in question. The publicity will all blow over and –" I took a deep breath, this was the crunch, "should you ever want to see her again, say in ways more in keeping with her career … she would have gained a respectable cover. I mean, it must be hard…." Richard's eyebrows disappeared into his fringe and I moved swiftly on. "Meanwhile, I can disappear off the face of this earth and get myself a life. The wicked stepfamily will be told to keep away from me – that is Tilly – and set me – her – up in an independent flat. If they don't, they get leant on: you've got the power for that, surely, and the last thing they'd want to risk is prosecution. They'll never see me again and need never know the truth. I get to be free, Tilly gets 'well done by' and you get – er – well, whatever you want. And we all live happily ever after. What do you reckon?"

Richard looked at me. Then he looked at Tilly who arched her eyebrows and smiled. She was very pretty. He looked back at me and stood up.

"Come into the study a minute, will you? I want to ask you something in private."

I went, feeling nervous. He hadn't made his mind up and I couldn't blame him. On the other hand it couldn't be easy for a man with his background to get casual sex with no repercussions. Not these days, with this media. And if Tilly was game who was I to moralise? But was he game, that was the question.

In the study he walked over to the mantelpiece and leant on it, gazing at the unlit fire.

"It's been a long time since I last read Cinderella," he said when he was ready, "but I seem to remember it had a different ending."

I smiled. "They fell in love at first sight, got married, and lived happily ever after. Or so the story says."

"You don't believe it?"

I shook my head. "Pure Hollywood."

"Which, I take it, means that you don't – fall in love at first sight, that is – and all that."

"Oh no!" I exclaimed. "Certainly not."

"Right." He looked relieved.

"Why?" I pressed. "Surely you didn't want to?"

Instead of answering my question he looked me in the eye.

"You are extremely refreshing," he said. "Spontaneous, witty, resourceful...."

"Mendacious," I continued, embarrassed. "Conniving, tactless, hot-tempered...."

"You're right of course," he interrupted, hopefully agreeing with my outline rather than the self-analysis. "But do you really want it to happen, this plan you've worked out? Is it truly your choice?"

I realised I hadn't really thought about it.

"I haven't really thought about it," I said.

"Well then I suggest you do." He smiled. "Because, from a personal point of view, I'd like you to know that I'd be just as happy to act out your arrangement with the real Ella Fitzgerald as with the impostor."

I thought about it. And the more I thought about it, the more I realised what a brilliant plan I'd come up with. My idea had been only to save us all from ruthless publicity, but the result genuinely did get me what I wanted.

"If it's all the same to you," I said finally, "I prefer things the way they are. And I don't think the real Ella Fitzgerald would be nearly so 'convenient' as the impostor."

"Ah. Well, that is rather a consideration." He smiled again, eyes twinkling with a laddish charm that took away all offence. It was decided. "It'd be nice to see you again from time to time though. Catch up on your adventures?"

"That'd be great," I agreed. "God will always know where to find me." Then, at his look of bewilderment: "Gordon – Gordon O'Dare. We call him God for short."

He nodded.

"Let me know what you want to do," he told me, opening the door. "I'd like to help you out." I nodded in turn. I may be proud but I wasn't stupid. If you're going to have powerful friends you may as well use them.

We left in one of Henry's private cars a few minutes later. Gordon, like the fairy godmother he was, would put me up until I got sorted. Tilly stayed. I watched the house recede out of the rear window, then turned around, tucked Gordon's arm through mine and looked ahead.

The future beckoned.

Jerzi

It was a day like any other. Men worked slowly in the scorching heat and the few animals left dozed in back yards and the small empty fields beyond. Distant explosions were ignored. Only the shot of an occasional sniper from the town above brought a jerk of life to the lethargic bodies – a state of alert that soon slumped back into apathy when it became clear the danger was not for them.

The cease-fire had been holding for months now, to everyone's surprise, the days stretching into weeks and beyond, despite the media's dire warnings and civilian expectations. It was a cease-fire in the modern sense, entailing a few daily deaths rather than none, but for the citizens of Brezdebach it was good enough to be going on with, and infinitely better than before.

The sudden slam of a door sent a lizard scurrying for shelter. Jerzi paused on the veranda blinking owlishly in the bright light, then stepped carefully over the empty bottles from his drinking session of the night before, and slowly descended the sagging wooden steps to the cement-hard earth. He headed straight for the trough, cleared the dust and insects from the water's surface, then plunged his head in and kept it there.

Just when any observer would have started to worry, he reared up, gasping for air. He shook the drops from his hair like a shaggy dog, sending iridescent shards of rainbow in an arc around him, then plunged his head back in again. When he came up this time he began to groom. Ignoring where the water had soaked the collar and shoulders of his shirt, he ran his fingers through his hair, smoothed down his moustache, and ran his sodden neckerchief over his face before tying it once more around his scraggy neck. Jerzi always wore a neckerchief. If not fully camouflaging his lack of substance, it at least gave him a creative, slightly artistic air he could often turn to his advantage. And right now he was going to need all the advantages he could get.

Finished, his wet clothing already beginning to dry in the late morning sun while sweat darkened his arm pits in counterpoint, he gave a final look towards the front window. She was there, watching him. He could make out the darker grey of her silhouette against the dim interior, distorted and hazy through the pale dust that smeared the glass.

He raised a hand and smiled in cheery farewell – as much to annoy her as for the benefit of any onlookers – and called out, but not loud enough to be heard:

"I'll see you later, you old bitch," then turned and headed for the barn.

The cow seemed as reluctant as he to get started.

"Too fucking right," Jerzi murmured as he tied the cord around its neck. "You'd be better off in the barn, wouldn't you, and I'd be better off in bed. A long walk to market is the last thing either of us needs, heh?" And he glanced involuntarily back to the window before jerking the cow into movement with a pull that sent a lowing protest from the skinny beast.

"Yeah, yeah," Jerzi replied. "Tell me about it. You think you got worries. You ain't got no worries. You got a long walk and death at the end of it, that's what you got – that's facts, not worries. Now me, I've got worries."

He paused where the gap in a piecemeal fence marked the entrance to their smallholding and put up a hand to shade his eyes. The field opposite was ploughed and ready for planting. "See that?" he continued. "You know what that is? That's a problem, that's what that is. If this cease-fire carries on much longer, people are going to start farming again. And then where will I be, eh? You tell me that." The cow lowed again, and with a sigh Jerzi started forward once more. An old woman was standing at the bottom end of the far field and he raised his arm in salute as he approached her.

"Good morning Old Katya," he said respectfully. "And how are you today?"

"Same as any other day. See you're selling your cow?"

"Mother thinks it best." He kept all annoyance from his face. A trader who couldn't fool people was no trader at all. "You're planning on keeping yours then?"

The woman burst out cackling. "Darn right, I am. I'm keeping it and I'm fattening it up. Won't be long before I'm growing crops again too." She gestured over to her field lying ready. "The war's over Jerzi, might as well face it. The stealing days are running out. Won't be long before soldiers are going to have to *buy* food again. And when they do," she thrust her ugly old face close to his and whispered, smirking, "I'm going to have the food to sell 'em." She nodded to herself twice, in satisfaction. "What d'you make of that then?"

Jerzi didn't bat an eyelid. "I wish you all the best," he said smoothly, "though I can't agree with you. But I can't spend all day chatting, Old Katya. I've got a cow to get to market."

"Bit late in the day for it, aren't you?" Katya retorted as he jerked the cow into action for the third time. "Market will be over by the time you get there."

Jerzi didn't answer. The old woman watched him part, then spat onto the dry hard earth at her feet. "Scum," she said quietly. "What are you going to do when the war comes to an end, eh? Who are you going to steal from when there's no more dead men's homes to ransack?"

Jerzi was thinking much the same thing. His back to Katya, he let his face fall into the heavy scowl that was its norm. He hadn't been bringing much into the household lately and although Brezdebach had escaped the worst of the fighting, the unseasonably dry heat, compounded by the odd bomb, refugees, and fleeing or advancing troops, meant that there was very little food left for anyone, his mother included. There would always be a role for people like him, his father had shown him that, but the fact remained that successful crops and secure homes would severely damage his business.

He hadn't got far when a stranger stepped out onto the track in front of him: tall, ragged, exhausted, but with an aura of class around him, for all that. Jerzi reached for his knife.

"I come in peace," said the stranger, holding out both arms palms upwards and using a formulaic greeting from the North. "Tell me, where am I?"

Jerzi stepped back to keep the cow between him and the stranger, and looked around warily for an ambush.

"Who wants to know?"

"Piotr Tsadenach," the stranger replied promptly, confirming his northern origins. "I have been fleeing the Troubles with my family. I wish only to know into what territory I have brought them…"

The request was innocent enough, and nicely put. The man was educated – and the ruins of his clothes showed that he had once been well dressed. Jerzi made up his mind.

"Brezdebach," he said.

Tsadenach frowned. "That is Jant territory, is it not?"

Jerzi gestured to the top of the cliff that towered above their path. Squinting through the heat haze it was just possible to separate rock-coloured buildings from the rock that supported them. "It is up there," he confirmed. "Down here we're mostly Dzjitans."

"Ah-ha." The stranger nodded, remembering. "Brezdebach – the split village of High Traders and Low Farmers...." He realised instantly his mistake. "Or so the ignorant say. I say that in times of war, a farmer will out-feast a trader any day."

He looked at Jerzi levelly, placatory but not afraid. Jerzi decided to let it pass. The man was obviously a talker, best then to make him talk: there was always the chance of a deal. He settled his feet and began to chat, to put the other at his ease.

"Try telling that to the Jants," he retorted. "The way they act, you'd think they were still the lords of ancient times and we the serfs. Take this cow for instance. They need food, I have food, I'll sell 'em food. But do you think they'll be grateful? Do you think they'll cough up, first time, the price I ask? Will they fuck. Once a trader always a trader. They'll make me play their bargaining games for the rest of the day, even though we both know from the start the price they're going to give me. As if I didn't have better things to do. Bah!" And he spat into the dusty ground as proof of his contempt.

"You are selling your cow?" The man confirmed. He seemed surprised.

"Did you think I was taking it for a walk?"

Tsadenach was unoffended. "It just seems a strange route. I don't know the area, but I would have thought there were more direct ways up the mountain than to come around the back ...."

He let the words hang there. It was a dangerous business, these days, to question someone's path, but again Tsadenach didn't seem afraid, merely curious. Jerzi looked at him searchingly, and concluded that he was not a man to be bullied: there was something about this stranger, for all his openness, that implied he could take care of himself. He decided to answer the implicit question.

"There were," he confirmed, "before the bombing. Direct hits and landslides destroyed most of them. The rest were landmined by the Jants themselves. Didn't want those dirty Dzjitans getting uppity ideas now, did they? Felt it safer to pull up the drawbridge. The only route up there now is the High Road – which means a dozen roadblocks and half a day to get to market – if you're lucky – not to mention the insults. Though they're for free," he added, with bitter humour. "Even the Jants know where to draw the limit."

"Hmm." Tsadenach considered the information then came to a decision. "I'll buy your cow from you," he offered. "What do you want for it?"

Jerzi's heart leapt. His instinct had been right.

"It's a good cow," he started, "and she'll get me a good price at the market, despite the hassle. Can you do better?"

"I can save you the journey," replied the stranger. "And give you something that's worth more than money to some."

Jerzi sniffed. "Show me," he said. "But don't waste my time."

The stranger checked the horizon for stray eyes, then put his hand into his pocket and pulled it out again, fist clenched tight.

Despite himself, Jerzi felt a pull of excitement. If he was going to lose the cow then at least he'd get something good for it. Maybe the old woman would even be pleased with him for once. Besides, who needed a cow anyway? He could always steal old Katya's if push came to shove: throw a hand grenade in the stable, plant a bloodied old bone or two and tell her it had been blown up. She'd never know the difference.

Approaching cautiously, Jerzi watched the stranger open his hand, then sagged in disappointment. It looked like a handful of beans.

"Don't judge too quickly," said the stranger, reading his mind. "Never judge a bomb by its appearance."

"A bomb!" Jerzi laughed. "Yeah, and this cow is the Queen of Sheba." His tone turned ugly. "Do I look like a fool?"

"No," Tsadenach replied, unruffled. "Indeed I quickly saw you were the kind of man I could do business with. These," he continued, before Jerzi could disagree, "are primed explosives, new out, the smallest, most powerful yet. Each one of them could blow up a house – with a timer so safe you can make sure you're never around when it goes off. All you do is throw them. The impact on landing releases the timing mechanism – you've got as long as you set. These ones are set for twelve hours, just to be on the safe side, but you could make it a few seconds if you wanted." He held them out in front of Jerzi tantalisingly. "There are," he concluded, "certain people who'd give a lot of money for a weapon like this."

It was true. With those tiny bombs Jerzi could blow up Katya's stable and buy five more cows to boot. Which meant there must be something wrong with them.

"So why give them to me?" Jerzi asked. "All that for one measly old cow. Do you think I was born yesterday?"

"Because I have no money and I have no time," the stranger replied. "Near here my wife is ill, possibly dying. Her milk has dried up and my baby will die too if I don't do something. I am a stranger in a time of war. No-one will help me, and I can't wait to find an army to buy these for their proper worth. Give me your cow to feed my family and I will give you these willingly."

Put like that it sounded like a deal. Jerzi hesitated one last moment, then, with a show of reluctance, pocketed the bombs and handed over the cow. It looked like his luck was finally turning.

The cry of an eagle awoke him and he jerked his eyes open quickly, afraid he had overslept. The long shadows and a touch of softness in the air reassured him; he had timed it well. Had he gone to market for real he would have arrived home at just this hour. He drank deeply from his canteen, then stood up looking absently around for the cow before he remembered. The bombs. Tentatively he put his hand into his pocket and pulled them out. There were still there, still looking absurdly inoffensive – almost like the kidney beans they used to eat before times got hard. He shook his head in amusement: it was hard to believe that a thing so small could be so deadly. The thought didn't worry him – he'd learnt how to smell out a deal from the best and he was sure of his instinct. He was sitting on a gold mine.

Whistling, he started off for home.

His mother was cleaning out the barn. He raised a hand wearily in greeting, as if tired after a long journey, and went straight into the house. He had scarcely poured himself a glass of cold tea when she arrived at the doorway. Silhouetted against the light her figure, even in her shapeless old dress, retained much of its former glory: tall, willowy, yet strong, it was easy to believe she had once been a beauty. Then she stepped forward into the room and her features told a different story. Her nose was bent and swollen, her teeth few, her right cheekbone irregular from an ancient break. Lines of sadness had slowly hardened into bitterness and her eyes, though bright and enquiring, were suspicious, enquiring now only after treachery and disappointment. It was, as Jerzi knew to his cost, all she had learnt to look for.

"So?" she said.

He took a sip before answering.

"I got a really good deal." Even to himself the words sounded false, despite their truth. She had the ability to make him sound in the wrong whatever he did.

"How much?"

"Oh – about 2000 Slavti." The amount was vital. Tell her too much and he'd lose any profit he could make on the side. Too little and she'd suspect.

"About?"

"I mean nearly – nearly 2000." He smiled to cover his mistake. "About sounds more than nearly, eh? Still, that's not bad for these days – even with inflation."

"Well, let's see it then." She held out her hand. Jerzi ignored it and took another sip. This was the moment he had to get right.

"I hid it."

Her eyes narrowed. He sat down in order to avoid her gaze then, before she could consider too much, leant back on the chair and began his spiel.

"We sold the cow to get the money, right? Rather than have it butchered and taken by the guerrillas for nothing. Even though I have contacts with the guerrillas, even though the cow was still good for milk, you decided that we should sell it – just to be on the safe side. Right?"

"Right," she agreed, watching, taking a cigarette from her pocket. "And when I die, if I die before you, then you can make the decisions – right? If I leave you the farm – right? If I think you're up to it … right?"

She looked him in the eyes and left the threat hanging in the air. It was Jerzi who looked away first. She lit up.

"So," he continued, moving on. "It makes sense not to leave the money here for them to plunder either, doesn't it?"

"Maybe." She inhaled deeply, watching him carefully all the time. "So where'd you hide it?"

"Better not to say." He raised his tea for another sip, an attempt at nonchalance to compete with her cigarette. "The fewer who know the better, eh?"

She slapped the glass from his hand, sending it rolling on the floor.

"Do you think I'm not up to your little games? Hide it so you can gamble it away with your idle friends – that's your plan, is it? Two thousand Slavti? In your dreams! What did you really get? A thousand? Five hundred?…."

"I – I bartered it." He should have known he wouldn't hold out. "I need to trade on – that may take a few days – but the money'll be good, believe me."

"Believe you?" She said it softly, with infinite scorn. He tried to meet her look defiantly, but her poison seeped into him, crumbling his resolve.

Then, without warning, she too seemed to crumble, shrinking into her clothes, and before she turned away he caught an expression on her face that was almost vulnerable. She walked to the window, keeping her back to him, the smoke from her cigarette trickling gently upwards.

"What are we going to do?" She said it so quietly, so seriously, that for a moment he thought she was genuinely consulting him. He stood up and approached her hesitantly, his mind already searching for conciliatory words.

"I might have known you'd make a mess of it." Her voice cut in, hard, merciless. "You're useless like your father. Useless. I should have gone up there myself…."

"What! And leave me in charge of the farm?" Disappointment rose up in him like a physical sensation. "Impossible. How could you trust me not to sell it from under your feet while you were gone!"

"Trust…. You barter the cow away behind my back and you reproach me about trust. Come here," she added, before he could remonstrate. "Come here, come on, here, to the window. Look out, and tell me what you see."

Jerzi came, curiosity outweighing rebellion, and scanned the arid rocky land that stretched out below them. Their farm was one of the highest, nestling just below the foot of the mountain in a position that offered better defence than fertile earth. He had an unblocked view of the broken-down stone walls and occasional fence post that delineated their two fields from their wealthier, more fertile neighbours.

"I see gold," he said stubbornly. "Minerals, riches, wealth beyond anything farming here could ever bring you…."

"Ah, Jerzi, Jerzi," she sighed, and then, as if he weren't there: "The boy wants to take over the farm. He begs me to let him run it. And for what? Is it to farm? No – what does this boy know about farming? He can't even sell a cow without fucking it up."

"Mother –"

"But because he has some crazy idea that it's 'worth something'. Well let me tell you my boy – this land is worth the sweat and blood I put into it – and I mean *blood*. And while I'm alive no-one – *no-one* – is going to sell it from under my feet. *Do you understand*?"

"No." It came out as a bellowing wail. "What d'you think everyone is fighting for? Do you really think it's because they hate us? The Jants were perfectly happy with us so long as they had everything. Now they've found out we might have something too and they want us out so they can get it. This isn't about having a homeland, mother, it's about power. I don't want to sell your stupid fucking land, can't you understand? I want to keep it. I want to make us rich!"

"Always you want to make us rich. Everything you do is to make us rich. Just like your father. And look at us. Are we rich? Bah! Even your father could do better than you."

It was the ultimate insult. She turned away from him, and walked out the back door to the small patch of land between the homestead and the cliff that dominated them, where a few scrawny chickens scratched desultorily for food.

He followed her out. "Mother – you're making a big deal out of nothing. Look." He dipped his hand into his pocket. "I can exchange these with the guerrillas for a small fortune…"

She looked.

"Beans!" she shouted, snatching them from him. "You exchanged our cow for a handful of beans! No wonder you didn't want to tell me!"

"They're explosives," Jerzi explained, trying to get them back. "They just look like beans. They're state of the art."

"And you believed that. You – you –" She shook her head. "And you want to run this farm. There. That's what I think of you and your exploding beans. Ha!" And she threw them with all her strength, sending them scattering as they arced out towards the cliff.

"No!" Jerzi moved to run after them but she stopped him with an almighty backhander across his face.

"You do realise, don't you," rage flecked her lips with spittle, "that we are finished. That cow was our last asset. We have three chickens left. Three chickens between ourselves and starvation. And it's your fault."

"Mother," he cowered holding his cheek, but stood his ground. "You don't understand… Forget the chickens – those bombs are our fortune. Once I've sold them all our problems will be over. I promise you.…" And he stepped forward to go find them.

"If you go after those beans now, after all you've done, I swear I'll go down and sell this farm to Old Katya tonight." He hesitated, looking her over with disbelief and she grabbed his arm, digging into his sinews with her strong, scrawny fingers. "I tell you, I mean it." Her voice had an hysterical edge. She meant it. Defeated, Jerzi turned to go back indoors.

"You can peel the potatoes for supper," her voice followed him, taunting. "It's all we'll be eating from now on, thanks to you, you great oaf."

Jerzi stopped, feeling his heart fasten with hate and fury. Women's work. On top of all the other insults she wanted him to do women's work. If anyone found out he'd be a laughing stock

– and if he became a laughing stock it wasn't just his status in the village that would go, but his power on the black market. To get a good deal you needed respect. The thought gave him strength.

"No," he said, making up his mind. "No, I won't. Do your own work."

His mother stared at him as if he had gone mad. Perhaps, he thought, he had. He flinched, waiting for her blows, but she seemed to realise that he meant it and switched tack.

"Right then." Her voice became stony and she turned her back on him. "Then you may as well go to bed. There'll be no supper for you today – nor any other day you don't help out – and you'd be best to learn it." She raised her voice as he went back in. "There's no point leaving the farm to an incompetent idiot!"

Jerzi shut the door to his bedroom on her, then leant his back on it, breathing hard. She made the threat about the farm more and more these days. Was she playing a game or did she mean it? Jerzi wouldn't put it past her. She was capable of anything. He had to impress her; he *had* to gain her respect. His whole livelihood depended on it.

First though he had to regain his bombs.

He waited until the shadows had gathered into darkness then climbed quietly out his bedroom window. It was now dark enough to search without risk of being seen – the only disadvantage being that it was likewise hard to see. Each bomb was tiny, literally the size of a bean and their dark brown camouflage didn't help. They would have scattered towards the foot of the mountain where it rose steeply up to the High Road and the Jants above, and where mini landslides had filled the ground between the boulders with scree, small rocks and pebbles. How would he ever find the bombs in there?

He tried for two hours, often on his hands and knees, picking up objects one by one and feeling their texture for clues. Finally he gave up, weary, dispirited and scared the stranger might have been wrong about the timing.

He was woken in the night by the earth trembling, the worst he'd known yet. The very house seemed to shudder beneath him.

"That'll be the bombs," he thought, and he was so depressed he just lay there, danger or not, until the rumbling stopped and the shaking subsided. Then he went back to sleep. What was the point of worrying now it was too late?

He was awoken in the morning by his mother's shouts and banging on the door.

"Jerzi!" she called, her voice almost friendly in its urgency. "Jerzi, come and look. It's incredible!"

Curious despite himself, and responding to the hint of a truce in her tone, Jerzi went to look. Then he looked harder, concentrating to grasp the details.

It was amazing. The bombs had unleashed a new series of landslides which, for the first time, had destabilised the olive copse at the top of the cliff. Trees, uprooted but for the most part undamaged, had fallen down the slope, piling up on top of each other as they fell. It was like a waterfall of small, robust olives growing upside down, a mass of grey-green cascading down the mountainside from top to bottom. Leafy branches swept the floor, building up to gnarled trunks that stretched out into roots that in turn snatched and caught at the branches of the tree above.

"It's beautiful," murmured Jerzi.

"How did it happen?" wondered his mother.

Jerzi gave her a look of scorn. "The bombs," he said. "I told you they were bombs. Now do you believe me, you stupid woman?"

And instead of replying sharply, his mother looked flustered.

Jerzi stepped forward quickly to the bottom-most branches. He had called his mother stupid. He had dared to call his mother stupid to her face – and she hadn't answered back. For a second he felt he could anything. Exhilaration gave him strength and he swung himself up into the first tree for the sheer joy of it.

"What are you doing?" His mother called, and he noticed with satisfaction a slight note of anxiety in her voice.

"Climbing the tree," he said easily, as if he'd been lipping her all his life. "What does it look like?"

"But it's not stable!" She walked towards him and he saw her feet appear under the dense, dark leaves. "The whole lot could go at any minute."

"I'll be all right." For a glorious second he saw himself as a hero in his mother's eyes, strong and bold before her trembling concern.

"You'll kill yourself, you little idiot – and destroy the farm too. Come back right now before you bring any more rocks down."

Jerzi climbed a little higher, out of her reach.

"No," he said. It was becoming easier with practice. "I won't."

"All right," his mother gave up. "Kill yourself then, if that's what you want. That'll show you." And she went.

Jerzi sat perched in the tree, grasping at his lost image of glory. He hadn't really meant to climb all the trees, but he'd have to now. He'd show her. He'd climb all the way to the top and come back safely. That'd piss her off. A thought occurred to him. Maybe there'd be some good loot up there. Everyone knew how rich the Jants were. And with all tracks destroyed but the blockaded High Road there'd been little chance for looting. No-one knew about these trees yet; he was the only one. If he could bring back some booty, something valuable, his mother would see him in a completely different light. That would convince her.

As dreams went it wasn't much, but a poor dream is better than no dream at all. Reaching through the foliage for a handhold, Jerzi began to climb.

He reached the top nearly an hour later, staggered a few steps away from the edge and lay down amongst the few remaining trees to get his breath. Dealing, charming, drinking, and dodging chores on the farm required little fitness, and he hadn't made such sustained physical effort for a long time. He was hungry and very thirsty. His rashness had cost him his breakfast and, more importantly, his canteen – and the day, though young, was already hot. He would need sustenance, as well as booty.

As soon as he had recovered he concentrated on getting his bearings. In the old days he had sometimes come up to the top village with his father, who had considered the Jants far more interesting dealers than the plodding farm folk they lived among. Fighting had since scarred the landscape, levelling some landmarks and raising others, such as lookout towers and search lights, but the olive grove he knew to have belonged to one of the richest families of the area. Fertile land up there was hard to come by, and the olives were a loud statement of how much irrigation water they could afford to divert and pay for. Whether that particular family was still around, and still rich, was another matter. Hard facts about the Jants had been difficult to come by since tensions had mounted and the lines between territories hardened, and what news he gleaned had to be well-strained for gossip and misinformation. There'd been an elderly man, he thought, and several wives. If he remembered rightly, there'd been rumours about a son: that he was slow-thinking. There'd been other stuff too, though Jerzi couldn't now remember what. If he were lucky the old man would be feeble or dead, the son a pushover, and he could as good as walk in and help himself.

It was as good a place to start as any.

The grove backed onto what had once been landscaped gardens, now faded and partially given over to agriculture, and it didn't take long for Jerzi to make his way to the back of the house. A small yard had taken over what must have once been a herb garden, separated from the rest of the land and outbuildings by a low, ornamental wall. The back door was open, as everyone's was in this harsh country where even now the tradition of hospitality had not been completely worn down by the newer habit of suspicion. Jerzi crouched down behind the wall and waited a while, listening for sounds of work in the kitchen or on the far side of the house, but heard nothing. The place seemed empty. Standing up he walked forward at a slow, confident pace until he reached the door. Always look as if you're supposed to be there, his father had told him, and nine times out of ten, people think you are.

Once at the door he knocked perfunctorily, just in case, a story ready at his lips. He surveyed the kitchen hungrily as he waited. Like every house he'd ever known this was the heart of the home, where family gathered and talked and sang and lived their lives, but what a difference there was between this rich scene and his mother's shack. A huge dresser of solid wood, elaborately carved and inlaid with ivory, held gold-rimmed crockery and crystal vases; copper saucepans hung from the ceiling; pictures, ornately framed family portraits and religious scenes cluttered the walls. Even the chairs and table were comfortably shaped from ancient, imported oak. Everywhere he looked were signs of wealth and solid, lasting comfort. He almost salivated in his hunger. One day, things like this would be his.

He knocked again and stepped in. If no-one came he would take some of the smaller objects and be off – there was an old potato sack in the corner he could carry them in. He grinned to himself, they would even provide him with the means to transport his loot – yet at the same time he wondered: such a careless show of wealth in these dangerous times was reckless in the extreme. Was there no end to people's naivety? He walked forward to the dresser to choose his pieces.

"Hello?"

He froze for a millisecond, then turned, his rehearsed pretext already dropping smoothly from his lips.

"I'm so sorry to intrude, only –" he stopped, and this time froze completely. She was beautiful. He stared, analysing her as his father had taught him. She was pretty, but it was more than that. She was young, healthy and – fresh, that was the word – in a way only money can buy. It wasn't just the silk ribbons in her long, dark hair, or the kohl round her green eyes, or the rich fabric of her dress; but the dainty hands that didn't labour all day in the fields, the flat stomach unstretched by a constant diet of potatoes, and firm breasts not yet sagging through endless child rearing. There was something else too, something in keeping with this wide-open, vulnerable house, which he had already pinned down: naivety – an openness that posted emotions over her face in a way that no-one ever showed these days. It made him vaguely angry. She had no right to be so exposed – and certainly no right to be vulnerable, pretty and rich. Pretty young women at the bottom of the mountain didn't stay pretty for long – and they certainly didn't stay vulnerable if they wanted to survive.

"Can I help you?" Her look was surprised and enquiring, but not afraid: as though a stranger calling at her back door was more bizarre than frightening. That reaction itself, in this time of war, was intriguing, and Jerzi quickly adapted his tale to try and find out more.

"I am a stranger to these parts," he said, mimicking the accent of the northerners with whom he often traded. He pointed to his dirty, sweat-soaked clothes and stubbled chin as if they were rare and distasteful to him. "I have walked many days. The cease-fire in the North – it is not working so well. At last, this morning, I could walk no further, and my supplies – my water – everything is gone." He put on a proud but needy look he often used with success.

"I wanted to know if you could spare some food and water – and, if possible – a place to wash." His instinct told him that a need to be clean, with its implied sense of refinement, would pull at her more than the usual sob story. "I knocked a couple of times, but no-one answered…." He trailed off and looked at her, finally meeting the gaze of her deep green, startled eyes.

After a long pause he realised she had not spoken.

"I'm sorry," he said, taking her silence for a rebuttal. "I have intruded in your home. It was unforgivable." He turned to go. He could always come back later.

"So you don't know about him then?" she blurted out.

"I'm sorry?" Jerzi knew about many people, he made it his business, but she'd got him there.

"My – husband. You haven't heard what they say?" He noticed the slightest pause before husband, the wildness in her question, and for once he was drawn enough to give a straight answer.

"No."

"Oh." Her gaze slipped to one side. This, the dealer in him knew, was decision time. Would she tell him? Would she send him on his way? Or would she….

Hope like he had rarely known flared in his heart. Would she, this beauty, this rich innocent woman, be kind to him; treat him as an equal; believe him to be good? The idea was ridiculous. Of course she wouldn't. Quickly, he moved to leave while he had the upper hand.

"Wait!" Her face, when he looked, was almost composed, but there was something in her eyes – fear? loneliness? sorrow? – that he couldn't quite grasp. Used to eyes that reflected a narrow range of despair, victory, hate or sheer fatigue, Jerzi had grown rusty at reading nuances, but he knew enough to read a mystery and it intrigued him. He waited.

"I have little to offer," she continued hesitantly. "But water we have in plenty. If you would like to make use of the bathroom… we have soap and you could shave…. Meanwhile, I could prepare you something to eat – a simple meal."

She mistook his silence for reluctance. "Unless you would rather eat first…"

"No, no." Jerzi remembered he was supposed to have manners and gave a small, clipped bow. "To get clean would be the best feast of all. I only regret I have no clean clothes to put on. One shouldn't appear as I in the presence of a lady."

"Oh!" She almost blushed, and looked away. "I'll see what I can find you. I'm sure my father-in-law wouldn't mind. My husband – well – they wouldn't fit." She put her hand to her mouth, as if she had said too much, then continued: "I will show you the bathroom. Call me if you need anything."

In the bathroom Jerzi could hardly wash for wonder. Hot water came out of shiny taps. Soap rested on porcelain dishes; tiled walls gleamed their worth. He couldn't believe it. This was the wealth he dreamed of. How could anyone vaunt it in such times? Or, rather, how could anyone vaunt it yet survive?

As he shaved he tried to concentrate his mind on what he had heard of the family. The father, a martinet, had amassed his fortune in the traditional way, building on what his father had left him. Then there was the idiot son, a simpleton who, by all accounts was good for nothing. So had there been a second son? He hadn't heard of one, but that didn't mean it wasn't true – indeed with several wives it was more than probable. The woman had talked of her father-in-law. Men obviously talked of her husband or she wouldn't have asked him what he had heard. Perhaps the old man had adopted a nephew or cousin in order to have a decent heir. The woman had implied his clothes wouldn't fit – could he be a giant of a man? A soldier hired to protect the homestead in return for inherited booty? The idea made sense.

If it were true then Jerzi would be best to take what he could now, while he had the chance: although he knew his fair share of dirty tricks, he was no match for a professional fighter. There was stuff in this bathroom that would fetch plenty of money and prestige down below without him bothering about the gold-plate in the kitchen. There was so much clutter indeed it might never be missed.

Yet something made him hesitate. The trader in him sniffed a bigger deal, something less tangible but more rewarding, that might reveal itself should he play along. Something that might change his fortune for real, for ever…. Besides, there was the woman. If he took the money and ran he would never see her again. And to look on such freshness – to feel, even for a moment, that soaring hope – to be seen as a real man and treated as honourable…. In the end it was these feelings even more than his nose for a jackpot that led him back empty pocketed into the kitchen, smartly dressed in her father-in-law's clothes.

"It smells good," he said, retying his newly rinsed neckerchief.

"It's nearly ready."

"My name is Jerzi," Jerzi said, moving forward and presenting himself to her formally. "Jerzi Vladowski." He had a surname for every occasion. "I am delighted to make your acquaintance."

"Ania," she said, flustered, as he bowed over her hand. "Ania Krol," and she blushed red and looked away.

Jerzi had never been with a woman so rich who was so shy and unworldly. Rich people were the arrogant bastards who tried to screw him – whose place he'd like to take – but this woman wasn't like that at all. Rather, as the meal progressed he discovered he was trying to put her at her ease – and that as a result Ania was finding him amusing, even interesting – a concept so far from his mother's view as to be almost unthinkable. Astonishingly, he was enjoying himself more than he could remember – and if his instincts were right, so was she.

A couple of tentative questions brought him quickly up against her reluctance to talk about herself, and he changed the subject easily to him instead, making up and recounting adventures that expanded as he discovered how little she knew of the real world. Time flew. It must have flown for both of them, because when they were disturbed by a great roar outside she was as surprised as she was frightened.

"My husband!" she cried, starting up as though they were guilty lovers. "Quick! Go! Hide!" and she looked around frantically and ineffectually for a means of escape.

The roar came again.

"But I'm just a poor stranger," Jerzi protested, trying to convince himself as much as her. "I've done no harm – you've helped me out, that's all. Why should I hide?"

"Oh you don't understand." She was almost weeping. It was true; he didn't.

She grabbed their plates and threw them in the sink, leftovers and all, then ran to him and tried to pull him to his feet, casting around for a hiding place. Catching sight of the curtain to the larder, she dropped his arm and ran to pull it back.

"Here," she ordered. "He won't look in here. There's room if you breath in." And there was, just, amongst the shelves and the sacks on the floor. Bewildered and wrong-footed, both by the roars and her evident fear, Jerzi allowed himself to be pushed inside.

"Don't move," she whispered as she dropped the curtain to hide him. "He has very keen ears."

Jerzi was frightened. His theory of an adopted cousin brought over to protect the home was obviously right. And judging from Ania's reactions this was a fearsome fighter who attacked first and asked questions later. Had it been left to him – had he had a chance to think – Jerzi would have escaped through the front door as the husband came in through the back. But her panic had disconcerted him just as her naivety had disarmed him and he was stuck now. The only thing left was to get the best out of the situation. Positioning himself so that he could see through one of the tiny gaps between curtain and frame, Jerzi prepared to wait, listen, and if necessary move quickly.

The roar came a third time and Ania rushed to the back door.

"Hello dearest," she said, making an effort to talk calmly. "Have you had a good day?"

"No." The answer was shouted and seemed to Jerzi to be full of woe. It was the sound of a man in despair.

"Oh sweetheart, what happened?" Ania's voice, far from sounding frightened at this, had become reassuring. "Come here darling," she said as a mother would to her child, "and tell me all about it."

There was the sound of stumbling, uncoordinated movement and the scrape of wood across the stone floor. Then into Jerzi's view came a giant of a man. A good seven feet tall, he had a head the size of a rock and a hand that engulfed Ania's palm as she led him to his chair.

"They – teased – me!" he bellowed, forcing out each word. "They – laughed – at – me! They – don't – like – me!" and he raised his enormous hands to his monstrous head and wept, tears sliding down his cheeks in abandonment and saliva dripping from the corners of his mouth.

Jerzi was stunned, but Ania seemed to find this normal.

"Oh my darling," she comforted him, wrapping her slight arm around his massive shoulders. "Oh my poor darling. Were those bad men mean to you again?"

He nodded his head, too distressed to talk.

"Did you –" she hesitated, and this time Jerzi caught a flicker of fear, immediately smoothed over as she spoke again. "Did you do anything back to them?"

"No." Jerzi could almost feel her relief. "Only – throw – stones. But – they – were – too – far – away. Cowards. They're – cowards." He was working himself up and Jerzi could sense, as much as see, Ania working to calm him back down.

"That's right, they're cowards," she soothed. "Bad, nasty cowards. We don't want them, do we poppet? We don't care about them? We have each other, don't we? You have me. I love you. I'm not mean to you."

"Ania – not – mean! Ania – nice! Ania – lovely. Ania – good – to me…"

"That's right," Ania interrupted what promised to be a long list. "And to show you how much I love you I'm going to make you your favourite dinner. Would you like that?"

"Yes." He nodded, calming slowly.

"And while I make it, I'll get your favourite game – would you like that?"

He nodded again. Giving his shoulder a final squeeze, Ania disappeared from view for a minute then returned with a large leather purse.

"Here you are," she said, letting it fall with a thump onto the table in front of him. "You count the money in there and tell me how much there is."

Laboriously, with much prompting from Ania as she prepared her second meal of the day, the husband counted more gold pieces than Jerzi had ever seen in his life.

"Finished," he called at last. "Fin-ished."

"Hide your eyes then," she said in response. "No peeking." And he put his hands over his eyes as a child would and waited patiently. Carefully, as silently as possible, humming to cover the chink of gold, Ania put all the money back in the purse and tied its strings.

"OK," she called gaily, "you can look now."

"Pee-bo," he called, as he took his hands away. "I – can – see – now." All his former distress seemed to be forgotten. He looked at the table, then looked around the room with the exaggerated moves of a familiar game.

"It's gone," he said in delight. "It's all gone. Where's – the – money – gone?"

"I don't know." Ania played. "I don't know where it is. It's disappeared."

"Disappeared," he echoed. "Gone."

"It's just as well," Ania continued, "that you've got a magic purse."

"Yes," he smiled. "Just – as – well."

"Why don't you empty it," she suggested, "and see how much money you've got this time?"

So he did, with great joy. Again and again while she prepared dinner, Ania chopping and cooking and helping him as if it were normal, as if Jerzi didn't exist – while he grew stiff, sweaty and impatient in her father-in-law's new clothes. So she had married the simpleton. There were things here he didn't understand, but that at least was now clear. Yet while he told himself he had nothing to fear from an idiot, still something kept him behind the curtains. Perhaps it was the monster's size, her terror at his arrival, the animal anguish in his roar. Or perhaps it was something else. But each time Jerzi thought of opening the curtain and striding out he looked once more at Ania; watched her clean, tapered, unspoilt fingers chopping, mixing, soothing – glimpsed her face full of tender concern – and didn't move.

Finally the meal was over, the game played out and it was time for their siesta.

When they had gone Jerzi left the larder and stretched, trying the regain the dignity he had found with his wash and now lost with the sweat darkening his new shirt.

"I'm just going to the bathroom," he heard her call. "I'll be back in a minute sweetheart, don't worry."

And she was back in the kitchen.

"Go," she said urgently, when she saw him standing there. "Go now, quickly – and don't come back."

The 'Go', Jerzi had expected, but not the corollary. Of course he must come back. She had enjoyed his company. She liked him. She *needed* him. How could she bear it, here alone with her idiot husband?

"How can you bear it?" he asked, stupidly, and was rewarded by a flash of pain flickering through her eyes.

"You don't understand," she said fiercely. "No-one understands," she added. "You're all the same."

"No. I'm not," he protested, hurt in turn. She had treated him as if he were different. She had listened to him, laughed with him, fed him with kindness and generosity. He must be different.

"Your hospitality," he stammered awkwardly, in an attempt to remind her of what they had shared. "How can I repay you? How can I help you? What can I do?"

"Oh." And for a moment yearning washed over her liquid face. She caught herself quickly, covering her need with another gift. "Here, take this." She reached for the sack of gold that lay on the table. "There are many dangers out there and you are a stranger, alone and empty-handed. This will help you make your way."

Jerzi couldn't believe it. This would make his mother sit up and take notice. This would be the making of him. So why didn't he go? Why did he instead move closer as she handed it over – so close he could smell her skin and feel the fear beating in her heart?

"But –" he protested insanely, "but – the – your husband. He'll notice – he'll miss it. You'll get in trouble."

"Oh, he's got plenty more where that came from," she answered carelessly. "He doesn't even know how many. That's no problem."

"Ania!"

His call, sleepy, demanding, made them both jump.

"Go, for God's sake," she insisted. "He'll come and find me if I'm any longer. Go – and never return."

He tilted his face down to where hers looked up at him and took the kiss he sensed was his – the kiss she'd give because she thought it sealed their goodbye – a kiss that turned out to be tender and sweet and far too fleeting.

"Oh I'll be back," he said. "Don't you worry about that." And he left, not knowing himself if it was a threat or a promise.

Jerzi ran all the way back to the treefall, climbed down the first few branches until he felt he had truly left that strange land above, then sat down to catch his breath and think.

Except that he found he couldn't concentrate – the images swirling around his head far too vivid and unfamiliar to leave room for thought. Her hair, her eyes, her face – those liquid features, where emotions rippled across the deep pool of her privacy. She'd liked him. She didn't know about his mother, his father's legacy, his marketeering, the other women…. And in her not knowing it was as if they hadn't been. He became a new man, a free man, released to be however she saw him. She was different. She had kissed him almost like a sister – their tongues hadn't even met – and yet he could still feel the electric sweetness of her lips on his.

Then there was the gold. He hugged it to him, feeling the comfort of its sagging weight, then opened the strings to check as suspicion grabbed him. No. It hadn't been a cruel joke. It was all there, the 129 pieces of gold her husband had counted out so many times. Automatically he took out a handful and put it in his pocket. His mother might finally be pleased with him, but that didn't mean she'd share any of the benefits. Better to keep some back for himself.

Descending the trees took almost as long as climbing them and he arrived at the bottom in mid-afternoon, after the siesta.

"Oh," his mother said as she emerged from the kitchen door. "You've decided to come back, have you?" And she turned her back on him and trudged out to the far end of the upper field.

He followed her, saying nothing, waiting until she reached the dry irrigation ditch. Then before she could start to clear it he said quietly, to her back:

"Mum." He had never called her that before. It sounded odd, almost tender, and it stopped her in her tracks.

"What is it?" she asked turning round. "What have you done?" She searched his face for signs of what she should worry about. His new clothes, plus something new in his manner, some bravado, made her suspect the worst.

"You've killed someone?"

Jerzi felt a stab of disappointment. He was tempted, almost, to keep the money to himself. That'd pay her back for her lack of faith. But he'd come too far now to change his mind: he wanted to see her face when he showed her the gold; see her eyes light up with pleasure and greed and know it was all because of him. Slowly he pulled out the sack from under his jacket and almost reverently handed it over to her.

"For you," he said, watching her closely. "You could say it's what we got for the cow."

She gave him a last, long, hard look, then turned her attention to the purse before her. It was obviously money. But Jerzi knew she would never dream of the type or how much. He held his breath as she undid it, watched her hands delve inside, then stop at the enormity of what they found, waited for her to look back at him.

Her eyes, when they returned to his, certainly glittered with something. Her cheeks flushed red and she took a step towards him.

"Where did you get this?" she hissed. It wasn't anger, but it wasn't pleasure either. "Quick, tell me."

"Up – up the top," he blurted out, taken aback by her ferocity. "I found it."

"Did you kill anyone?"

Again he was hurt by her assumption. "No!" he yelled, and his anger spilling over in contrast to her tight, urgent questions, carried conviction. "No I didn't kill anyone! I found it! There was a bombed out house – it was dangerous – the roof was falling in. I thought I might get some loot. And I did. It had been hidden in a wall that collapsed when I went in. I could have been killed!" He warmed to his theme. "I could have been killed, bringing that money back for you – and all you can do is stand there and accuse me. Well if that's what you think…." He made to snatch back the purse and storm off.

She pulled the bag quickly into her stomach, shielding it with her hands.

"I was worried for you," she said quickly. "Frightened they might come and get you. They're dangerous, that lot up there. Dangerous and powerful. Are you sure no-one saw you?"

"No-one saw me." He said it too quickly. The glitter in her eyes hardened into cunning, then finally softened into the pleasure her son had hoped for.

"I was so worried," she said again. "I thought you would die. And instead my big boy has brought home some treasure. More treasure than we ever dreamed of." She smiled at him, the ugly grimace of a woman who has forgotten how, and patted his arm. "I am very proud of you." At last Jerzi's heart soared with satisfaction. "Tonight," she continued, "we will celebrate. I will cook you a special meal, you will drink the last of the whisky and we will party – and you will promise me never to go up there again, eh? It is too dangerous. We have all we need now. Why risk losing my only son for any more?"

Even though Jerzi didn't trust her, he couldn't help basking in her words. Tonight the unthinkable would happen, all because of Ania.

His mother wined him and dined him as she had promised and tried to get him talking, but some instinct helped him to thwart her, for once keeping him to his story even after a whole bottle had lubricated his insides. Ania was his – all his – and no-one, not even his mother, would take her from him.

The next few weeks were some of the best Jerzi had ever known, bolstered by money in his pocket, thoughts of Ania, and the respect of a mother no longer sure of her ground. His vow to never return was easily given, empty words they both recognised as such, but for a while he was content to act as though he meant them. He enjoyed her new manner too much to disappoint her quickly. In any case, there was no point in going back to Ania until she was ready to see him. She needed to miss him, to believe he had obeyed her command to never come back, and to understand how she dreamt of his promise that he would. She needed time to feed on the hunger his visit had awakened and to be ravenous by the time of his return.

There was another reason too – the one downside to this moment of triumph – for while his mother treated him better, she also watched him more closely, as if she could tell that this was something different. Just as Jerzi revelled in her new found deference, so he shrank before the depth of her perception. She didn't give a fig for the local sluts he sometimes visited, he knew that, they posed her no danger. But another woman, a real woman, could take him from her – and Jerzi was aware enough to know that, while his mother didn't particularly want her son, she certainly didn't want to lose him to another.

So it was that two months passed before, his mother safely off to market, Jerzi climbed back up the treefall.

He was approaching the door cautiously when she came out, bucket in hand. She stopped as soon as she saw him and a rapid pattern of emotions shifted across her face: shock at seeing a stranger quickly turning to joy as she recognised him. She took a step forward, a step that filled his heart with something he'd never known before – something tender, proud and warm – then she caught herself and stiffened into coldness and formality.

"I told you not to come back," she said.

"And I told you I would."

She looked around instinctively for watching eyes.

"Go away," she said, hardly faltering. "Go away. Now."

She waited for him obey her order. Instead he took a step forward.

"I said 'go away,'" she repeated, her voice rising in panic. Then, "Please. Please...."

But she wasn't begging him to leave. Jerzi, who had seen her joy and hugged it to him like the rare possession it was, understood what she meant, and was ruthless.

"No," he said and took another step forward. "You don't want me to. Not really." He paused and watched her, holding her gaze with eyes more intent, more serious than they had ever been. This was the biggest deal of his life. "Do you?"

In response she gave a half sob and turned back to the kitchen.

After a pause he followed her.

He found her facing the wall, shoulders tight with the tears she was fighting to control, and he didn't even think about it. He went up to her, reached out one finger and gently, tremblingly, followed the curl of her hair where it escaped from her bun down the nape of her neck. Then his other fingers joined in, caressing the back of her head where it fitted so perfectly into his palm, before continuing round over her small tight ear onto her cheek. He spread his hand out, across and down on to her lips as she turned to meet him – and then she was in his arms, sobbing, her head in his chest until he lifted it for another kiss. This one was even sweeter, mingled with the salt of her tears and the juices of her mouth, so that his tongue moved to explore and savour it and hers moved up to respond and suddenly he felt an erection so strong it almost hurt. He pulled her body towards him and she froze, then pulled away.

He reached out, terrified at what he had done; furious at himself for blowing it – and at her for making him. She spoke before he could touch her.

"Would you like some tea?" and the question, so bizarre, startled him out of the moment.

"Yes," he replied after a pause, following her lead. "That would be very kind."

"Please sit down." She indicated a chair then went about her work in silence.

For a while he watched her. Watched how her body moved, how her dress swung, how her shoulders slowly relaxed as the familiar task helped calm her. Then, when she had sat down beside him and poured them both tea and they had sipped, once or twice, politely, he spoke.

"You look well," he said, keeping his tone carefully formal.

"Thank you," she replied in kind. "So do you. Indeed," she added after a long pause, with a touch of a smile, "you look much better than the last time I saw you."

It was true. Jerzi had taken great care in his appearance and had climbed the trees slowly and carefully so as not to spoil the new clothes with dirt and sweat.

"The gold that you gave me...." Jerzi kept his tone neutral and glanced to see if he was stepping on forbidden ground. She didn't react. "It has been very useful."

"I am glad." She dismissed the subject. "So, tell me. What have you been doing since I last saw you? How come you are still in the area?"

She spoke as if she didn't care, as if the question were purely polite, a part of the formal conversation she was obliged to make with visitors. But he had other plans.

He shook his head and looked her in the eyes with a half smile that echoed her own.

"As for why I am still in the area," he answered, his tone relaxing, "that is surely obvious." He waited for her to understand his meaning then continued as her eyes widened. "As for what I have been doing...." He shook his head again. "I told you much about myself on my last visit. This time is for me to learn about you."

He had planned his approach and was well-pleased with it. This way he could avoid having to remember his former lies – always a risky option – and at the same time perhaps get to the bottom of the mystery and fear that surrounded her bizarre marriage.

"You don't have to tell me much," he insisted as she hesitated. "Just whatever you choose. After all," he sipped his tea and watched her with eyes intent with such desire they were almost menacing. "It is only right."

Which, while deeply unfair, was strictly true. In their code of hospitality confidences had to be reciprocated. Jerzi's gamble was that she would be too unworldly – or perhaps too hungry – to think of using empty words and superficial lies to fulfil her duty. He was right. She began, instead, to tell him about herself.

"I am an orphan."

He nodded. She had to have been.

"My parents died when I was very young. Apparently I had no relatives, no friends or family to take care of me – so I was sent to the orphanage." She paused and looked him full in the eye for his reaction, her chin tilted proudly. Jerzi absorbed her gaze without reaction, held it and looked past it to the hurt that lay below. He understood her defensiveness. In the traditional, close-knit village communities they'd grown up in, neighbours looked after each other. Orphanages were for huge impersonal cities – or for outcasts. He longed to lay his hand on hers. Instead he nodded.

"Yes," he said.

She took a deep breath like a sigh, and continued. "My parents had foreseen my situation," she said with difficulty. "They had put by some money to pay for my education when I was old enough – the best money could buy. Naturally this meant the church." Again she paused, but this time only to drop her formal tone as she appealed to him.

"The Sisters said only a fool would waste all his money on my childhood, leaving me no dowry for marriage. They told me my parents were selfish and cruel. But they weren't! They did it because they cared! They knew what happens to children – to girls – who grow up illiterate and coarse, educated only in milking and crops. They knew what kind of a husband a dowry would buy a girl like that. They didn't know how I would grow up, what kind of advantages I might have – I was only a baby. But they decided, rightly or wrongly, to give me all they could for my childhood and leave me as an adult to find my way. And they were right. Surely they were right!"

She was near tears again. Jerzi didn't fully understand what reassurance she needed, but did understand how very odd their choice had been – how completely unheard of it was to look to your daughter's needs in any context but that of marriage. Some instinct, sharpened by his concern for her, led him to say the right thing.

"It must have been hard," he said slowly, considering, "for your parents to make such a decision. And even harder for you to live with it." He remembered back to his own childhood, so very different, when he too would have given anything to be approved. "A child, after all, just wants to fit in." She threw him a look of gratitude, of complicity, that filled him with satisfaction.

"It was hard," she agreed. "The Sisters were honest – they taught me everything my parents had stipulated in their will: languages, geography, history, art, needlework, music…." She lingered over the word and for a moment her face grew dreamy. "But at the same time they were always pointing out how useless it was. A woman without a dowry or relatives, they made very clear to me, has but two futures: to become a mistress, if she has the looks and the cunning, or to become a governess, which in this country of course is almost the same thing only with less pay. Since I had no looks to speak of and even less cunning, my fate was laid out remorselessly before me."

"But you are beautiful!" Jerzi protested. She hadn't said it coyly as bait for a compliment, but simply, factually, as a universal truth.

"Oh no!" She looked surprised. "My brow is too wide, my eyes and hair too dark – blondes have the best chance naturally, they are so rare – my figure is too thin, my feet too big, my arms too long and angular, my –"

"Stop!" Jerzi stood up in frustration and walked round the table staring at her until she shifted uncomfortably in her chair. "They told you this," he asked. "The Sisters?"

"Oh yes," she agreed, "and they said that –"

"They lied!" Jerzi surprised himself with his vehemence. "Why you – you're -" he stopped and looked at her, the look turning into an appraising stare as he calmed down so that she blushed and looked away in confusion.

"Stand up!" he ordered, his tone almost bullying.

Slowly, blushing even more deeply, she stood.

"Your brow," he began, looking at her brow, "is wide and clear and generous like the thoughts within it. Your eyes are like rapids that drag a man into and over every emotion that crosses your face. Your hair," and he remembered the touch of his finger as he traced her errant curl, "is like the midnight stillness, and your figure...." Words failed him and she moved away quickly, busying herself at the sink to shield herself from the thoughts he was so patently thinking.

He coughed, then moved to sit back down at the table and sip his tea in distraction.

"You *are* beautiful," he repeated, careful now to keep his tone dispassionate.

She looked at him uncertainly, but with a glimmer of belief, of understanding. Quickly, before she could feel ill-at-ease, or guilty, he moved her on.

"And then?" he asked.

"Yes?" she was confused.

"So you were educated, you grew up, you had no dowry. And then?"

He realised as soon as he had spoken that he had been too precise, too brutal. His words carried a flippancy that was far from his intent.

"I got married after all," she said simply. "Now you must go," she walked to the door, dismissing him. "And I must feed the hens."

"I will help you!" He stood up quickly, keen to regain his lost standing, and blocked her path. She looked at him patiently, with dignity, waiting for him to move out of her way, and he felt a strange sense of shame. He stepped aside. "Please," he said instead. "I'd like to help you. If I may."

This time it was her turn to give him a slow, appraising stare and his turn to shift uncomfortably under her gaze, wondering if she read the many parts of his character that lurked beneath the surface. But he must have passed because suddenly, without even a nod, she handed him the bucket of chickenfeed and led the way.

"Jesus and Mary!" If his mother had heard him she would have boxed his ears, but he was too excited to care. "Black Zabistas! Hundreds of them! People would pay a fortune for these...." He was exaggerating, but not greatly. The coop was full of healthy-looking hens of the most valued type in the country. Eggs of any sort had become rare since the war had turned serious, and eggs from this breed were a rare treat indeed.

"My father-in-law likes them," she explained. "They are difficult to care for, but he considers it worth the effort." She looked up at his face and saw, even in the half-light, how it was alight with enthusiasm. "You are a farmer," she stated. And because it came from her, and was just a fact, said plainly with neither scorn nor implicit contempt, he didn't deny it, rather nodded his head.

"Take one," she offered. Like the last time he hesitated, worried about the consequences for her.

"We have more, many more than we need," she reassured him, reading his thoughts. "The people of the village will not eat our things, and with my father-in-law and his family away …." She trailed off. "Take one and welcome," she reiterated. "They're no good to me."

"Why….?" He knew he was back on dodgy ground but here, protected in the semi-darkness, he felt he could take the risk. "The villagers…," he started again, groping for a more subtle approach, "you'd have thought they'd be glad to buy such luxuries…." He trailed off as she had done, leaving her to fill in the gaps as she desired. She hesitated, opened her mouth, but before she could say anything they were disturbed by a familiar roar.

"Ania!" There was a dull thwack like a rotten branch hitting a tree.

"My husband!" She reached out and clenched his arms with fingers tight with fear. "Stay here. Stay here until I get him inside. Wait until I've had time to calm him a little – to be sure he'll stay put – then go."

"But –" he held her arm and she shook him off fiercely.

"Do as I say," she hissed. "If you value your life then you must leave me." Something in her voice, the ugliness of her hissing, made him submissive. He stood back, making room for her to leave, and waited for her to tell him never to return.

Instead she approached and, almost before he knew it was happening, had kissed him.

"Thank you," she said. "Thank you for coming back." Then she walked out to meet her husband.

Putting his fingers to his lips, savouring the touch, Jerzi hunkered down to watch through a chink in the wall. He caught sight of Ania trying to hurry the simpleton in through the back door, but he was agitated, reluctant to move, gesticulating with the large branch in his hand. Or was he? Even as they disappeared inside Jerzi stiffened, straining for a better look. Had it been? It couldn't possibly be... but it looked like.... The glimpse had definitely looked like the trousered remains of a human leg.

His mother was happy with the Black Zabista; the eggs would fetch a pretty price on any market, let alone the black one – but her delight was soiled with suspicion. She told Jerzi it was fear for him that tempered her pride, that she was worried now he'd broken his promise that he'd do it again – that instead of more riches, next time she'd get only his corpse. But he knew she was lying.

His lies to her too, were less than convincing. The hope Ania had aroused in him, confirmed by the response of her lips, was becoming a passion and he thought of her, dreamt of her, burnt for her in a way that words, however cunning, could not hide.

At nights he slipped out to the prostitutes that could be found following the straggled army encampments. Sometimes the walk there and back was long, but never long enough to exhaust his desire. He fucked energetically, some would say violently, repeating to himself as if it were a mantra that sex was for them and they were for sex: that Ania was apart – too pure for such thoughts, such acts. But he knew it wasn't true. He knew there was an act of sex as yet unknown to him, as pure as Ania and as beautiful too – and knowing it was barred to him did nothing to decrease his need for it.

His mother let his behaviour pass for the most part without comment. She would have preferred to contain his activities to the village but he had, after all, made them rich. The balance of power had shifted subtly, and if she wanted to be sure not to lose him completely she needed to be cunning. She knew he had someone else – she could smell Ania's influence on him like fox on a dog – and the fact that he might have somewhere to run to made her cautious.

As for Jerzi, cautions of a lifetime were finally losing their hold. Unsettled by this new, glorious passion, his desire was given urgency by what he had seen just before leaving. The more he tried to tell himself he'd got it wrong, the more he knew with a terrible certainty that he'd got it right. It all added up: the fear in her voice, her surprise that he hadn't heard, the villagers attacking the husband – from a distance, the dread in her voice when she'd asked if he'd retaliated, the fact that no-one bought their eggs, the fact they didn't secure their home…. Of course they didn't, it was guarded by an idiot monster who ate humans for breakfast – and who was married to his Ania.

He didn't know when the 'his' had snuck in – nor did he care – it was so obviously right. What was less obvious was how to make it come true – how to make real, in real life, what he tried to exorcise at night – and it was that detail that kept him from going straight back up to her. He knew he no longer had to stay away to make her realise she needed him. He understood that, once aware of her needs, she would play no games. But he saw also that her dignity and pride went hand in hand with a moral code he could only guess at. And while it was obvious to him that they should run away together, living off the monster's riches, it was likewise clear that she would be difficult to persuade. Ania cared for the person she thought Jerzi was and with such high stakes he couldn't undeceive her. Better rather to deceive himself that he really was the person she thought him to be. And wasn't that in fact so, when he was with her? She brought out the best in him just as his mother relentlessly brought out the worst. That was what was true, that was what counted, that was what he held on to.

With that in mind, their future blindingly clear to him, how to achieve it stubbornly remote, he came to a decision. He could bear it no longer. Instead, before dawn put an end to another sleepless night, he got up, head buzzing with frustration, and sneaked out to the treefall.

He would put the problem to Ania and await her solution.

He climbed more skilfully now, practice making him reasonably sure-footed in the dark, and arrived well before breakfast. A light shone in the kitchen and walking swiftly up to the window, he peered in to see Ania in her nightdress, preparing the fire for the morning meal.

For a while he watched her as she moved in the dull lamplight, absorbing the folds of her nightdress where they touched her skin, the sway of her hips as she moved, the fall of her heavy black hair down her back. He knew it was a moment of privilege and drank it in, watching her with an open desire he couldn't have shown had she been conscious of his gaze.

"Ania!" He jumped. So intimate had been the moment, he had all but forgotten the husband within. "An-i-a!" He turned to look for a hiding place and saw that dawn had crept up on him while he gazed. In the clear grey light he could easily make out the different outbuildings that dotted the once symmetrical grounds. He hesitated, then headed for the hen coop. The hens might make a noise, but that risk was offset against the fact that it was woman's territory. There was no danger of the monster going in there. Turning back to the window for a farewell glance Jerzi saw Ania looking at him, alert with surprise and fear. Colour was seeping into the light quickly now, making him more visible than he had realised. He smiled quickly, reassuringly, then before she had time to gesticulate the warning that was so clearly written on her face, he went to hide.

An hour later, a smelly, dirty hour in which he had plenty of time to regret his choice, Jerzi heard the back door open and put his eye to the chink in the wall. The simpleton and Ania were standing on the step. She handed him his lunch, which he stowed away in a pocket, then he leant down to give her a massive embrace.

Ania said something that Jerzi couldn't hear, but the idiot's voice was clear as he boomed out his reply.

"I – won't," he promised, followed by, "I – will." Then, "See – you – later."

He took a few steps then turned and ran back to give her another bear hug, swallowing her up in his huge bulk.

"I – love – you," he boomed. "I – love – you, Ania."

She said something back. As the idiot released her, Jerzi saw that she was smiling. She reached up and touched the monster tenderly on his cheek with the back of her hand. He held still a moment, absorbing her affection, then reached up to take her little fingers in his. He kissed them gently, returned them to her, then, with a great whoop of joy, almost skipping with his long strides, he turned and left.

Ania put up her hand to wave goodbye to him, then kept it up, turning it towards Jerzi as a warning to stay put. Perhaps the fool came back many times to say goodbye before finally leaving. Once again Jerzi chaffed at the indignity of his hiding place, and for a moment anger fuelled his courage. He took a step forward to end this farce, then hesitated: he hadn't got where he was now through taking unnecessary risks.

Finally Ania lowered her hand and came towards the coop. He left it hurriedly so as to meet her standing tall in the fresh air, and walked forward to meet her. She stopped a few paces from him. Her face had none of the cold formality she had tried to muster before, but neither did it show any joy. Instead she seemed ill at ease.

"Hello," she said.

Jerzi stopped too, wrong-footed by her attitude. In his mind their relationship had developed so far together he was unprepared for any hesitation.

"I have come," he started, then paused. It was the speech he had repeated a hundred times on his way up to her. Only now it didn't seem right.

"Yes?" She genuinely didn't know. Her face expressed expectation and curiosity, but only superficially. Underneath she was troubled. It was a welcome that undermined Jerzi unlike any protest could have done.

"I have come," he tried again, "to –" He met her eyes full of denial and resistance, and he knew he couldn't go on. "I have come," he finished instead, shrugging weakly. "Am I welcome?"

"Of course," she said, and she smiled – a sweet, generous smile, but not, he felt for him alone; it was a smile she would give anyone who requested hospitality. "Come in," she continued. "We've just had breakfast. Would you like some?" Her conventional welcome, combined with the 'we', that pronoun of intimacy and exclusion, undid him. He could be cautious no longer.

"We!" he groaned, the word torn from his belly. "We! How can you say that? You are not his – he is not yours – there is no 'we' between you. Ania...." He stepped towards her, his arms stretching forwards, the longing wild on his face.

"No." She put her hand out to him as she had to her monstrous husband, but this time she used it to cover his lips. "No," she repeated, and in a flash of hope he understood that she wasn't denying his emotions, but his words. He stopped speaking and reached to take her hand, again as the monster had done, to kiss it, to draw her towards him and speak a sweeter language than that of words. She smiled, a tight, sad smile that was at least for him and him alone, and turned away.

"Come in," she repeated. "It is better to be inside."

Bewildered, Jerzi followed her.

As soon as they entered she busied herself making more porridge, a task that gave her an excuse to keep her distance.

"This is wrong," she said, her back to him.

Jerzi was filled with a calm joy. So that was what it was. Her unease with him wasn't a change in feelings, merely a woman's moral qualms. Sure of his ground once more he brushed away her objection with the brutality it deserved.

"No," he disagreed. "This is right."

She turned to look at him then, her unease changing to wonder. He returned her gaze confidently, knowing once more with a certainty that came from deep within his guts that he was right, that *they* were right – and it was Ania who dropped her eyes first, turning back to stir the porridge.

He gave her time. His renewed conviction had brought back his caution and sense of timing, and he waited for her to absorb this new perspective at her own speed. Finally she spooned the mixture into a dainty porcelain bowl, poured some tea, and came and sat opposite him. When he was slowing down on his third bowl, she said:

"I am an honest woman."

He stopped and looked at her.

"People said I would never be an honest woman," she continued. "The Sisters filled my ears, every day, with what would become of me. They were wrong. I have succeeded in becoming an honest wife to an honest man of an honest family. That is very important to me. My father-in-law has treated me generously. I don't want to do anything to betray that trust."

Jerzi struggled not to react. He pushed aside the porridge and turned to the sweet tea, holding it in his mouth to savour the taste while wondering how best to respond.

"Your husband," he said finally, stressing the word despite himself, "is an honest man." He had meant to repeat the sentence neutrally, but again his voice betrayed him, ending on a note of contempt that was beyond his control. He saw the defensiveness spring into her eyes and spoke again, quickly, before she could forestall him. "And that – thing – I saw in his hands last time, before I left. Was that honestly come by?"

Again he had been brutal. Again he had aimed true. This time he had struck the core of her unease: she hadn't been sure if he had seen. Well now she knew.

"It's not his fault." She slumped back in her chair and shook her head from side to side as if trying to shake the problem from her. "Really it isn't."

Jerzi waited.

"When he was a child," she stood up and began to pace around the table, the story in her too powerful to be told sitting, "about ten or eleven in years but no more than two or three in his head, there was a fire in the stables. It was the start of the Twenty Day War, and his mother and father, thinking themselves in times of peace, had gone to Diev for the day, leaving my husband in the care of his nurse. But my husband didn't like his nurse; he liked the groom, who let him help with the horses – and when the mortar that started the fire struck, he was in the stables, helping."

She paused and composed herself.

"The groom was killed instantly. The nurse had been sleeping and didn't know where her charge had gone. My husband, though bewildered, had the good instinct to let the horses out, and in the confusion that followed it was some time before he was found. Frightened, scared that perhaps it was all his fault, he had hidden himself away in the orchard. When he was hungry, he instinctively returned to the groom, his friend, for help. But the groom was dead – and his charred body, neglected in the frantic search for the boy, had merely been covered with a blanket. The boy smelt meat. Moving the blanket, he discovered meat. What more does a simple mind need? When they found him, he had eaten part of the thigh."

She stopped and gazed into the fire. A long, quivering sigh shook her whole body. Finally, with an effort, she lifted her head and looked at him squarely for the first time since she had started her story.

"He acquired the taste," she finished simply. "He has no sense of right or wrong. Just the memory of that sweet meat that fed him in his time of need – and now – whenever he is frightened, or angry, which is often – or even hungry – his natural instinct is to find the taste that helped him before."

Jerzi met her gaze but couldn't focus, his head fuzzy with the enormity of what he'd heard. The details of her face dissolved into her burning green eyes and instead of seeming naive and vulnerable, she suddenly seemed to be a woman of impossible strength, a woman who drew her wisdom from knowledge of the bottomless pit – and who yet walked on. For a moment he was powerless before her.

"Come into the music room," she said, turning abruptly. "I need to play." Leaving him to follow, she walked quickly to the front of the house, past bathroom, bedrooms and the sitting room into a small room furnished only with a simple sofa and more instruments than he had ever seen. Guitars, fiddles and flutes festooned the walls; a piano in front of the window took advantage of the best light, while in the corner, standing on a ornate pedestal, was a small, simple harp.

Ania gestured him to the sofa and continued on to the harp, settling herself to it as if Jerzi wasn't there. For a moment she just sat, head bowed, hands still, then, slowly, she began to play.

At first Jerzi watched her, seeing how at home she was with the instrument, how completely she abandoned herself to it. Then, as the notes she picked out fell into a tune, his attention moved to the room they were in, marvelling again at the richness of it, a richness that seemed, in the context of what he had just heard, to be soiled with horror. Finally, as the melody picked up and rounded out and began to seep into his blood, he gave himself over to it – until all else was blotted out and he had attention only for the music she made.

Jerzi knew about music. There was scarcely a person in the country who couldn't handle a fiddle or tin whistle, and every public event was an opportunity to play: weddings, funerals, births, festivals, saint days, beginnings of wars and ends of wars – all were marked by the folk songs and melodies traditional to the occasion. But this was different. This wasn't peasant music – this was Ania's song, the harp's strings moving as she bid them to echo the emotions that stirred her soul – and Jerzi drank it in until he was dizzy on its raw power.

When she finally stopped he was hardly aware of it, listening to the silence as if it too were part of the music, absorbing it as avidly as the notes. Then, slowly, he realised that the silence was silence, a thing apart, and he lifted his head to look at her. She had her eyes closed. Her head leant against the frame of the harp as though against her lover, her fingers still touching the now spent strings.

Slowly, careful not to break the bubble, Jerzi stood up and moved towards her, placing each foot deliberately in front of him like a drunk. He put a hand onto the dark mane of her head and she looked up at him, eyes dreamy from another world, face flushed with emotion. He reached out his other hand and drew her to him. She came willingly and he held her to him, feeling her delicate back through the linen nightdress, running his hands down to her small buttocks and then up and round to her breasts. Then her hands too were moving – undoing his buttons, fumbling with his belt – until slowly they made love, there on the music room floor, they made *love*, together, him and her, and Jerzi knew a dream come true.

Afterwards they lay for a long time in each others' arms. He dozed. When he awoke to see her lying there, still, quiet, sorrowful, he pulled her close to him and kissed her cheek tenderly.

"I love you," he said.

"Yes." It was a statement of fact, not of passion, but he wasn't worried. She had given herself to him and he had tasted the fire that lay beneath that shy exterior.

"And you love me too."

"Yes." Again it was a fact, tinged with sadness. "Yes, I suppose I do."

He kissed her again, guessing at her concerns. "Don't worry," he whispered. "I'll make it all right. I'll make everything all right. Soon you'll never have to see that husband of yours again."

She turned to face him, her body tensing in shock. "What?"

He sensed her moral qualms getting ready to interfere and his fear that she might protest made him rush on, ignoring his instinct for caution.

"I'll take you away from here," he elaborated. "We don't need to harm him. We can even leave him enough to live on. We won't take much, just what we need to set ourselves up. After all, you've earned it."

He didn't realise at first the enormity of his mistake. Her easy way of bestowing her husband's gifts had made him think she could take easily, as well as give, and all he saw was that now was his moment. If he didn't seize it, he understood clearly he'd never get another chance. What he didn't understand was that he'd never had a chance at all.

"Earned it," she repeated. "So you too see me as only a mistress, selling myself for the comfort of riches. Well," her voice was heavy with bitterness. "I suppose you have more right than most."

"Of course I don't." He was answering her first statement, not the second. "You know what I mean. After all, you work hard here – looking after the hens and house and caring for the – your husband. A nurse would be paid – a servant – so why not you?"

"Because I am a wife!" she snapped, pulling away from him and getting up, "and because wives do these things for free, because of their vows, because of their family ties, because of their – love." She turned away from him and pulled back on her nightdress.

"Love," Jerzi's scorn was easy. He thought the words were just her conscience flapping around in its last throes before death. "Love," he repeated. "This is love, you and me, here, what we've just done – and will do again – and again. That's love. We belong together," he continued. "Can't you see it's obvious? How else could a virgin like you have been so sure of yourself, so perfect the very first time? It's because you belong to me."

"Virgin?" She repeated the word softly and turned to look at him, her face perplexed. "How could I be a virgin?"

"But – but...." He faltered, beginning to sense his mistake, though still not its magnitude. "The Sisters," he stammered, "the nunnery, your moral principles.... How could you be otherwise....?"

"But I am married," she stated. "Of course I'm not a virgin."

Jerzi stared at her. The truth was so far from his assumptions that at first he couldn't believe it, obvious though she felt it to be. Then, as the first gut-wrenching inkling of despair touched him, he too stood up, the better to protect himself from these mortal facts she threw at him so callously.

"You sleep with him?" he exclaimed. "That – monster? That drooling, shouting, moronic – cannibal! You sleep with him?" And before he knew it he had slapped her, hard, across the face. "How could you?"

She staggered under his blow, then straightened again to meet him, cold dignity blazing through her eyes.

"He is my husband," she repeated. Then, softening in the face of his misery, she explained. "My father-in-law needs an heir. The land goes to the eldest son born of the first wife, as it always has – that is how they maintain their riches, you know that. My husband is the eldest son. I am his first wife. He needs an heir – it is essential that the line continue. I am quite clever," she continued impersonally in a seeming non-sequitur. "My father-in-law felt that, with my brains, our son might be of normal intelligence. That was his hope, and a risk he was prepared to take."

"He was prepared to take," Jerzi repeated. "A risk *he* was prepared to take. What about you?"

"Yes," she nodded, "me too." Then, understanding his confusion, she elaborated. "My father-in-law explained everything to the nuns and insisted they make my duties clear. He made sure I understood exactly what I was being asked to take on. He has always been completely honest with me. If he had wanted a mere nurse for his son he could have hired one. What he needed was a means to beget future heirs."

"And you?" It came out a sneer. "What did you want?"

"I wanted a husband," she said, struggling to control her voice beneath his scorn. "I wanted to be an honest woman. I wanted to stay off the streets. Oh Jerzi," and she went to him. "Was that so much to want? I never dreamt so far as happiness. How could I know it might come my way and ruin everything?"

"No." Jerzi clasped her to him, then pushed her aside as he hurriedly pulled on his clothes. "No," he repeated. "We won't let it ruin everything. We *will* be happy. You'll come with me, far away. I forgive you. I forgive you, I promise, but you must come away with me right now. Forget about him, never mention him again. Be mine, be mine now, and we shall be happy for ever."

"But I can't!" She gesticulated at the room and all it represented. "Don't you understand? I can't. My father-in-law trusts me. He has left his son here in my charge. Without me to look after him he wouldn't last a day. And my vows – my wedding vows, made before God – and his heir, the son he asks of me...." She broke off as a thought occurred to her, and looked at Jerzi with a new concern.

Jerzi understood.

"Frightened you might beget my child?" he asked gruffly, hurt to the quick. "What a tragedy that would be, eh? To have the child of a lover who loves you." He looked at her for a moment, then hit her so hard that she fell to the floor and kicked her in the stomach as she lay there.

"There," he shouted, wild with grief. "That'll sort you out. That should get rid of the little bastard. Make you bleed. Is that what you want? Is it? *Is it!*"

"No." She brought her knuckles up to her mouth, and wept as she lay curled up on the floor. "No, please God no. It's not what I want. I don't know what I want – I can't have what I want. Oh dear God, please help me...."

Filled with remorse Jerzi threw himself down beside her and held her, covering her tears with kisses as he pulled her to him tight. He got another erection. Urgently he fumbled with her nightdress.

"No." She turned away from him. "No. Please don't." But he was crazy now, exploding with a mêlée of emotions that he had no choice but to release into her, the cause of all his pain.

This time it was over quickly. Afterwards, spent, yet still filled with inchoate yearning, Jerzi finally understood that he had lost her. Like his mother though, that didn't mean he was willing to let her go.

"Come on," he said, doing himself up then pulling her roughly to her feet. "Get dressed." Instead she backed away until she bumped against her harp in the corner of the room.

"I said get dressed." She shook her head, touching the harp strings as though for comfort and strength.

"Jerzi," she began. "Please. Try to understand...."

Instead he wilfully misunderstood. "So it's your music, is it? You don't want to leave your music. Well, I can understand that. A player like you.... A talent like yours.... Such a musical soul...." He trailed off, then held on stubbornly to his brutality. "We'll bring it with us." He picked it up, barely feeling its weight in his anger. "Then you can play it to your heart's content."

"No!" She ran in front of him, hands fluttering, as if to protect a baby from harm. "Please..." She struggled to regain a semblance of calm, to not fan the fire of his rage, but he could see the misery and fear in her eyes and the knowledge aggravated his despair. To have never known happiness, that was one thing; but to have known it – to have its promise dangled before you, to have taken it, seizing with both hands the offered fruit, only to have it withdrawn as soon as you had tasted the bliss of its flesh. That was unforgivable – and if he was to suffer he'd make sure she suffered with him.

Pushing her out of the way, still clasping the harp to him, he began to walk down the corridor back towards the kitchen. She followed anxiously.

"An-ia!"

They both stopped in astonishment. Home already? For a second there was almost the old complicity between them again, the need for secrecy against a common enemy. Then suddenly, while Jerzi was still under that illusion, she betrayed him finally and utterly.

"Help!" she screamed. "Darling, help! Come quickly. He is stealing my harp!"

For a moment Jerzi stood quite still, his face drained white, his eyes staring at her, fixed with horror.

"You choose him?" he said quietly in wonder. "You choose him over me? How could you?" And his bemusement stung her to reply.

"There was never any choice. Don't you understand? He is my husband – and I love him."

Her voice broke at the revelation and she sagged back against the wall.

Jerzi reached out a hand slowly, and traced a tear with his finger as it ran down her cheek. He followed it under her chin, then brought his thumb round to the other side, tenderly, as though caressing the hollows in her neck. Then gently, so gently, he began to squeeze.

"An-ia!"

The roar was closer now, the wailing bellow of an animal in pain. "An-ia! I'm – coming. Where – are – you? An-ia!"

The sound jerked Jerzi back into the danger of the moment. Letting her go he shifted the harp's weight back into both his arms.

"You won't get away that easily," he hissed as he prepared to run. "You'll come to me. You'll come begging – because I have this – your music – your soul. I have your *soul*!" he shouted, and his chest vibrated with the sound of his victory. *"I have your soul!"* Then he ran through the kitchen and out the back door as her husband reached the yard.

"An-ia's – harp!" the idiot shouted and he turned, reaching out one of his enormous arms to stop Jerzi as he passed. He was powerful but slow, while Jerzi was quick with cunning and strong with madness. Dodging the massive hand he leapt over the low stone wall and began to race through the grounds to the remaining olive trees. Behind him he heard the pounding feet of the monster's heavy tread and for the first time fear entered his madness as he realised what would happen to him should he be caught. The adrenaline gave him extra speed and he reached the treefall still in front, but only just. The monster was so close behind him now that he could hear his breath, could almost feel his fingers reaching out to touch his collar. Then they did touch his collar, yanking him to a halt. With a wrench Jerzi tore the material and threw himself over the edge of the cliff into the branches and roots of the trees below.

He landed so hard he was winded, almost losing the harp as his muscles relaxed their grip. For a moment he lay there, struggling to regain his breath, then he realised the branches above were shaking and trembling under an enormous weight. The giant was following him.

"An-ia!" The idiot bellowed again. "An-ia's – harp!" Then, faintly in the distance, another voice called: "No, come back. Sweetheart! Stop."

The shaking was getting closer. Tightening his hold on the harp Jerzi forced himself to move and began, more falling than climbing, to descend the trees. Stones rattled down past him, gaining momentum as they fell, occasionally a tree slid as it took his weight – and he realised that the treefall, always precarious, was suffering under the extra weight. Fear of a landslide sped him on – and the idea of a landslide gave him a plan.

He hit the ground running, shouting to his mother for help – though all that came out of his mouth was a wild, incoherent cry – and raced to the shed where he kept the grenades. Dropping the harp, he picked one up, pulled the pin, and threw it just as the idiot came into sight amongst the tangled branches of the bottom-most tree. The bomb seemed to sail in slow motion towards the rock face, everything falling momentarily quiet, then the blast hit him with a wall of sound and he fell back as the treefall collapsed into an avalanche of rocks, debris and broken giant.

For a moment Jerzi lay where he'd fallen, watching. Then a stray stone struck the harp, twanging a string with a sharp discordant noise that turned his attention immediately from the rumbling landslide. Ania. Scrambling to his feet he pulled the harp to him and looked wildly for a way through the cascading boulders. Dust smarted his eyes and he stumbled backwards instead, searching for a viewpoint to the cliff edge above.

"Ania. Ania! *Ania!*"

But there was no-one. Only the pounding of settling rocks and far off, yet also close and remorseless in his head, a high-pitched keen that could have been the call of an eagle – but that he knew to be the despairing scream of a woman, crying "No".

Wolf

Mum and the woodcutter had an affair of course, but it didn't last. It wasn't love. He was the hero and she was the victim-by-proxy, and once those roles had been played out they didn't have much in common.

I was kind of glad. I was very grateful to the woodcutter, but feeling grateful all the time isn't comfortable, and having him around kept reminding me of things I'd rather forget. Anyway, things got sorted pretty quickly once the fights started. She said he 'didn't understand', he said she was 'fucking weird', and that was that.

I told Grandmaman the next time I saw her. She raised her eyebrows at the language and her face went hard and tight the way it does when she's cross, but she didn't tell me off for eavesdropping. Instead she sighed, looked me in the eye as if working out what to say, then told me they were both right – that of course he couldn't understand mum when she didn't even understand herself, and that there was nothing weirder than a woman who denies her nature.

I asked her what she meant, which was what she'd been waiting for. She patted the sofa next to where she was sitting and jerked her head for me to come on over. I took my time, savouring the moment. Grandmaman had three sides: her stern, strict, sarcastic side – frightening when turned on you, but wonderful when aimed at someone else; her wild, eccentric side, full of magic and adventure when I was younger, though more embarrassing these days; and her cuddly side, like now, the side I liked best – when she would put her arms around me, lean her chin on my shoulder, and make me feel entirely loved. When I was finally settled, my back snug in the corner of the sofa, my feet up on her lap, she began.

Instead of explaining about mum though, she started talking about wolves. I stiffened, guessing what was coming. Sure enough it wasn't long before she asked me to tell her all about it.

To my surprise, I did.

I'd known I could trust Grandmaman not to give me sympathy, and I knew she could get angry, but I still wasn't prepared when I'd finished my story, for her thin-lipped fury.

"Come on," she said, shaking my legs off her knees and standing up. She got our coats and held out mine.

"Come on," she said again, "let's go."

"Where?" I asked.

"Home, of course. To your mother's. You want to know why she's like she is? You want to know why the wolf got you? Well – it's time you found out."

I knew her anger wasn't directed at me but it was scary all the same. I wasn't sure that I did, after all, want to know why mum was weird – not if it got Grandmaman so riled up. As for why the wolf got me – I'd assumed it was just one of those things; it got me because I was there. That was bad enough without adding any more sinister reason.

We walked back in silence. I knew better than to ask questions and in any case Grandmaman walked so fast, striding ahead in fury, that it was all I could do to keep up. We shot out of that hollow and over the crooked bridge quicker than I walk it alone at dusk. She slowed up on the long hill that led over the ridge to our house, her breathing heavy, but as soon as she'd recovered she stormed off again, blasting into the clearing where our track joins the path from the village. I love it here. There are tree stumps to sit on, wild flowers growing in the extra sunlight, and an old water trough left over from the days of horses that's normally full of rain water. If you're really quiet as you approach you can sometimes see a wild animal having a drink. I'd once seen a brown bear, often saw deer, and marmots were two a penny.

All we saw today though were some butterflies and a startled blue jay, flapping noisily up into the trees from where it watched us – a short, chunky, white-haired old woman racing along, with a supposedly fit, long-legged girl trailing behind her.

When we arrived home Grandmaman threw open the door, stomped into the front room and stood there, glowering. Mum looked up in surprise. She was curled up in the comfy chair with a book in her hands, still in the t-shirt and leggings she wore to bed now the nights were colder. She didn't look like she'd been doing much reading though – rather her face was soft and blotchy, as if she'd been crying.

"Your daughter," Grandmaman spat out, "would like to know why you're so weird. I think – don't you – that it's about time you told her."

Mum went pale.

"No," she said. It wasn't an answer, it was a plea. She stood up, the forgotten book falling to the floor, and took a step towards us. Her eyes were dark with panic. Still puffed from the hike, I pushed past Grandmaman and went to her.

"No," I agreed. "No, I don't want to know. I don't think you're weird anyway, mum – it was just the woodcutter. I overheard the woodcutter...."

I put my arms around her and tried to make her sit down again, but she'd tensed-up, too stiff for me to move. I'd never seen mum like this before – not even when Dad left. I was used to her being grumpy – that was normal, that was healthy. This was frightening.

I turned to look at Grandmaman.

"We don't want to know, do we Grandmaman?" I pleaded. "You were just joking...."

"No I wasn't." Grandmaman stood fast but her voice softened. She came forward, gently now, and stood close to mum, looking her in the eyes. "The girl has to know," she told her firmly. "There are others where that wolf came from, you know that. Do you really want her to –"

"No!" It was almost a scream. My mother put her hands to her face. She was shaking. "No," she repeated. "No – don't – I can't...."

Instinctively Grandmaman put her arms out to comfort her, but mum stepped back as if it would hurt. "No," she said again, and this time it was a low snarl of anger. "Stay away from me you – you – witch!" Then she started to cry, sobbing violently.

Grandmaman turned to me.

"I think we could all use a cup of tea," she said calmly. "Would you mind?"

I wouldn't. I knew I was being got rid of, but this time I didn't care – this was too scary for me. As I left I saw Grandmaman steer mum, now limp and unprotesting, back into her chair, then sit down opposite her and start talking.

I stayed away as long as I could. Mum's a lousy

housekeeper, so the kitchen was a mess and the dishes needed washing. It's a job I usually hate, but today the chore seemed reassuringly normal. I got stuck in and waited until they called me.

When I went back in Grandmaman was still sitting on the sofa. Mum was standing up, gazing out the front window over the autumn-touched forests and across the valley to the mountains beyond. It was our favourite view, one of the reasons we lived here. She turned when she heard me, smiled a ghost of a smile full of recent tears, and held out her hand.

"Grandmaman's right," she said, in a resigned voice that wasn't like her at all. "Come and sit down and we'll tell you all about it."

I looked at Grandmaman, who nodded.

I wasn't sure I wanted to hear 'all about it' but I was sure I didn't have much choice, so I sat down. Grandmaman poured the tea. Mum added a slug of whisky to hers then cleared her throat, took my hand, and started.

"Your Grandmaman," she said, "has … special powers."

I looked at her, then across to Grandmaman, who nodded again encouragingly.

"That's right," she confirmed. "And when that wolf-shifter got you it was because of that. It could tell you were part of my family – and that you hadn't yet come into your power. It was new in the region or else I'd have known about it, but as it was…." She must have seen the confusion on my face because she stopped, and tried again.

"When you trusted that wolf on your walk through the woods," she explained, "something in your heart melted and fused with its. It was able to use that – that trust, that affection – to get through my defences. That was why it suddenly rushed off – to use its power while it still had it – to catch me unawares. It pretended to be you – and for that vital moment I believed it. If that woodcutter hadn't come along…."

Her voice caught and she stopped.

I looked from her to mum, then back again. I wasn't too sure about this. Then I remembered mum's insult.

"Does that mean you're a witch?" I asked.

"Well," Grandmaman's laugh was slightly false, the put-down

of a specialist for the layman. "That's not what I would call it."

"Though it's as good a name as any," mum chipped in, throwing her a sharp glance. Grandmaman let it ride.

"If you're a witch," I tried to think this through. "A *nice* witch, of course." Mum snorted. "Does that mean mum and I are witches too?"

"It does," Grandmaman said. This time mum said nothing, then nodded reluctantly.

"Then why doesn't mum act like a witch?" I asked. "I mean, now that I know Grandmaman, *you* being a witch kind of makes sense. At least it explains why you live in that horrid swamp and make all those yucky soups and everything – no offence. But mum – well, mum – you're so *normal*. You know – shopping, TV, your job…." I trailed off.

Grandmaman looked across at mum, giving her the chance to answer, but mum shook her head and gestured for her to carry on.

"Your mum doesn't want to be a – witch – as you call it." Grandmaman explained. "She rebelled when she was a teenager – said she just wanted to be normal, that just because I had stupid powers, it didn't mean she had to have them too." She smiled to show she understood, but I could hear the undertones of resentment. "Most adolescents rebel, of course," she continued, "only your mum here never came back on track. She went off, married your Dad and pretended she was just an ordinary woman."

"Why?" I asked. I couldn't understand that at all. "No moonlit rides on broomsticks? No cheating at exams? No best tickets to all the gigs? Why would you choose such a thing?"

"I was scared." There was a trace of a whinge in mum's voice, nestling within the anger. "Being one of us isn't about broomstick rides, you know – it's about power – real, potent power that others don't have and don't understand. Discovering that power can be terrifying…." She stopped, remembering, then stared at Grandmaman with open hostility. "Your grandmother," she continued bitterly, "comes from the sink or swim school of education. She left me out in that forest when I was five – *five* – all night long, alone, to 'come into my powers'. Can you imagine what that feels like – to be abandoned, surrounded by danger, with only my five-year-old wits to keep me alive?"

"I was there all the time," Grandmaman cut in wearily. They had forgotten about me now, back in the throes of an old feud. "And you survived very well. Do you really think I would have left you, my only daughter, to the mercy of –"

"Of course I thought that – it was what you meant me to think!" Mum stared at her, then made a stabbing motion with her arm, both a rejection and a truce. "Anyway, that's all over now. The point is, whether it's because of that or not, I was afraid to own such power. Afraid of the evil that might track me down because of it, and afraid, very afraid, of abusing it to do wrong. We all have a capacity for darkness, you'll learn that – and my role model wasn't exactly sweetness and light...." She looked back at Grandmaman, then stopped before she could crank herself up again. She sighed deeply.

"It seemed to me that with such power I had only two choices – either to be stalked by evil or to turn out evil myself. So I decided not to use my powers at all."

"The problem is," Grandmaman took over, speaking as though to me, but really at mum. "Having powers you don't use isn't the same as never having powers at all. That's why your mum gets so unhappy and bad-tempered at times – and why the woodcutter thinks she's weird. He's right – she is weird – because she's never come to terms with who she really is."

It may not have been the whole truth, but there was enough there for mum to accept it.

I looked at her. For the first time in my life she seemed small, even weak. Then I looked at Grandmaman where she sat with her tea, a faint look of victory on her face. And suddenly, unbidden, I saw the wolf as I did so often these days, and felt myself pulled again into its stinking maw. Only this time, instead of feeling the cold sweat of fear, I was filled with such fury it was like a white-hot fire in my head.

"This is about you two," I said. "*I* was used, *I* was attacked, *I* was nearly killed, and all because of *you*! What about me?" I turned to mum, my voice rising. "Why didn't you *tell* me!" Then to Grandmaman, shouting. "Why didn't *you* tell me instead of using me as a pawn in your stupid games? Don't you care? If I'd have known then I'd never have...." My voice broke and I couldn't go on.

Mum stood up. She reached out to touch me, yet held back as though I'd bite her. I realised I was standing in my rage but was too angry to sit back down. Instead I turned my back on them and walked out onto the veranda to look out at the same view that had soothed my mother. An infinity of trees spread out across the ancient mountains. In a few days I would be looking at a fire of yellows and reds, the leaves spitting back the sun they'd absorbed all summer. In less than two months I'd be going to Grandmaman's on skis. If I still went.

Behind my back mum's words reached me, low, deadened by sorrow.

"I made Grandmaman promise," she said. "I told her that if she wanted to see you, she had to be normal – and let you be normal too. I said she'd ruined my life with all her magic nonsense, and I wasn't going to let her ruin yours...."

She let the words hang there, stark, without excuses. It was Grandmaman, following us out, who came to her defence.

"It sounds dramatic, I know," she said, "but your mum meant well. She only wanted the best for you. Because she loves you – as I love her."

I turned around then and stared at them.

"I've spoken with your mum," Grandmaman continued, as if that wasn't obvious. "And it's all right with her if I – we – teach you how to defend yourself. In fact, now the wolf-shifter's had a go at you, you don't have much choice. You've been touched by evil and that leaves its mark."

"I suppose you didn't really have a choice anyway," mum said, trying to make it easier. "Once a witch always a witch, as your Grandmaman would say. It just took me a while to find out."

I'm still not sure she really knows.

I go along with her and Grandmaman for now, it keeps them happy, but I'm not convinced I believe them. In fact I'm not convinced about anything in this crazy new life they've thrown me into.

Sometimes I think I'd rather break away, leave these 'fucking weirdoes' and go back to Dad and the normal life I had before that awful day – a day that only happened because of their lies and incompetence. Sometimes I think we're all three just playing a game – a game of Grandmother's Footsteps, where any step is good only so long as it heads in one direction – to Grandmaman and all she holds true.

And sometimes, when I feel my power flexing within me, I think I'd like to change that game and try a new one. It might not be popular, but it would be mine. There's one in particular I haven't played for a while.

It's called 'What's The Time Mr Wolf' – and I think it might be fun.

Hogan and Gabi

The fan had broken again. Lying on his mattress, beads of sweat lining his face, Hogan remembered the job he'd done where there'd been air-conditioning. He concentrated on the memory, for a moment almost feeling the soft chill on his skin, the urge to put on something warm, then the blanket covering his door frame was pushed aside, stirring some of the hot, dry air, and Jonah stuck his head round.

"The boss wants to see you. In the ops room."

For a moment Hogan just looked at him, too lethargic to care, then the meaning behind the words sunk in and a gleam crept into his eyes. He nodded, both an acknowledgement and a dismissal, then waited for Jonah's head to disappear before getting up. His leg was still sore from the last mission and he didn't want Jonah to see how awkwardly he moved when stiff.

He took his time to get dressed. The camouflage trousers were far too big for him, but they'd been too good a find to pass up – virtually unspoilt, with only a tear near the zip where the bullet had killed their previous owner, the blood almost all washed out. He rolled the legs up carefully so that the folded hems were equal on each side, and pulled the belt as tight as he could against his skinny waist. They still slipped down when he walked – he had no hips at all to snag the sinking waistband, but he had developed a hands-in-pockets swagger that allowed him to look cool while keeping them up. Not ideal should they be attacked, but the rest of his accessories should help him out there.

It was too hot for a jacket – even a cut-off t-shirt – and he swung the strap of his AK-47 directly over his sweaty skin. The Beretta went in the holster on his right and the hunting knife in the sheath on the left, the weight of both conniving with gravity against his thick leather belt. The whole lot was heavy, the rifle not much shorter than he was, and he wasn't likely to need it – a surprise attack here was impossible – but he had learnt to always be prepared. Besides, the weapons had become part of his everyday life and he felt naked without them. Lastly he wiped the sweat off his face with a big red bandana, tied it round his neck, and went in search of his sister.

Gabi was waiting for him, her gaunt face almost tender in the half-light of dawn. Her clothing was similar to his, but for the khaki vest that covered the slight protrusion of her pre-pubescent breasts and the great clunking army boots she always wore, no matter how bad the blisters or hot the day. They were the first pair of shoes she had ever had and no-one was going to take them from her. The others joked she even slept in them, but only Hogan knew that to be true. The first – and last – soldier who had tried to find out had ended up with a bullet in his brain and his throat cut. Gabi didn't do things by halves. The others hadn't been so curious after that.

They were a pair of contrasts, their similar weapons only emphasising the differences between them. Hogan's baby face – as far from tough as Gabi was from sweetness – gave him an image of innocence that was compounded by his reluctance to pull the trigger. It wasn't that he couldn't use his kit, he'd killed before and would again. But whereas Gabi had killed more than she could remember, Hogan could remember each and every one of his victims, their faces coming back to haunt him at night. Only Gabi knew what each death cost her brother. Only she – and now the boss – appreciated how deeply his skills lay in thinking, not doing, and how that was where he should be deployed. Hogan questioned the meaning of life, Gabi got on with it. Together they made a great team.

"Ready?" There was a hint of concern in Gabi's question. She knew how closely run the last job had been.

He nodded.

"OK." She smiled, and ruffled his wild mop of hair, the gesture safe in the privacy of her room, then slapped him on his bony shoulder. "Let's go."

Their sleeping quarters were in the remains of bandas – part of a large complex that had once belonged to one a white landowner who had long since fled their land. It must have been an impressive outfit at one time – horses for trekking, the individual bandas for the tourists, a large main house for cocktails, socializing and planning the following day, a sunken rectangle of cracked cement that had once been a pool, still surrounded by white plastic loungers – now cluttered with the soldiers who'd failed to get a banda, stable stall or mattress. And best of all the view. Here, high in the broken foothills, they could see all the way across the Udebi Plain to the edges of the

Umtezi forest. Tourists from all around the world had flown here for this view – and now the boss had brought them up the hard way – scrambling up mountain sides and past gorge-sheer valleys, to keep them safe while they planned the next move.

Angling past the stables and skirting the pool, Gabi and Hogan turned their backs on the huge sun that rose from the plains and headed into the main house, where the old office had been kitted out as the ops room. Here, the fan worked – and here the boss was waiting for them.

"The People's Army have acquired a witch." He tapped a key on his laptop and a face leapt into view on the once-white office wall. It was a proud face, majestic rather than beautiful, the long slim nose and high cheek bones sitting uneasily between her low brow and short square chin. She was looking at the camera, so that her eyes sought them out and her expression seemed to say: *I know you. I know what you're doing. I am not afraid.*

Gabi, on the other hand, felt a shiver snake down her spine despite the already oppressive heat. Not only were witches bad news, this one was….

"She's like me," she said.

The boss looked away – a smile would have hurt her feelings – but despite the fact there was no real resemblance between the witch's clear features and Gabi's scarred and savage face, he knew what she meant. They were both mixed race – with all the assets and disadvantages that entailed.

"She's been working some *major* magic for them," he continued. "The others don't know this yet, but on top of holding us at the river, they've beaten us back at Sundulu and Ngarta. No bodies were recovered."

Perched on his swivel chair Hogan swung his feet as if this meant nothing – but Gabi pursed her lips, looking both fierce and shaken. She knew what that meant. The spirits of their dead soldiers would be trapped within the witch's spells, condemned to do her evil no matter how loyal they'd been when alive. Even worse, any prisoners taken would increase her power with each live sacrifice, their drained bodies returning as the living dead – traitors whose familiar features would reinstall them in positions of trust.

Before the boss could continue Hogan slipped down from his chair and went over to his desk.

"You got any of that chocolate left?"

"I have." Opening the bottom drawer, the boss pulled out two bars of the local dark chocolate that had been sold as fair-trade before the war had put it into his hands. In the early days he'd have struck Hogan for such insolent non-sequiturs – had done even, once, before Gabi had stepped in. But now he understood that Hogan worked in mysterious ways. If eating chocolate helped Hogan think, then chocolate was what he'd get – because when Hogan thought he thought uniquely, despite his youth, and the results so far had been impressive.

Hogan gave the second bar to Gabi as the boss had intended, but she put it to one side, habits of starvation ensuring she never ate now what she could eke out till later. Hogan unwrapped his slowly, licking the melted bits off the wrapper as he walked back to his chair, then biting off a chunk and spreading the taste around his mouth before turning his attention back to the witch.

"So," he said. "What do you want us to do?"

The plan was low on detail, high on risk. Get caught by the opposition, stay alive long enough to find a way to kill the witch, then escape. Gabi would be the hunter and Hogan the bait – such a young boy would make powerful medicine, his dreamy, unworldly air and odd ways adding to his value – and the witch was likely to fall for the trap.

Beyond that, things got harder. She couldn't be killed like a normal person; she had charms to stop bullets, powers over animals, eyes in the back of her head. For them to have even a chance of killing her she must be unprotected, which meant stealing her nkisi, the sack of power she kept tied around her neck and guarded more fervently than any treasure. On top of that, her body, once killed, had to be destroyed to stop her ghost from coming back to haunt them, burnt until its cinders turned white and were scattered to the four winds. All this in full view of several hundred troops. As the boss never tired of telling them – no-one said it would be easy.

So much for the plan. The risks were different for each of them. Gabi's weren't that she would be raped – that wasn't a risk, it was a certainty – rather that she wouldn't be docile enough to carry it off. Given she knew Hogan's life depended on her however, the boss was gambling that her motivation would carry the day. Everyone knew what her job would be – and if she could make herself amenable and refrain from cutting too many throats, she'd probably be left pretty much to her own devices between demands – which would put her in a prime position to study the witch and help Hogan when the time came.

For Hogan, the danger was that he'd be killed before they found a solution – but the odds against this were good. Small boys were too valuable to waste as bullet fodder on routine missions, and while the witch might take an odd toe or finger should a war lord request it, she would keep the whole boy to sacrifice for a major operation. To increase his chances, the boss would arrange for a sustained attack while the two made their way into People's Army territory, lending cover both to them and their story. He would then pull back his troops, ostensibly withdrawing to lick his wounds and effectively instigating a ceasefire. Without any major battles there should be no need for major medicine, ergo Hogan's safety.

Of course if the People's Army had plans the boss didn't know about – well, that was another risk they had to take.

The 'had', as always, was both optional and inviolate. Although the war was officially fought on ideological grounds, in reality ideology split along tribal lines so that Gabi and Hogan, half-Usate, half-Mbinde, had been outcast from the beginning – suspected by all, wanted by none but each other. Only the boss had embraced them and seen their worth, and while the demands he made on them were heavy, the place he gave them in both his hierarchy and his esteem was high. The boss valued not just their mixed blood, but their unique skills and flawless teamwork – and to be so valued, to know he asked them because they were the best, because no-one else could do it so well – and that if they turned down his 'request' they would turn down also their place in his heart … well, there were some risks that just weren't worth taking.

The children, dressed in civilian rags, looked tired and hungry – mainly because they were. Whilst having great faith in their ability, the boss favoured the method school of acting – injecting a little reality into their cover being, in his opinion, a good way to inject a little safety. Kids were only kids after all, for all their worldly experience, and the less you gave them to slip up on, the less they'd slip up. Hogan and Gabi didn't question this: they'd been tired and hungry all their lives before they'd met the boss and now they were only tired and hungry on a job. It was a big improvement.

"Our troops destroyed this village here – Kinta – five days ago." The boss drew a cross in the mud. "Here," another cross, "ten days walk to the east, is the refugee camp you're trying to get to. Here, in between them, is the forest, the People's Army – and the witch."

Gabi looked up from the scratches in the mud to the trees across the river. The land here was flatter and wetter, the dense forest providing valued cover and resources for the other side – and currently helping them too. The boss had brought them as far as he could, deep into the enemy's stronghold.

"Their leader is a man called Shimbabo. He's ruthless, but more or less sane and keeps his troops in order. You should be OK with him." He flashed them a smile, as though the information was reassuring. "I'll have men here watching for your signal. If you can make it back this far after you've killed her, we'll get you out."

And if we can't? Gabi thought. But she didn't say it. Instead she nodded, stood up, and turned with Hogan to the shore. All they had to do now was cross the river and get caught.

They were captured the following afternoon, though it took a while – the two resorting to blundering around in circles, stamping on cracking twigs and telling each other to be quiet in loud, hissing whispers to attract attention. The troops who finally chanced upon them were so stoned Gabi worried she might have to kill a few just to get them moving, but a couple had kept their senses and the leader, Antoine, handcuffed the children's hands behind their backs, tied a rope around their necks and led them back to camp, his soldiers stumbling to keep up.

After a couple of hours, as they were approaching the boma – a palisaded village that was Shimbabo's HQ – the trail skirted a clearing that had been hacked out of the trees. Through the branches Gabi could see a large round hut, roofed with banana leaves, next to a small, neatly kept garden. Further away, closer to the far side, was a solitary flame tree, its short trunk and wide branches supporting what might have been a tree house. Hogan didn't notice it, his head bowed, eyes almost shut, closing out the approaching reality, but she took in everything, hungry for any detail that might help. As they passed, a woman came out of the hut, turning to see what made the noise, and Gabi immediately recognised her majestic features and the proud tilt of her head. She was tall too, something the photo hadn't shown, and dressed simply in an orange and black kitenge. Their gazes met, a timeless moment where they seemed to be sizing each other up, eyes frank and curious, then Antoine pulled at Gabi's rope and she stumbled, turning to watch her footing. When she looked back, the witch was gone.

The boma was big and had been made well, although tilting logs and broken spikes in the high palisade indicated recent neglect. The soldiers in it seemed disciplined enough however, drawing back to watch the children's arrival in silence. When they were near the centre Antoine stopped and dismissed his men with a few scolding words, then he led Hogan and Gabi slowly forward to a large hut where a guard stood outside the door. They exchanged a few quiet words, the guard went in, and a few minutes later Shimbabo, the warlord, came out.

He was tall, so tall he had to bend almost in half to get through the door, and when he stretched up he seemed almost as high as the surrounding fence. He was big too, more heavy than fat, with a wide, acne-pitted face and huge, fleshy hands. His eyes though were small and hard, and as Gabi met them she felt her courage stumble, past memories threatening to rise and choke her. She shook them off and lowered her gaze, but the warlord had seen the flicker of fear in her eyes and was pleased with it.

"Do you know where you are?"

Gabi glanced at Hogan who was staring down at his feet, as though the question couldn't possibly be aimed at him.

"No sir," she answered. "That is, somewhere between Thwate and Kinta, sir."

"And what are you doing here?"

"Nothing sir. That is, we were hoping to get to the refugee camp, sir...." She let her voice die off and flicked a glance at him. It was a tale he expected.

"The *refugee* camp? Why?"

"Everyone was killed, sir. They came five days ago and killed my uncle and older brother and took my sister. We were out in the forest – collecting firewood...."

"So everyone was killed. Yet rather than fight for revenge, you turn your cowardly tails and run to the foreigners?"

"Yes sir. I mean, no sir. That is, I don't know sir." She looked at him now, hoping that confusion showed on her face. "We didn't know what else to do, sir."

"Well today's your lucky day." Shimbabo's mouth was smiling but his eyes gleamed spite. "Because I can tell you." He walked around them then, a well-practised swagger, letting the pause build until he faced them again. "You can help us," he spelt out finally. "Help us to fight those who killed your family. Serve me – and my men – in the ways that will help us best. Isn't that what you would like to do?"

"No sir. I mean, yes sir. But – my brother sir. He's not – right, sir. He can't do much. He needs me to look after him, sir."

Shimbabo frowned. She was going to be awkward, was she? Casually he reached out and cuffed the boy on the head. Hogan staggered under the blow, then caught his balance, eyes never rising from his feet.

"Look at me!"

Hogan didn't. Gabi put her hand in his and whispered something in his ear so that he slowly raised his eyes to look at her and then – at her urgent gesture – at Shimbabo.

"So." Shimbabo nodded to himself, suddenly pleased. "The light's on, but nobody's home. Well, we have uses for dim lights too." He nodded, decision made. "Take them both inside," he ordered Antoine, gesturing to the hut behind him. "I'll test drive these two personally."

Gabi clenched Hogan's hand hard, her heart pounding. It was all going wrong. Hogan's simple-mindedness was supposed to increase his value for the witch, not make him bum candy – and if it wasn't going to work then she couldn't face it. She couldn't. Not again. Despite the precautions she'd taken. Once more flashes of the past stabbed her vision and she bowed her head, unsure if her eyes would reveal fear or hatred. Antoine gave her a push, knocking her forward, and as she caught her balance she turned back to face him, all passivity forgotten.

"Wait." The shout was loud, authoritative, stopping activity and turning heads. It was the shout of a woman. Twenty metres from them stood the witch, her kitenge now partially covered with the feathers and bones that marked her trade.

"If you would be so kind, Musoja Shimbabo," she added, her tone harsh despite the words, then she walked slowly up to him and waited. There was a pause, a momentary struggle of power, then Shimbabo cut the air with his hand so that Antoine left and their audience returned to work, talking loudly as they pretended not to listen.

"I apologise for interrupting your plans," the witch said once they were alone. "But the boy has special powers." Gabi saw Shimbabo's eyes widen and felt Hogan stiffen beside her. The witch knew. "I will need him for your venture."

"Very well, Chiremba Rose." Shimbabo nodded as if the decision were his. "You may have him." He nodded again in farewell, grabbed Gabi by the shoulder and turned to take her inside.

"The girl too."

He stopped, his fingers digging hard into her tendons.

"I have a great deal of work these days," the woman continued. "And have long felt the need of an assistant. Unfortunately all the girls you've brought into the camp have already been – tainted. If this girl escaped the fighting, if she is still untouched, then she is just what I need. A little old, perhaps," Gabi felt the witch's eyes on her, appraising, "but still young enough. I'll warrant she learns quickly, don't you girl?"

Gabi started at the unexpected question, then risked a look at the witch's face. "Yes Chiremba," she nodded her head rapidly, copying the soldier's honorific. Who knew, maybe she even was a real doctor. "Very quick."

Shimbabo tightened his hold. "She will run away," he protested. "Once outside the boma there is nothing to hold her here. She would reveal our position. I cannot risk it."

"She will not leave. Not so long as I have her brother"

"And when her brother is – used?"

"That will not be for sometime. By then, if I have done my job well, she will be mine."

Gabi swallowed, the icy certainty in the witch's voice more chilling than any man's hectoring tones. But at the same time her heart began to pound to a different beat. She was being saved. Not only saved, but taken into the witch's lair, and all this brought about by the very witch herself. Did that mean it was all tricks and mirrors? that she really believed Gabi a virgin? that she knew nothing? – or did it mean, conversely and disastrously, that she knew all?

"And if you have not done your job well?" The question was angry, frustrated.

"I have not failed you yet. But if the girl escapes then I will answer for it."

Shimbabo nodded, a glint lighting up his hard little eyes, and he pushed Gabi back towards her brother.

"It is agreed, Chiremba Rose. I will hold you to your word."

"Of course." She pulled the two children towards her. "In the meantime I will make an offering to the spirits in your name – to thank you for your generosity." A hand lightly on each child's shoulder, she turned and led them back through a wide path and sudden silence as the soldiers pulled back and watched them leave.

Gabi's first job was to put her brother in a cage. It was an old primate shipping crate that had been fastened in the branches of the flame tree she'd seen when passing. Originally intended for a chimpanzee, an adult would have been painfully restricted, but Hogan could sit comfortably enough so long as he didn't want to stretch his legs and back at the same time. Though old and well-used, it was still strong, the stains on the metal turning out to be blood rather than rust, and it was barred with an army padlock far too sophisticated for Gabi's basic lock-picking skills.

"Won't the animals get him?" She asked once she'd fastened him in and climbed back down. The cage was scarcely three metres above the ground, well within reach of a hungry lion. It was an ingenuous question – if the animals got her victims the witch would have long since moved the cage – but Gabi was curious to know what tricks she used to keep them away.

"So you are hungry to learn my skills?" The woman looked at her with a cool level gaze and Gabi found herself nodding, the keenness in her eyes no act. Such knowledge, she realised with a sudden stab, would finally give her – the eternal misfit – a place that she could call her own. Chiremba Rose seemed to understand.

"You can belong nowhere," she said finally, "or you can belong here, with me. The price will be your brother. The rewards will be beyond anything you have ever dreamed of. It is your choice. Now go and prepare the evening meal."

Her education began the next morning.

"They will all hate you," the witch told her over a breakfast of mealie porridge. "It is important you understand this. Our power is based on fear, not respect. The more they need us, the more they hate us for that need."

"But they can't touch you," Gabi probed for information, pleased with her subtlety, "because of that power?"

"Precisely." Chiremba Rose's steady gaze seemed to see right through her efforts at cunning. "But never rub your power in their face," she added. "Use it, hold it over them, but always give them an opening to keep their pride. They will still hate you, but less clearly, with no desire for revenge. And never – *never* – make an empty threat or fail to keep a promise."

"So if I run away…." Gabi's mind flashed back to the witch's promise to Shimbabo. "What will happen to you?"

"Firstly I will curse you so that your skin crawls and your eyes explode and your blood pours from every opening – and yet you do not die. Then I will bring you back, tear out your heart and offer it to the spirits of vengeance. Then I will go to Shimbabo and pay the penance he demands."

Gabi was silent. She had heard many threats in her lifetime, and seen many of them carried out, but this was different. This wasn't a threat, it was a fact, stated in her calm voice as if it were just another piece of information. For a moment she faltered as the fierce rage in her chilled. She was used to fighting anger with fury, violence with more so. What weapons did she have against this cold, sure power?

As if he sensed her hesitation, Hogan rattled his cage above them, clamouring for food and attention. She met his gaze and nodded, reassuring herself as much as him, trying to ignore the flicker of fear she saw in his eyes. He would think of a plan. His inward turning eyes would see things she could not yet guess at, his silent brain would plumb the witch's depths. They were a team. No-one, not even Chiremba Rose, could change that.

Over the next few days Gabi analysed the witch's defences and looked for openings, but she may as well not have bothered. Chiremba Rose had her vulnerabilities locked up as tight as Hogan's cage – the key for which, to Gabi's dismay, was handed over to Shimbabo for safe-keeping. "It is a sign of mutual trust," the witch explained and she laughed, a short soft exhalation that was more a look of amusement than any real noise. "Besides, I don't need a key to open locks."

Nor, it appeared, did she need ordinary weapons to protect herself – or if she did, she hid them nowhere that Gabi could find them. No rifles, no grenades, no pistols – nothing but the knife she used to cut plants from the garden, and this she gave to the girl freely to do her chores. Gabi would finger it thoughtfully sometimes, out of the witch's sight, but even if she could out-manoeuvre her nkisi and kill her, she'd never be able to get Hogan out of the cage before the soldiers came. And whilst their mission required only the witch's death for success, the boss had surely understood that Hogan's life would not be offered in return.

Meanwhile no-one suffered. That is, of course Hogan was cramped, bored and frightened, but he was well-fed too – on moambé and cassava, plantain and papaya, even fish – unlike Gabi, whom the witch put on a basic diet intended to clear her head, strengthen her soul, and purify her for the knowledge soon to come her way. And while Gabi was hungry the rest of her life was good – important even – for while the witch still didn't teach her any witching craft, she taught her a great deal of its related skills. Every day Chiremba Rose talked to her as they worked together, handing out information in her composed way, treating her as both a potential equal and yet also as just a girl, allowed to make mistakes and learn. And learn Gabi did, her hunger for this knowledge easily outstripping that for food.

Gabi had never been treated like that before, and as the days passed by she found she was starting to act as though it would last for ever. She still looked for opportunities obviously, but a small part of her realised she was beginning to go through the motions. Likewise, just as she told herself that Hogan was fine, another, more honest voice knew that, for him, every day of waiting grew more terrible. Each time the witch came with the knife to cut off a curl of his hair, he suffered a thousand fates worse than death. Each night he lay awake, alone with the spirits of those he had killed, knowing that the witch could call them down on him at any moment, was a night of no dawn. Gabi knew this – knew it and yet, rather than working harder to release him, found instead that she was visiting him less often, talking to him less when she did, and avoiding his eyes that were full of a message she didn't want to see.

Meanwhile she put what she learned to the test. Every time she went to the boma she tried out the effect of different stances and words, watching how the soldiers treated her now she was a sorceress's apprentice – and seeing, with growing understanding, how it added to her power.

She had never been a child that adults made a fuss of. Even as a toddler circumstances had made her aloof, suspicious, her hawk nose and fierce eyes opening none of the doors available to a prettier girl. But now she noticed something different in the soldiers' indifference. They no longer ignored her because she was of no use to them – but because she made them uncomfortable, even a little nervous. All this without a single shot fired. She realised it wasn't her own power of course, that it was because she was the witch's proxy – that if they treated her well it was because they feared what her mistress could do – but if she could get all this at just the start of her apprenticeship, imagine what the future would hold if she knew it all. If only she could get Hogan safely away, she thought, she might almost be content to live without him for awhile – so that later she could keep them both from harm for evermore.

The thought scared her, seeing it for the thin end of the wedge it was – and that fear made her bold.

They'd been there two weeks when Chiremba Rose sent Gabi to the boma with a charm for Antoine. It was a task that upped her status considerably, since only the witch or the owner could usually touch such a thing, and sealed her position as official apprentice. Gabi understood this and couldn't help a fierce sense of triumph as she took hold of the charm, even as another part of her knew she should dread what if foretold.

Antoine's hut was on the far side of the boma, near the back palisade. Shimbabo liked to keep his henchmen spread out, each keeping an eye on his own group of men so that the encampment, small though it was, had the sense of being made up of suburbs, each with its own distinctive atmosphere. Antoine's was the druggie's quarter, a status Shimbabo tolerated so long as Antoine kept his men under control. Gabi found him sitting outside his hut, legs stretched out, head leaning back in the shade of the trees that stretched over the high wooden stakes, sweat lining his skin and staining his stinking clothes.

She stopped before him and stared at him calmly, saying nothing, waiting as Chiremba Rose would have done. Feeling her presence he looked up from his spliff, a stoned smile fading as he saw who it was. When he was thoroughly uncomfortable, but before he had time to show it, Gabi held out her package.

"Chiremba Rose sent me to give you this."

"Ah?" His eyes widened in pleasure then narrowed in insult. She hadn't brought it herself. Gabi could see the dilemma playing out on his face as he decided how to react it, apathy more than caution winning out.

"Good." He reached for it, examined it, then put it around his neck. "Send her my thanks."

"I will." Gabi didn't move.

Antoine's face creased in annoyance, but he spoke patiently. "There was something else?"

"Yes." Again she let the pause drag out, meeting his gaze calmly. Again she spoke just before it grew too long. "She said you could send back payment via me too."

"Ah." Antoine sighed out a long stream of smoke. "OK." He felt in his pockets, but finding nothing that suited, stood, caught his balance on the door frame, then went into the dark space beyond. "Come on in, then." It was a display of manners Gabi would never normally have merited and she went and stood by the door, blocking the light as she waited for her eyes to adjust.

Antoine was by the bed counting a stash of notes, his rifle leaning up against the far wall. Beside her, a row of hooks supported his few spare clothes, amongst them an army kit bag, poorly closed, with one side sagging open. As Antoine turned his body to shield the money from her view, Gabi reached into it and pulled out the first thing she touched – a grenade, she could feel that immediately, probably a variation on the RGD-5. Quickly, she thrust it into the side pocket of her dress, thanking the stars it was small, and praying to the moon that no-one would dare ask what made her hip stick out so.

"Here you are." Antoine was holding out a wad of cash. "Tell Chiremba Rose that I've included an extra note for you." He smiled. "Transport duty."

"Yes." Gabi's heart was racing. "I will."

She took the money with her left hand, right arm dangling to hide the bulge at her side, gave him a curt nod and left abruptly, half-expecting to see Shimbabo and his men waiting outside. But no-one was there, no-one had seen what she'd done, and no-one challenged her as she left the boma. The power of a witch's actions, she realised, wasn't just in the moment, but in the general fear that created so much opportunity. It was an important lesson and one she intended to make the most of. Meanwhile she hid the grenade high up in the branches of a young mahogany tree and returned to Chiremba Rose, feeling that now, at least, she could look Hogan in the eyes without shame.

She took him the grenade that night, going up to speak with him while her mistress slept. Although the witch's hut was big Gabi was made to sleep outside, something she was used to on campaign but had never done alone before. At first she had spent most of the dark hours up the tree with Hogan, holding his fingers through the bars, reassuring him with her presence, keeping the night fears at bay. More recently though she had slept through the night, tired out from all the work she did each day. Or so she told herself. Tonight though, with a full moon rising through the forest, turning it into a mosaic of black and grey, she climbed back up to him. Ignoring the stench of his evacuations that were scattered against the tree trunk, she hunkered down in front of the cage and took the grenade from her pocket.

Hogan was leaning against the side, legs bent at the knees, head lolling as though he were asleep, which he wasn't. He looked at her once as she arrived, then closed his eyes and turned his head away. Gabi's heart stopped as she saw what she'd done to him, guilt and shame sending her blood thick and heavy. Then it started up again, pounding in compensation as she stretched her fingers through the bars, trying to reach his hand.

"Hogan," she whispered.

"Go away," he said, his eyes still closed.

"No." She said it with all of her old fierceness, recent doubts forgotten, and at the sound he opened his eyes, their gleam a question mark in the moonlight.

"Look, Hogan. I've brought you this." She opened her fingers, guilt making her over eager. "You can keep it here, hide it in your clothes."

Hogan looked down to where it was clearly visible in her hand, but made no move to take it.

"What am I supposed to do with that?"

The resignation in his voice stung her more than any bitterness. That, along with the realisation that she didn't know – hadn't thought it through – that her offering was an empty gesture.

"If – if something happens to me," she created wildly. "If they come for you – to do terrible things. If I can't save you...."

Hogan closed his eyes again, the crease in his forehead the only sign of his pain. Gabi stopped, ashamed and helpless. But what else could she do?

"You could blow her up," he said, reading her thoughts. "Now."

"And the key? The key to release you? Do you think I haven't thought of that?"

The anger was back in her voice again, ringing true, and for a long moment he stared at his sister, taking her measure.

"Perhaps the soldiers would give it to you," he suggested finally. "A witch's apprentice so powerful she can kill the mistress no-one else can touch. They'd be afraid."

"They'd be afraid," she agreed. She thought about it. "But it wouldn't be the right kind of fear. They'd more likely tear us to pieces for what we'd done."

He shut his eyes again and Gabi realised his hopelessness had become physical – that despite the good food she brought him every day he had barely the strength to stay awake. She knew that – more than the cage, the night fears, the suspense of what would happen, of knowing as only Hogan's imagination could know, how terrible it would be – more than any of these things it was her own wavering, her abandonment that had caused this despair. She had caused his spirit to fade from his body as his hope waned, and soon there would be no brother worth saving.

"Hogan," she let go of his hand and shook him hard. "Hogan, listen to me. I will get you out of here. Soon. Very soon. I don't know how, but I will, I swear I will. Hogan, look at me."

With a sigh he looked at her, then sat up a little, his neck growing firm as he saw the resolution in her eyes. She took back his hand and grasped it firmly in their special hold. "Whatever happens Hogan, trust me. I will not let you down. I swear this on our mother's soul."

For a moment he was still in the darkness, then he squeezed her hand back tightly. "Good." A ghost of a smile flittered around his lips. "About bloody time."

She smiled back, almost laughing in relief, then, as she shifted position, the smile froze on her face. The moon had just risen over the edge of the clearing to show Chiremba Rose, clear as day, standing in the doorway of her hut. She was looking up at them with her serene gaze.

"Hogan." But even as she turned to warn him, the witch was gone.

"What?"

Gabi blinked and strained her eyes, but saw only shadows. "Nothing." She put the grenade in his hand. "Keep it safe. I will come when I am ready."

"Yes." And it was the yes of old, full of unquestioning trust.

Once back down, when Hogan was no longer looking, Gabi examined the earth by the hut. There were no footprints. Perhaps she had invented the witch, panic and shame lending her Hogan's imagination. Perhaps. She hoped so. But it was a weak hope, jostled and buffeted by fear, and it took a long time before she finally fell asleep.

"Wake, child."

For a moment Gabi thought she was still dreaming, that her mother had come back to talk to her in gentle, mothering tones. No-one had called her *child* for a very long time. But her mother didn't speak again, the image disappeared, and slowly she realised she'd left sleep behind. Opening her eyes, she saw the witch standing over her, looking at her with an expression that made her heart stab with fear.

She had run out of time.

Quickly she darted a look at Hogan's cage. He was still there, still alive, kneeling to look down at them intently, sensing the different energy in the air.

"Yes, Chiremba." Gabi scrambled clumsily to her feet, urgency making her seem keen to please. Then, as she met her gaze, something in the woman's face made her freeze, her limbs becoming heavy and awkward. She couldn't quite understand the sadness she read there, but understood immediately it was for her.

"It is time to make a choice, child."

Gabi said nothing.

"I must begin the sacrifices for the next offensive. Much magic will be needed." She stopped to see if she had said enough but Gabi just stared at her, shaking her head a little – not at the information, but at this moment that she had convinced herself would never come.

"There is too much power in your brother to be wasted in just one kill. Every part of him is useful – every finger, every toe, his penis of course, his testicle sacs…. I will harvest each part separately, one at a time, keeping him alive throughout, ensuring the power of his spirit continues to nourish every element – so that together they create a magic more powerful and terrible than one mere body could ever do. When I have finished with him, the power I unleash will win us the war – and once we've won, my place in the new order will be undisputed. My place – and yours too if you are with me. So choose, girl, for there is no place here for the half-hearted. Help me with this sacrifice and I will begin to show you secrets you cannot imagine. Refuse me and I will return you to the soldiers. They won't harm you now you've been touched by me."

She waited patiently for an answer, her gentleness more terrible than any rage could be. Gabi backed against the wall of the hut and leant against it, unsure if her legs would hold, then stared up at Hogan, her head shaking. But the stare Hogan returned was firm.

Come on, his gaze said. *You can do it. This is our chance. Seize it. I trust you.* And suddenly she saw it all, understood his plan, and her legs stood firm.

"Yes." She nodded her head, as though to herself, then stepped away from the hut and turned her back to Hogan as she met the witch's gaze. "Yes," she repeated. "I will do this thing. I choose you, mistress, and the power you give me."

"Good." For a moment the woman smiled at her, her eyes soft as a caress, then her face was back to normal and she reached out to give Gabi the knife.

"Make a fire," she ordered. "When it's ready put this stone in and leave it there until it's hot." She handed her a pale wedge-shaped rock, rounded at one end, thin at the other, the round end covered with dark spots and stains like a speckled egg. "While it's heating, sharpen the knife. Make it as sharp as you can. The sharper it is, the quicker the cut. Then, when you've finished, go and wash in the river." She didn't wait for an answer, but went back inside her hut to prepare for the ritual, leaving Gabi to her tasks.

Gabi made the fire. She sharpened the knife. She did everything slowly and deliberately without once looking at Hogan, conscious all the time of his eyes on her, watching her every movement, fighting his fear. Then, when everything was ready, she walked out into the forest, down to the river where she performed her ablutions, and took out the fake blood capsules she kept hidden in her vagina.

She had first come across the capsules during an ambush – when the boss had set up a fake massacre – and had quickly seen a use for them he would never imagine. Since then, like the razor blades in the heels of her shoes, she had always kept some about her, hidden for no better reason than that they might come in useful. And while the razors might conceivably be found before she could use them, the capsules were in no such danger. When a man checked out her vagina it was with his penis, and more often than not when he felt the lumps there, they frightened him off without further ado. If not, if he was forceful, the resulting sheets of blood generally did the trick. It was a good way, she had discovered, to put the other men off.

Gabi checked the capsules over for leaks, put them in her pocket, then washed carefully as instructed. Then she walked back to the clearing where the witch was waiting for her.

The sun was high now, high noon, the hour at which nothing usually moved. The heat in the clearing was physical, rays of light bouncing off the dry earth, Hogan sweltering beneath the sparse shade of the flame tree's leaves. Even without the fire the stone would have been hot, but now the flames added to the heat like an extra layer of hell, on the far side of which Chiremba Rose watched her approach. Gabi walked up to her slowly, more solemn than reluctant, and stopped in front of the blaze. For a moment they stared at each other, the air shimmering between them, then the witch nodded.

"Take the knife and climb the tree," she ordered. "Cut off the little toe of his left foot. When you have done this, I will pass you the stone." She indicated the thick wad of material she would wrap around its 'handle'. "Press the rounded end against his stump – it will heal it quickly and stop the blood. Do you understand?"

Gabi nodded. "I understand."

"Are you ready?"

She nodded again. "I am."

"Then go."

Slowly, carefully, heart pounding and vision fuzzy as if she watched through someone else's eyes, Gabi turned and climbed the tree.

Hogan cowered away from her.

"No," he said, limbs curled up tightly, as far as possible from her reach. "No."

"Yes," she said, and the word was a savage hiss, full of ferocious certainty. "Yes," she repeated. "You will do this thing."

For a long moment Hogan stared at her. She didn't waver. Slowly, his eyes never leaving hers, he stretched out his left foot.

"Stand up," she ordered. It would be easier to push the knife down against the floor of the cage. He stood and she smelt the acrid scent of his pee as he soiled himself. Ignoring it, she lowered her eyes and reached to hold his ankle.

"Don't move." He didn't move. He was incapable of moving and suddenly, swiftly, she brought down the knife as if she were slicing a yam, and severed his little toe.

Hogan screamed.

"Quick, seal it." The witch was right beside her – how long had she been there? – handing her the stone. Gabi took it, fumbling clumsily at the thick cloth, then held the red-hot rock against the bleeding stump. Hogan screamed again and tried to pull his foot away but she held it mercilessly, her strength seemingly without limits, until she could smell the scorch of burning flesh. Then she let go and Hogan shrunk from her, his trousers soiled now with more than pee, the stink vying with so many other smells that Gabi turned in sudden disgust, turned her back on him and handed his toe, the little brown toe with its tiny pink nail down to her mistress.

The witch took it, then looked back up at Gabi.

"Good," she said. "Very good. Now come into the hut and I will prepare you for the ritual."

Gabi followed her, leaving Hogan without a backward glance – and leaving the blood capsules hidden amongst the stains on the floor of his cage.

When they came out the sun was low in the sky and Gabi was exhausted. There was so much to do, so much to remember. For a moment she stared at the clearing, at the tree in it, at the cage, at the boy in the cage, as though they were in another world, a film perhaps, something false and shallow – meaningless compared to the spirit world she had just touched with Chiremba Rose. Then the blazing sunset tried to seduce her with its colours, sending tints of orange and pink through the flame tree's leaves. But not that pink, surely? Not red?

"The boy." The witch saw it immediately. "Something is wrong." She pushed past Gabi and climbed up for a closer look, her face for once troubled, to find Hogan collapsed on the floor, seemingly lifeless. Around his left foot, dripping out of the cage and onto the tree, where it trickled past the bright red flowers in a sticky red line, was a great deal of blood.

"What is this?"

Gabi thought the woman was speaking to herself but she turned, face twisted with rage, and repeated the question slowly and clearly. "What is this?"

"It's – I – that is – I don't know. He often bleeds a lot – whenever he falls or bumps into things. Uncle called him his little bleeder – but he couldn't help it. Does it matter?"

"Haemophilia." Chiremba Rose jumped back down, graceful and light, her emotions back under control. "He has lost too much blood to live – it has spoilt the sacrifice. We will not be able to proceed as planned."

"I'm s-sorry." Gabi backed away. "I didn't realise – I thought your magic...."

"My magic must know what it deals with to work well." She looked away to think, recriminations unimportant, all her energy going into saving the situation, then she decided. "Very well, we will drain him – take his blood like a stuck boar. It will work just as well. We can take the parts afterwards and soak them in his blood." She turned to Gabi. "We must work quickly before he wastes any more. We must take him from the cage and hang

him from the tree, tying his arms to that branch there – you see."
She pointed to a lower limb they used as a hand hold to get up.
"We'll put a bucket beneath his foot to collect the rest of the
blood. Go. Quickly."

Gabi turned and headed for the boma.

"Stop. Where are you going?"

"To get the key."

"As if I'd need their key." She held up the nkisi she kept
round her neck. "Get the rope and bucket from my hut. I will
deal with the cage."

When Gabi came back the witch had got Hogan out and
heaved his listless body over her shoulder, the blood on his
clothes glistening in the slanting sun.

"Quick, help me tie him."

Dropping the bucket beneath the tree, Gabi ran to support
his weight while the witch secured first one wrist, then the other.

"Put the bucket beneath his foot, the one that's bleeding."

Gabi did, brushing the blood from Hogan's trousers so that it
splattered noisily against the black plastic.

"That's strange."

Gabi looked up to see the witch peering down from the tree.
"What?"

"It doesn't sound right."

The witch strained forward to see his foot, but night had
fallen in the last few minutes and everything was cast in
shadow. Swinging herself down, as balanced as a cat – was
she a cat? would she turn into a lion? – she went to investigate
Hogan's leg. Gabi moved back to give her room and, as she
bent forward Hogan kicked out at her throat with all the strength
left in his little body, crushing her pouch of charms with the ball
of his foot.

She was fast. Terrifyingly fast. Something in her – her third
eye – had sensed his body coil and was pulling away from the
bucket even as he lashed out, so that he only knocked her off
balance. But Gabi was behind her, knife in hand, the newly
sharpened blade sliding between the woman's shoulders as
easily as it had cut off Hogan's toe. Chiremba Rose's
momentum slammed her body up to its hilt where she hung for

a moment, her full weight in Gabi's hands, then she fell to the earth, pulling the knife from Gabi's grasp.

Quick as breathing Gabi took out the extra rope she had brought from the hut and tied the witch's hands and feet. Only then did she remove the knife from the woman's back and stand over her, breathing heavily, looking down into the whites of her eyes.

"Untie me," Hogan said, as if from a great distance. Gabi didn't move. "Untie me Gabi, untie me now." His voice was the calm before the storm, his firm order more urgent than any scream.

Slowly, as if not quite sure what she was doing, Gabi stood up, walked over to Hogan, and untied his wrists. Instead of falling to the ground though, he twisted himself back up into the tree, disappearing into its branches, then returned holding something small and hard which he handed to Gabi. It was the grenade.

"Quick," he said. "Do it and let's get out of here."

Gabi looked at it then back at Hogan.

"We don't have to," she said. "We could just –"

"No."

She stopped. He was right. She had to make a choice. She had made her choice.

"OK." She took a deep breath, then let it out in a shuddering sigh.

Chiremba Rose's face was tight with pain, but her eyes clear with understanding as Gabi slowly leant down and opened her mouth. She didn't struggle, didn't argue or beg, didn't fight to keep her jaws clenched shut – she didn't even curse. She just let Gabi open her lips and put in the grenade, like a child giving a sweet to its mother. When only the safety pin protruded Gabi took the last bit of cord from her pocket and carefully, almost tenderly, tied it around the witch's head to force her jaw closed.

"I'm sorry," she said. "I'm sorry." Then the woman's face blurred and shimmered as something wet and strange fell from Gabi's eyes onto her cheeks. Slowly she lent over and kissed her on the forehead, then she stood up, pulled the pin, and they ran away.

When they heard the explosion they stopped, ducking down to avoid the fragments of her spirit as it scattered away into the night. Then they walked west, away from the rising moon, Hogan limping, Gabi supporting, until they could walk no more.

Dawn found them curled up in the branches of the understorey, snatching at sleep before they set off once more. A day's hike should get them to the river. By this time tomorrow they'd be safe in the boss's hands – except that safe didn't feel quite the right word any more.

Hogan stirred and Gabi put out her hand to hold him safe, tenderness swelling up in her as she saw the shrivelled stump of his toe. Gently she soothed his forehead with her other hand. Hogan stiffened, then relaxed, then without opening his eyes, said, "She had another key."

"What?"

"She had another key. In her nkisi. She used it to open the cage while you were in the hut."

"Ah."

Hogan sat up, leaning against her while she cradled his head. "You know that…" he hesitated, swallowed, then said it anyway. "You know that I nearly lost you there. With her."

Gabi stopped caressing his head. "Yes," she said at last.

Hogan said no more and for a long time they sat there, together and alone. Finally, just as Gabi resolved to get going, he spoke again.

"I've been thinking."

Her heart took an extra beat. "Don't," she said. "Please don't."

"It's important."

Gabi sighed. The one luxury she had right now was being too tired to think. Hogan was going to take it away. "It's always important," she said. "But does it have to be now?"

"Yes." Hogan's voice was fierce with conviction. It occurred to Gabi that she owed him this. Besides, far better in the long run to know what was going on in his strange, impenetrable mind. She sighed again.

"Go on, then."

"Well…." Hogan paused as if unsure how to continue now he had her ear. "Well," he said again, "before we met the boss, life was pretty hard – right?"

"Yes."

"We were hungry and beaten and it was hard to survive."

"Yes." Gabi felt herself relaxing. This didn't seem too dangerous.

"And what are we now?"

"Hungry, beaten and fighting to survive," she replied promptly, with a small laugh that sounded more like a sob. "But that's usual on a mission, you know that."

"Exactly."

Gabi frowned. There was always a moment in Hogan's explanations where she lost the thread. This time it had come quicker than usual. "Exactly what?"

"You realise that now we've done this – killed the witch – it will only get worse."

Gabi didn't, she hadn't thought about it. Now she did. After a while she nodded. "Yes."

"Well...." Hogan took a deep breath, pulled away from her and turned to look her in the eye. "I don't want to do it anymore."

"What?"

"I don't want to do it." He was icy calm now, his voice firm and level. "I don't want missions like this anymore – I don't want to get rid of people like her. Witches never bothered us before. No-one we met then was ever as bad as the people we meet now.... So I've decided – I won't do it any more."

Gabi stared at him. Rebelling against the boss was a new concept, and not something she would have thought of on her own. But that didn't make it unacceptable. Her numbness even made the idea easier, cutting out the need for any thinking but the most basic logic. She wanted to rest, she wanted everything to go away. If they stopped working for the boss, it would. It was enough. Hogan took a long time to come to a decision, but when he did he was usually right – she had relied on it more times than she could count.

"How do we stop?" she asked.

"We refuse."

"Oh yeah? We refuse. Just like that."

"Why not?" It was Hogan's turn to be surprised. He'd expected resistance to the idea, not the method. "We can run away to the refugee camps."

"Sure. But do you think he'd leave us there – that he wouldn't track us down? He'll tell everyone I'm a witch now – the destroyer of the People's Army's great witch Chiremba Rose. Everyone will want a piece of me – either to use me or destroy me in turn. But you know the truth. Without his power behind us I can't keep us safe – and if he can't use us, he'll make damn sure no-one else can."

"Then what can we do?"

Gabi never ceased to be surprised by Hogan's naivety; at how he could think his way through such difficult, uncharted terrain only to get stuck at the obvious.

"It's easy," she said. "We kill him."

For a moment they were silent, eyes locked, her words expanding out into the forest, then Hogan nodded.

"Yes," he said. "We kill him. It's the only way." He leant forward and they kissed, sealing their pact.

"Come on," Gabi dropped to the ground, then reached up to lower him gently down beside her. "It's time to go."

Slowly they limped through the trees, supporting each other. The thinker and the doer – together they made a great team.

Waking Beauty

"By the time you read this I'll be long gone. And if you ever try and find me I'll kill myself, I swear I will – and that'll teach you."

Princess Aurelie – 07:07:17

There was no name on the envelope. Everyone who read it thought it was meant for them – except the one person who knew they'd been found out. They, however, smelt a rat.

Queen's Diary – 22:01:00

They came to take her this morning, at dawn, and I let them. They told me she'd be safer like this – as if a daughter could possibly be safe without her mother – so I let them persuade me and they took her away. In truth I had no choice. It didn't occur to me I could have left all this – the palace, the King, my position – and hidden her myself. Their arguments were so convincing, so reasonable, so concerned.... How could I face the risk of being wrong when confronted with so much right? So much *might*. If only I had listened to my heart. And now I have lost her forever, the daughter I've hardly had – and my heart speaks no more, shrivelled with remorse and pain.

Edited Anthology of the King's Commentaries: Comment 2,497 – 08:07:17

There are two kinds of women: survivors and victims. My wife is a victim. When you find yourself in a position such as hers there are two choices: deal with your fate, preferably with dignity – or go under. My wife went under and wasted little time in doing so.

I sound unsympathetic? I am. A strong man needs a strong woman who lives by her decisions and has no time for regrets. The daughters of royalty are not teddy bears to be clutched at for comfort. They are commodities, land brokers, elements of deals to be negotiated for wealth, power… kingdoms. My daughter had an excellent childhood by all accounts, which turned out better than any of us could have hoped for. And what did she do with it? She threw it in my face – and in so doing lost me a friend, an ally, and a future kingdom.

My wife blames herself, and mourns and weeps for what might have been.

I blame nobody but my daughter, who tossed it all away when victory was ours.

Extract from *'It Shouldn't Happen to a Princess'* by Aurelie Regent

I always thought Mary Whither was my mother. The other two were like spinster aunts, kindly but aloof, and it was Mary who looked after my daily needs. She told me stories, sat me on her knee, played, listened. She was my real mother. My birthmother, this distant Queen I'd scarcely seen and knew nothing about, meant nothing to me. If I was lonely, well – that wasn't uncommon for an only child – and at least we had money. Having neither neighbours nor companions, I didn't think it odd the royal family were so much talked of, or that court etiquette was part of my lessons. I assumed all kids got the same. I felt hard-done-by that I didn't have a father, but we had a TV and I watched the soaps so I knew how common *that* was. I assumed the three Fairies were lesbians, happy in their a menage-à-trois.

The TV was well vetted though. Every time the news came on, or some other programme Mary disapproved of, "interference" would promptly cut out sound and picture – though there was no real need for me not to know. I heard Fern arguing with Mary once, asking what harm it did – and Mary saying that it was for my own safety – that the less I knew, the less I could give away.

"Oh, so that's why she gets lessons in Court Procedure," Fern retorted. "Very discreet that."

"That's not the same level of knowledge and you know it," Mary snapped back. "Any royalist might indulge in such ambitions. Knowing who you are is far more dangerous."

"Dangerous for whom?" asked Fallon, who'd been listening quietly. It seemed an innocent question, so I didn't understand why Mary went tight with rage and left the cabin. Nor did I understand the look the other two exchanged behind her back. But I did understand it was better not to let them know I'd overheard. And because I loved Mary with all my heart, I took her side without question and thought no more about it.

Until after my marriage.

Back in the castle, with so many new things to assimilate and so few of them pleasant, those memories came back to me. At first they arose unbidden, nostalgia to counter my unhappiness, but later I actively sought them out – eager for clues as to how I could have got in such a position. They were comforting, but gave me no real solutions – especially not to the one question that, once I had thought of it, I couldn't understand why nobody had ever asked. Nor why no-one, once I started asking it, would give me an answer.

The first person I tried was my new mother, the Queen. I found her in the smaller sitting room, still in her dressing gown, the pale pink towelling matching her washed-out complexion and faded hair.

"What I want to know," I asked, "is why I had to go away at all." The Queen looked worried. I knew she found these questions difficult, but she was the only one who even pretended to listen. I used her guilt as a lever.

"I mean, Millicent threatened me with death, via a spindle, on my 16th birthday, right?"

Mother reached for her cigarettes, but nodded. So far so good.

"Then Mary converted death into a mega-sleep, yes?"

She lit it, her long fingers trembling slightly, and inhaled deeply before nodding again.

"But even so, there was never any question of Millicent hurting me before I was sixteen?"

Another nod, more wary this time.

"So what I don't get is this – why couldn't I stay at the palace until I was – say – fifteen and a half, and *then* go into hiding?"

The Queen – my mother – looked like she was trying not to cry. "It was thought better, dear. Safer."

"I know it was thought bloody safer," I exploded. "That's what everyone keeps saying – but what I want to know is *why*? Why did intelligent, powerful, *sussed* people think it such a good idea when you knew *nothing* would happen for sixteen years? Don't you have the Secret Police? Couldn't the Good Fairies sort it – like they do everything else? Don't witnesses at the drug trials get hidden every week? What was the problem? Didn't you *want* me or something?"

My mother, her face collapsing into tears, got up and ran out of the room. It wasn't exactly the answer I'd been hoping for.

Pip came in as she left. He watched her go, stubbing out her fallen cigarette with the toe of his riding boot.

"Been stirring things up again, have you?"

Our marriage had never stood a chance. People seemed to think I should have been delighted – that I should have been dazzled by all the new discoveries, sensations and luxuries spread out before me – that I should have felt the luckiest girl in the whole world. A strong, handsome prince to marry, a kingdom to inherit, servants to fetch and carry, money to spend without measure, an adoring crowd who cheered and bowed and beamed and threw flowers everywhere I went. What more could a girl ask for?

Quite a lot, it turns out. Love, for instance – or freedom to do your own thing without your husband's permission. A husband, come to that, with a bit of kindness and understanding – rather than this daddy's boy who was charming only when you did exactly as he wanted, and a little tyrant when you didn't.

"Do you know why they sent me away?" I parried. "Why, when they knew I wouldn't be harmed for sixteen years, they sent me away as soon as I was born?"

He flicked his hair out of his eyes before replying – a delaying tactic I had come to know well.

"Because they cared about you, I expect. How would I know? I was only a little boy myself. Why do you have to go harping on about it, anyway? It's over now – and you know what they say...." He softened his voice in an attempt to win me over. "All's well that ends well."

"*Well!*" I exclaimed. "You call this ending *well*. I can't go anywhere, do anything, say anything. I'm not supposed to have opinions, concerns, emotions.... I spend nearly all my life *alone*, in the middle of a *forest*, without even a single *friend*, and then suddenly I can't *fart* without fifteen million people falling over themselves to smell it – and I'm supposed to be *happy*. I can't even go for a ride without half the cavalry chasing after me."

Pip sighed. We'd been here before. "It's for your own protection," he said wearily. "There are people out there who'd jump at the chance to kidnap you – or worse. You know what your father said."

"I didn't notice them all lining up to protect me in the forest."

"No-one knew you were a princess in the forest, as you fucking well know."

Pip rarely swore, he considered it common. It was a sign of his anger. There were other signs too: his face was white and pinched, his eyes hard, his breath short and shallow. I remembered we were alone and let it drop. I'd get nowhere with Pip, that was for sure.

Aurelie's Journal – 16:04:17

He woke me with a kiss. Everyone knows that, but surely they didn't think it ended there. I was deeply asleep, almost unconscious, and the first thing I knew was a stranger's mouth on my lips, kissing me. I didn't know where I was, who he was – what was going on. I hardly knew who *I* was, I was still so tangled up in dreams.

Then into those dreams came his tongue, softly at first then hard, pushing past my teeth. I gagged and moved my face away, gasping for air. He moved back and I breathed, trying to open my eyes against the haze of sleep that weighed me down. I caught a glimpse of sun and sky and the green of briars, then he caught my face in his hands and turned me to look at him, but all I saw was a blur silhouetted against the sun. He kissed me again, hard and ongoing. Then he climbed up onto the bier where I lay and stretched out on top of me, hurting, while he wrestled with his clothes and tore my dress. I remember the bird song. All the way through it the birds were singing as if spring had come. I suppose for them spring and screwing are much the same thing.

Afterwards he told them my clothes had ripped on the thorns. I didn't say anything, still in transition, not sure if the whole thing was real or a nightmare. No-one expected me to say anything anyway. It was my role to be grateful.

Later he told me his overpowering love for me had carried him away – that my great beauty had aroused such passion in him he wanted to bring me back to life in the most vibrant, positive act known to man. He was eloquent then. He asked what it mattered since we were to be wed, since I was his and had been ever since my fate was declared at my christening. He cooed and cajoled – then lost his patience when he saw it wouldn't work. He is silent now, sulky and angry. His eloquence is all for lies and hypocrisy – strip him of that and he has nothing left to say. He has plenty to do though. He is still my husband and master – his will law, his marital rights to be obeyed.

I, however, am no longer asleep. I am awake now, wide awake, and soon my time will come.

Extract from 'It shouldn't Happen to a Princess' by Aurelie Regent

It was like being in a conspiracy. All around me people were trying to shut me up, grind me down, make me conform – yet they all did it without any solid front I could rebel against. Rather, everyone seemed to have their own private reasons, against which Millicent's actions seemed increasingly irrelevant. Nobody seemed to care why she'd threatened me in the first place. Nobody was interested in what the King might have done to provoke her. Nobody, basically, despite everything she'd done, seemed to think her role in my life worth discussing at all.

My mother wanted me to pretend it didn't matter and 'start anew', now we were finally together. If she could pretend all the intervening years had never happened, then she needn't feel guilty and I wouldn't have to forgive her. Fat chance.

Pip just wanted a dumb blond: smile, look pretty, do what he said. He was a victim of his upbringing, of course, but that was hardly my fault. I think his heroic rescue was almost a dream come true for him, and that when he kissed me – asleep, quiet, virginal – he really thought he'd found the perfect bride. Awake, I wasn't so passive, and I don't think he ever got over the disappointment.

Mary was the only person I could talk to. Mary let me complain, cry, and rage. Mary was still there to soothe my brow, dry my tears, make me laugh and remind me of the good times we'd had together – and that might yet come again. Mary was the only person who made me feel good, but even she couldn't help me here. Mary, while insisting that my parents loved me dearly, that everything they had done was to protect me from the evil Millicent.... Mary, while taking their side as a loyal Good Fairy should, still couldn't hide the fact that really, deep down, she thought they hadn't wanted me either. I knew her too well. I loved her all the more for trying to protect me, but it was a love tinged with frustration. Why wouldn't anyone just give it to me straight?

I wished Fallon and Fern were still around. They'd helped me to settle in, but had then gone back to their official lives, even trying to persuade Mary to go with them. She'd realised how much I needed her though – how I couldn't bear to be abandoned amongst these strangers – and had stubbornly stayed on to look after me. The two F's had never been as demonstrative as Mary, never very vocal or affectionate, but they'd always been *there* – and when they'd intervened they'd generally been right. They wouldn't just pat me on the head and reassure me, surely? They'd tell me whatever they knew.

But they weren't available.

Which is why, bravely and foolishly, I went to see the one other person I hadn't yet asked: my father, the King.

Edited extract from Secret Police recordings of the King's private conversations. File D1384, Section 2. Recorded 20:07:17

I heard later she'd been causing a fuss for a while, but at the time I knew nothing about it. Afterwards I got the usual excuses about not wanting to bother me with petty affairs – the blithering idiots. If I'd known earlier I could have done something about it. As it was I found out too late. Too late to save a kingdom, an alliance, and a future legacy. The selfish bitch doesn't know what she's destroyed. All those years of work, pulling strings, negotiating.... She probably doesn't even care. Well, the strong don't cry over spilt milk. Another drink?

She came and found me in the garden. The prettiest little thing, all blonde hair and rosebud lips like her mother was when we first met. Made me indulgent, I admit it, so that I overlooked her shallow curtsey and forward approach. The young are always hasty. It's not wise, but it can show character – I didn't want to wait for anything much when I was younger either. Still don't, come to that. Must be young at heart, what!

She got stuck in straight away – wanting to know why I'd sent her away fifteen years before I needed to.

"What was your plan?" she asked, as bold as brass. Just like I'd ask a general whose strategy had failed. "You did as you saw fit," I'd murmur, "yet you lost 500 men and ten miles of border. What, exactly, was your plan?" Oh I can tell you, my men soon learnt to fear those quiet, polite questions – and here was my own daughter giving me the same treatment. Say what you like, blood tells. There she was, spent nearly all of her life a hermit in the woods, back in the palace for less than a year, and already she was treating her father with disdain. It tickled my fancy, I can tell you. I thought she was a chip off the old block. Wrong block. I might have guessed she'd turn out like her mother.

My mistake was to humour her.

"What was my plan?" I repeated. "Well, sit down next to me, my pretty one, and I'll see if I can explain."

She sat down. She seemed so demure then, in that long white flowing dress, her plump little breasts just peaking out.... Pity.

I started off with a little background. "You realise I had all the spindles in the kingdom burnt?"

She nodded.

"And all imports banned. Spindle smugglers got heavier penalties than the drug barons. And before you ask, of course I knew that if it had been prophesised, then it would happen – spindle-burning or not – but I still had to do something. I couldn't just take it lying down. It was good for technology actually. Putting the spinners out of business made way for plastic, which turned out more durable and less labour intensive. Saved me a fortune in spinning bills. I suppose I should be grateful to Millicent eh! Ha! Just my little joke, m'dear."

She didn't laugh, but I let it go. Stupid of me. I should have read the signs. Instead I carried on, ever the fool for a pretty face.

"Even if Mary Whither changed the curse to sleep, that was hardly practical – you couldn't marry Henry's son asleep. Besides, Pip's mettle was untested, he was still a boy. I had alliances to form, a kingdom to build up. I couldn't risk all that on you getting a bloody alarm call. Prophecy or no, Kingdoms and Empires are built on decisive men of action, acting when it counts, and you remember it."

"So?"

The question surprised me. "So I decided. One of the Fairies, Whither I think it was, suggested they hide you away to try and foil Millicent right from the start – and I agreed. Thought it was rather a good plan myself. I knew if they couldn't look after you nobody could. They'd certainly be better for you than your poor old mother."

"Didn't you mind? Didn't the Queen mind?"

"Mind!" I was losing my patience now. She didn't seem to understand. "Of course I minded. Nobody likes being buggered about. But you have to make the best of a bad deal – and when you're royalty you do it with your head held high. You have an example to give. Not like your mother, wringing her hands and sobbing her heart out – screaming mea culpa every night. Stupid woman. As if she ever had a choice."

"Didn't she?"

I snapped at that. "What kind of a question is that, missy? Of course she didn't. Who do you think wears the pants in this kingdom?"

She got up to go at that, the little hussy. I grabbed her arms and swung her back to me, growling down in her face. "Oh no you don't. I asked you a question."

She didn't seem afraid. I like that in a girl. She looked me in the eye quite calmly and said – I remember this well – "you're not a King, you're an ogre!"

Ha! I haven't been talked to like that for a while, I can tell you – and suddenly I found I had an erection. I held her to me, feeling her soft breasts against my chest, her young body struggling, lithe and warm-blooded. My god, if her mother had stayed like that.... What had that stupid prince been doing to leave her so full of verve and sex? I slipped my hand down between her thighs and kissed her on those rose-bud lips. If her husband couldn't keep her in order then her father would have to do the job – and the timing was perfect. We were in amongst the roses – no-one around except my personal guards – so I let go of one arm to undo my flies – and she, er, well – she kicked me. In the balls.

For a moment she just stood there instead of running, the little fool, screaming at me. Then she came to her senses and bolted. My idiot guards thought that her being my daughter had some bearing on the matter and let her go. By the time I'd recovered enough to bring them to their senses it was too late.

So that's the story old chap, from one ageing King to another. Well shot of the poisonous little bitch too, if you ask me, though of course we'll have to get her back. Not good for discipline. I've got Mary Whither on it now. Always said girls were nothing but trouble. Lucky you've got boys old fellow, I can tell you – honest bit of buggery never did them any harm, eh?

"Another whisky? Help yourself."

Extract from *'It Shouldn't Happen to a Princess'* by Aurelie Regent

When I fled my father's garden I didn't know where I was going. I hadn't been intending to run away, but I soon realised there was no going back. In fact, leaving suddenly like that had probably been the only way – taking the spies at court completely by surprise.

I ran until I was exhausted, instinct taking me to the poor side of town with its narrow streets and dark corners where I could hide. I had no money, of course, but at the time that didn't seem to be a problem. Rather the adrenaline surge of fleeing the King made mere petty theft seem almost like fun – a new experience in my hitherto stifling world.

The most important thing was to change my appearance. Outside the palace my flowing dress made me look more like a hippy than a princess, but only at first glance and I needed to get rid of it. I knew about shops of course, but it took me a while before found a supermarket that had everything I needed. TV did the rest. I may have been naïve, but I'd watched plenty of movies, and fifteen minutes later I walked out with dye, scissors, a change of clothes, snack bars and a great sense of power. I honestly think it was the first time I'd ever done anything for myself, by myself, without having to ask permission. It was exhilarating.

A first that wasn't quite so pleasant was the smell of public toilets. Trying not to breathe, I cut off my hair, dyed the remainder black, took off my dress, and adjusted the leggings and T-shirt I'd tried on underneath and never removed. I looked at myself in the mirror and liked what I saw – I almost looked tough. Resilient, at any rate. I hoped I could live up to the image.

My next job as I saw it was – well – to work out what my next job should be. The snack bars wouldn't keep off my hunger for long, but soup kitchens were out of the question. As a natural breeding ground for the disaffected, my father kept informers posted there as a matter of course. Far better to get out of town. But how? Train or bus? Plane or foot? Since I knew nothing about public transport, where they'd probably be looking out for me anyway, it didn't take me long to decide to hitch. I could always shelter behind a road sign if the police went by.

Where to go was a little harder. My natural inclination was to head out to where Fallon and Fern had last been stationed. They'd help me. but Mary would guess that straight away and so would my parents – and while I knew Mary would try to protect me, she was still part of the establishment. Short of mutiny and risking the death sentence, she was duty bound to bring me back.

Which for some reason got me thinking of Millicent, the woman who had started it all. Proud, evil Millicent who had issued my death sentence at birth only to have it rescinded by a pint-sized Good Fairy an eighth of her size. Of course I didn't remember her from my christening, and the few seconds I'd seen of her before falling asleep were a hazy, enchanted blur – but there was something about Millicent that troubled me and it was time I put my finger on what it was.

Why had she wanted me dead in the first place, for example? She'd demanded nothing from the King in exchange for my life. No-one had ever mentioned negotiations. If the King really hadn't done anything to set her off then what had been in it for her? What had been worth robbing me of my mother –

who, I began to realise, was as much a victim of all this as me – and risking the terrible fate that had finally caught up with her? Millicent's curse had provoked my father and Pip to destroy her and all her domain utterly. Why?

Her old territory seemed a good place to go and find out. On a more practical level, it was also the last place anyone would think to look for me.

Edited transcript of the rat's confession, extracted by the Secret Police between 09:07:17 and 21:07:17. Torture used in accordance with International Guidelines (Torture Act 314) Duty Chief: S.P. Maj. G. Hardson. Veridical Rating: 9.25 on the Truetale Scale

She arrived on the 6th. She looked a mess, like anyone would who'd hitched for a day then walked over a mountain in sandals. No-one comes near Millicent's old haunt and the closest village is ten miles away – well, you know that. She would have walked at least from there.

How did she seem? She seemed… Well – at first, coming up the hill, she seemed happy, stopping to catch her breath and turning back to take in the view. Have you seen it? Millicent used to say it was the one consolation of her exile, but then she was a city girl at heart. I love it out there though – mountainous, inaccessible – cliffs dropping down into the copper blue fjords; eagles soaring overhead … and that infertile soil to keep the people at bay. Just the odd fishing village out towards the coast; scattered highland farms; a few holiday homes for people with more money than sense…. I'd like to see it again one day.

It was a beautiful afternoon when she arrived. Sun burning out of a light blue sky. Puffy-white clouds floating over puffy-white sheep. Bird-song. You know the sort of thing…. The kind of day you get twice a year just to make you fall in love with the place, so you put up with rain all the rest of the time.

She gazed out over all that, seeming quite emotional. Then she did a little twirl like girls do sometimes, circling round and around the grass until she was so giddy she fell over, giggling like a six-year-old. Then she picked herself up, dusted herself down, and carried on over the brow of the hill.

Well, then she didn't look so happy. In fact I'd say that when she finally saw the ruins, aghast would be a better word. Lets face it – your young Pip and co didn't leave much for the looters to pick over, did they? A few charred walls the sheep use as shelter; the odd scattered boulder; holes in the ground from the blasted foundations…. Not much there for a young woman to get her teeth into. I don't know what she'd been hoping for, but I guess it was a lot more than that.

For a while she just wandered around the place as if she couldn't believe her eyes, as if there had to be more. Then, when she'd covered the whole area several times and seen the same charred remnants she'd seen each time before – well – she kind of drooped. She sat down on the grass, right where she was, leant back against one of those useless boulders and closed her eyes. I guess it was the exhaustion, but I'd say that right then she was feeling pretty low.

The time seemed about ripe to go up to her, so I did. She seemed startled. In fact she threw a stone at me. Missed. Rotten shot like most girls, and her heart wasn't in it. So I went up closer and signed for her to follow me.

Why didn't I talk? To stop her asking stupid questions, that's why. You know what humans are like – especially young women. Let them know you know something and they never let up. Besides, I haven't done much talking this last year. It seemed easier to just get her to follow me and let the truth reveal all when she saw it.

She didn't seem too keen at first. In fact, she was downright suspicious. Can't say I blame her. She may be a post-spindle seventeen, but young princesses can't be too careful – as far as she was concerned Millicent might have left a trap. And let's face it – Millicent could be a nasty piece of work when she wanted to. Not that you guys had exactly left her much choice.

She followed me on my third attempt and I led her to the well-shaft. The one you can't see no matter how many counter-spells you put on the place; the one Millicent put so much of her magic into protecting – the magic that, like all her spells, I don't know the first thing about. What did that register on your truth scale? Ten? I'll say it again just to up your average. I don't know the first thing about breaking any of Millicent's spells. Ten again? Oh, don't you just love a truth-teller....

So, I upped and overed the well wall and hurried down the shaft. She hesitated. I could see her from the bottom, looking down into the darkness. She seemed to be straining to hear something – perhaps waiting to hear the splash.... Then I realised she *could* hear something. Me too. A helicopter. One of your helicopters I suppose, unless it was a border patrol. Whoever it was she had to hide quickly, and since the only place close enough was down the well-shaft that kind of speeded things up for me. She climbed over gingerly, ready to hang on for dear life – and you should have seen her face when the stairs and lights appeared. For a moment she looked more scared than if I'd turned into a monster. But – well – she's a tough cookie, that one. After a final glance up at the helicopter, she followed the steps down to where I was waiting, and I led her to Millicent's study.

It sounds simple when I put it like that. I led her to Millicent's study. All those years plotting. The final battle. Leaving Millicent to die alone knowing she needed me to stay alive. Then the waiting, the long, lonely waiting – all for one thing – to lead Aurelie to Millicent's study. Pity I didn't stop there. I should have. That was my job finished, after all. If I'd stopped there I would be free right now – enjoying the rewards of my long and faithful service – stuffing myself on cake and whisky instead of your exquisite hospitality. Millicent always said I had more loyalty than was good for me.... So, what's new? She had more ambition than was good for her.... Everybody needs a fault. OK, OK. I'll get to it. Give me a second. What was I saying? Millicent's study? Right.

The first thing she noticed was the stuff on Millicent's desk, but I don't know what it said. I can't read, and even if I could I wouldn't have been able to read that – it was meant for Aurelie's eyes only. There was the book of spells, of course – she was brushing up on the dragon one just before she left.... But I guess what you want to know about is the letter left out in the middle with Aurelie's name on it – and underneath that, Millicent's diary....

The girl spent a long time reading. Then, when she finally got up, she seemed upset. Very upset. She strode around the room, hit the wall, threw things, screamed and shouted – you know the sort of thing. When she'd finally tired herself out I showed her where to eat and rest and left her to it. It seemed the kindest thing to do. Then the next day she sent me here with that note – the one everyone in the palace seems to think is for them. And that's all I know.

Honest to god, that's all I know.

Copy of Millicent's letter to Princess Aurelie – 05:03:16

Dear Aurelie,

Here are my diaries. I leave you to read them and to judge me accordingly. I swear that everything in them is true. I know I am going to my death – they could never afford to let me live now. I am so sorry for everything. Believe me when I say I thought I had no choice.

I place all my spells, books and magic here at your disposal. No-one else can access them. I hope they serve you better than they did me. Use them wisely.

My spirit is with you,
Millicent.

Extract from 'It Shouldn't Happen to a Princess' by Aurelie Regent

Well. What did I make of that? I pulled up her chair towards the desk and sat down. If this was a trap, it was certainly an odd one – although I'd seen enough of magic to know such a gift wasn't necessarily a blessing. Her diaries however, were all I could have wanted. I opened them, flicked through the entries to the time around my birth, and started reading.

Millicent's Journals

3rd November, 99

Bigwig visit from the Chief. I knew something was up when I got orders to settle in these god-forsaken sticks, but I never expected this in a million years. So now I know why I was really sent undercover – how all that crap about infiltrating the enemy was just a pretext....

It puts me in deep shit and that's a fact. I can't take this to the King – he and his advisors think I'm a genuine threat – it would be the Chief's word against mine. And since the Chief always kept me out of the loop, no prizes for guessing who'd win. What a sucker I've turned out to be. If only I'd been less ambitious. If only I'd had the sense to realise that someone like that could never sit back and watch me succeed, my every triumph a threat to their own position….

Oh, the arrogance of youth.

1st January, 00 – Princess Aurelie's Birth

It's settled then. I'm to invite myself to the christening and threaten her with death. It's either that, or death myself. I've been skewered on a load of trumped-up charges as long as my arm – all things I colluded with so as to infiltrate the other side. Why the fuck didn't I watch my back?

Poor little kid – what a life she's in for – though that said, I guess it's no worse than being raised by Attila the King. It's *my* life that's at stake. And I've got sixteen years to get myself out of it – which is better than the initial odds. A lot can be done in sixteen years, and I'm not exactly powerless.

Though whether I can beat *her*, remains to be seen.

22nd January 00

She's got the kid. The papers are full of it – the christening and all. 'Princess Aurelie Spirited Off To Safety.' I'm furious and afraid. Furious at the role I've been backed into, and afraid there's no escape. She'll leave me alive for as long as she needs a perceived threat, sure, but not a second longer. Which means once Aurelie reaches womanhood, I'm toast. Fallon or Fern, I might have been able to deal with – they're reasonable people at heart – just following orders. But I don't stand much of a chance against all three of them.

Why, oh why, did I ever trust Mary Whither?

Extract from 'It Shouldn't Happen to a Princess' by Aurelie Regent

There it was, in black and white. The name I'd been waiting for. The answer to my question. And once it had been written it appeared again and again throughout Millicent's diary, until I could read it no more.

Mary Whither had wanted a child. Since, like all Good Fairies, she couldn't have one, she'd used her position to get what she wanted.

Normally that wouldn't be so remarkable. A lot of the Secret Police got kids by proxy – informally adopting dissidents' children that they put down as servants in the paperwork. It was an open secret. But that wasn't enough for Mary. Oh no, Mary Whither, Chief of the Secret Police, Top Good Fairy, had to have it her way. She wanted the daughter of royalty – to become a mother who shaped kingdoms – so she did. She set up Millicent, advised the King, bullied the Queen and took me away. Easy.

Aurelie's Journal – 17:07:17

I feel a bit better today. The first few days were lousy and I still feel wobbly and confused – but not quite so raw. I wish I hadn't sent that note to Mary though. Talk about oozing melodramatic seventeen-year-old.

It wouldn't be so bad if they hadn't got the rat. He seemed so powerful here on Millicent's home ground, showing me all her magic – I thought he'd make the perfect spy. Wrong again. Which leaves him buggered and me not much better off. How can I make plans when I haven't a clue what they're up to at the Palace? How can I find out while I'm marooned alone up here? What do I do next? Questions, questions. If only I had some sodding answers.

I know what Millicent intended me to do – get my revenge. But why should I succeed where she failed? And more to the point, why should I try? Is it really what *I* want? Surely all I want is to be free from the whole damn lot of them.

Ha. Guess the rat feels the same way….

Unofficial transcript of the rat's rescue – 21:07:17. Recording started automatically by sound sensors on unscheduled opening of the door to his cell.

[Door opens. Footsteps cross the floor unsteadily.
Heavy breathing, grunts of effort, the dragging of a

weight. A thump. Brisk footsteps re-cross the floor. Door closes.]

Queen: Psst.

[Silence]

Queen: Psst.

Rat: Wwaah?

Queen: Psst. Wake up.

Rat: No. Please. No more.

Queen: Ssshh.

Rat: For pity's sake. I've told you all I kno– your *majesty*?

Queen: Ssshh. Is it true that you've come from my daughter?

Rat: What?

Queen: Is it true?

Rat: Well .... Yes. It's true. Ask Major Hard–

Queen: That note. The note you brought. Is it meant for me? Tell me, quickly – everything depends on that. If she wants me to leave her alone then I will, god knows I'll do anything she wants me to....   But if it was meant for another.... If I could help her.... Can't you see, I have to know!

Rat: Look. I've been over this with your thug. She never told me anything. Just said to leave it in the hall – said the person it was meant for would understand it straightaway.

Queen: Oh.

Rat: So I guess that means ... that it's not for you.

Queen: Oh!

Rat: In fact...

Queen: Yes?

Rat: From things I overheard... From things she said...

Queen: Yes!

Rat: I got the impression she didn't feel too good about the way she'd been with you. That...

Queen: Yes?

Rat: ... that she would appreciate having a chance to spend more time with you, ma'am. 'Give it another go,' I think was what she said.

Queen: Oh.

[Sound of undoing chains]

Rat: How did you do that?

Queen: Knocked out the guard – stole his key.

Rat: What!

Queen: Actually, it was quite easy. I was rather nervous to be honest, not being used to this kind of thing. But, well – I suppose having a reputation as a useless wimp has finally stood me in good stead....

Rat: Your majesty...

Queen: Oh, I know what they say about me. How could I not when it's put about by my own husband? Come on. Let's get out of here.

Rat: How?

Queen: How?

Rat: I'm deeply grateful for the idea – don't get me wrong – but there are a hell of a lot of security systems between here and freedom. Getting out of this room is the easy part. And if they catch me escaping... I really don't think I'd like what happens when they bring me back....

Queen: Have you been tagged?

Rat: Tagged?

Queen: Yes. Has your genetic code been put in the system?

Rat: Well...

Queen: Because I don't think it has.

Rat: But –

Queen: I know – it's the first thing they do. But you may be surprised to learn that your stay here is unofficial. It would appear that someone wants you, and what you know, kept secret. Very secret. You've noticed the guards' uniforms?

Rat: Secret Police, yes. So –

Queen: So why isn't it the Royal Guards? You were caught breaking into the palace, no? This is their territory. The Secret Police have no authority here. Unless....

Rat: Unless?

Queen: I don't know what's going on, but it's something very odd. And I think we could turn it to our advantage. I'm willing to bet that I could walk out of here with you in my pocket, just like that.

Rat: Oh you are, are you. On what odds?

Queen: Frankly sir, and I don't mean to be negative, but facts
    are facts – I don't think you have much to lose.

Report on the rat's escape. Submitted by S.P. Corporal G. Hardson

…… It would appear that her Majesty the Queen then placed
the rat in her pocket and left the palace without being
challenged. Indeed, knowing nothing about the rat, the Royal
Guards on gate duty had no reason to be suspicious.

The Queen – and the rat – have not been seen since.

Extract from '*It Shouldn't Happen to a Princess*' by Aurelie Regent

My mother's arrival with the rat was the beginning or a new
era. Alone, I'd been scared and guilty – blaming myself for the
rat, frightened to go outside in case they caught me too,
nervous to experiment with Millicent's spells – other people's
magic can be tricky…. In short, I was pretty useless. But with
their support all that changed – and not just in the morale
department either. The Queen hadn't survived the King all those
years without getting a pretty good handle on how he worked,
and the rat had picked up more than a few good tips from
Millicent, whilst as for me – I had something up my sleeve too.

It came to me when we first started planning. You don't
survive by reacting, as the King once said, you survive by acting
– by being on the ball and one step ahead of the opposition. So
taking a tip from his books, I insisted we make the first move.
We couldn't just wait for them to decide how to pluck out our
little thorn in their side. The problem was, while I knew we had
to do *something*, I wasn't sure what, and it was while we
thrashed it out, plotting and counter-plotting, that I began to
realise why Mary had insisted I learn chess – and with that
realisation came another – that I understood Mary, who had
taught me nearly everything I knew, better than anyone else
alive. Now, with a bit of luck, I could use that knowledge against
her.

We considered revenge, as Millicent had clearly hoped for,
then ruled it out. Mary was bad, sure. She'd lied, cheated,
robbed me of my intended childhood, murdered at least one of

her employees and probably many more. But then, as Millicent herself had said, my father was hardly any better – and at least Mary had truly loved me, which was more than could be said for him. My childhood, in all honesty – mum's feelings apart – had probably been better as it was.

Instead I decided to go for autonomy. Using Millicent's magic, we would turn her savaged castle and wild grounds into our own Queendom. A Queendom that was fair and open and not at all like my father's. One that would welcome all the disaffected from the King's and neighbouring lands. It was an ambitious plan, I realised, but not impossible if handled the right way – the right way being to never lose sight of Mary's big fat Archilles' heel – her love for me.

That was the knife I intended to twist in her twisted heart. Mary would do almost anything to avoid my death, I was sure – yet at the same time she knew if I told the King what she'd done, she'd be finished. But what if I didn't tell the King? What if I left Mary in power for as long as she used it to our advantage? What if she manipulated my father into leaving Mum and I alone, and we in turn let her be? She could do it if anyone could. And if I played my cards right, I could make it happen.

So we made a deal.

The rest, as you know, is history.